LIBERATION

A.L. CARTER

LIBERATION

For Nicki - You drink too much, you're sarcastic, and you're funny as hell. Thanks for being everything I needed in a friend. You're amazing.

CONTENT WARNING

This book is intended for adults 18 or older. It is a polyamorous science fiction erotic novel between one woman and three males. Reader discretion is strongly advised. This book contains content that could trigger people who have experienced trauma. It contains scenes of BDSM, violence, rape, profanity, and sexually explicit reading. Some of the chapters will be emotionally and intellectually challenging to engage with. The author does her best to make this book a story about survival and the power of women. While some of the content in this book may be difficult to read, please know that one in every six women in the US has been a survivor of sexual violence. We are survivors.

If you or someone you know is a survivor of sexual assault, please seek help: https://www.rainn.org/resources

On the Lutetian Homeworld

The Lutetian Empire is recovering from the unjust war waged by the high and mighty Nlyaxian matriarchy. It was not truly my intention to destroy their entire world, but my incompetent science offspring botched my weapon. I wanted a weapon to remove all animal life on a planet so that we could harvest resources. Instead of doing that, it caused instability in the planet's core, causing it to explode within an hour of its being fired.

I was watching, primed to revel in my victory over my enemies. Instead, I killed all my offspring on the command deck of my ship. I can always make more, but I wanted the resources on that planet. It was rich, and I would have taken it, vastly improving my wealth. I am not sad their world was destroyed. It was still exhilarating watching it explode.

Since my victory over the Nlyaxian, I have been rebuilding my empire. I have learned from my previous mistakes. Ravaging planets, not caring who it upsets. Ravaging worlds turned into a war with many species, and we were on the verge of losing. Destroying the surface of our homeworld was genius on my part since we have not lived on the surface for over a century. We are far below ground. They were all fools to believe they could best me.

Now I am rebuilding my power through influence. I inserted my spies in the slave trade and took it over within a year. All slave profit, in the end, comes to me. This profit is funding my new army. We have hit some roadblocks with my new soldiers. We need a new control mechanism, and I learned today that one may still be alive.

At first, I was livid that a member of the Nlyaxian royal family was still alive, but this has given me the possibility of regaining control of my army.

My intel states he travels with two women, possibly three, and one is his mate. They are wreaking havoc on my slave supply chain. The Cruxlin cowards are even trying to avoid them. Nlyaxians are incredibly protective of their mates', so if I can get my hands on her, we will have him. He will have to comply.

My plan hinges on their offspring. I need a generation of new Nlyaxians so I can program them. Once children are born, we put them into training camps to make them compliant with the Empire's needs, and our needs are complete domination. Yes, it is less elegant than the genetic splicing we were doing, but the results were spotty and expensive. Sometimes the low-tech way is the best. The Lutetian are a long-lived species. I am over two hundred years old. I have the time and the patience to breed the army I want.

So I send my newest spy Sitruc out to find them and bring them back. If not, bring her back... he will follow.

Dax

They stole my mate from me before I could touch her. I feel like a fool for not seeing her for what she was. Ronin says I am too hard on myself, but he is wrong. I met her as a child and immediately knew she was my mate. She was beautiful even as a child but lonely. Her red hair and green eyes captured me the first moment I saw her.

I was dreaming of hunting. It was the first time I felt her fear. I chased after the fear, and it drew me to end it. She huddled against a cliff so small, trapped by the crima beast I was hunting. I saw her and felt her fear. My battle fury burned through me. I had never felt it before, but it burst forth then. I roared with the fury that it would dare threaten my mate. It disappeared. She peaked at me from under her arm and then raced into my arms. "Thank you," she whispered.

"You are welcome. Are you alright?"

"Yes, it was very scary," still shaking from her encounter.

I hold her tighter, "I will let nothing happen to you."

She looked into my eyes, then gave me the brightest smile, "What is this place? It's so pretty."

"This is my homeworld. It is called Nlyax. This is the forest behind my home. I love it here."

"Will you show me around?" she asks with big green innocent eyes.

That was the beginning for us. For years we would see each other in our dreams. Not every day, but regularly. I prayed to the Goddess nightly to let me see her again. I could always feel her presence and find her in the forest when she was there. It became one of our many games.

As we aged, the dreams occurred less frequently, but we still met every few weeks. Once I was talking to Ronin and Aanon about mates and what ours would be like. I told them about her. They gave me a quizzical look, like they could not figure out what I was saying. I tried to explain dreams and how I had met her, but they brushed it off as my imagination, and we never spoke of her again.

A few years go by, and I come of age. I was going to start my military training with Ronin and Aanon. I felt grown up. A few days before we left for camp, she was in my dreams. She was growing, getting taller, and her muscles were becoming more defined.

"I missed you, Dax. I've waited in our valley several times, but you never came. Are you angry with me?" The hurt in her voice scraped against me.

"I am a male, and I have duties. I am going for military training in a few days. I am not sure you are even real anymore."

Tears start running down her face, and she whispers, "I am real, please, Dax. I enjoy being here with you. I have no one else."

Her pain was too much for me, and my anger flared, "I will not be back. Do not look for me."

When I turned away from her that day, my soul shattered. I knew she was real, but I had convinced myself she was not, so hurting her was nothing, but it was.

Years went by, and I was able, for the most part, not to think about her. That was until the Lutetian captured me. Every time they let me get even five minutes of sleep, I would search for her in my dreams, calling for her. I thought I could get through my pain if she were with me. Sometimes I could feel her, but she never manifested. By the time they rescued me, I was furious with her. She should have been there when I needed her. It was not till years later I realized how childish I was. I pushed her away. I did that, not her. She was not there because of me.

My mate, the one person destined to complete me, was gone forever.

When she pulled me into our valley after so many years without her, I was shocked and angry. I was convinced that the Lutetian had finally broken my mind. There is no way she would be willing to return to me.

She was the most beautiful thing I had ever seen. She had grown into her height and filled out in the most desirable ways.

When I saw her, the connection instantly clicked back into place. Her body and mind called to me like they always had.

She was naked, and I wanted her, but I was convinced she was not real. I was also confident that no female would ever want me. I was broken and scared. I stroked the mounds on her chest. It was a test in my mind, one that she failed. When she moaned at the contact, I knew she was not real because no female could find me attractive. I am a fool.

Now she is gone, and I still cannot touch the real June. I search for her every night in my dreams, but I cannot feel her, which terrifies me. Even when I tried to deny her existence, I could always feel her presence. Now, I cannot find her, and I fear what that means.

Ronin has been sparring with me daily to keep my mind busy, but it is not working. I like the training, and I can make him work for his wins now, but it only distracts me for a short time. I see the pain and worry on his face as well. We can feel her through the Kokoro on our arms, but for some reason, it feels muted, and she never responds. We assume they have her sedated, but we do not know for sure.

I have taken my own quarters because I cannot stand the idea of sleeping in her bed without her. I stay to myself mostly unless the crew is meeting on plans or information.

I am walking back to my quarters from my latest sparring match with Ronin when I round the corner, and something collides with me. I catch the little dark blur to make sure I did not injure it. I am so shocked by what I see I just stare for a while. "*Yes*, I am a Nlyaxian female. Can you let me go, please?" I release her, and she takes a step back but does not seem scared of my appearance.

"Who are you?" she asks.

I go down to one knee, so we are eye to eye, "My name is Dax. What is yours?"

"My name is Leena." She pauses for a second, then squints her eyes at me, "Are you my Mother's Dax? Her second?"

My shock at her statement lands my ass on the floor. "You are June's daughter?"

She gets a bit of a sad look, "Not really. My parents died. June found me on this ship and protected me from the monster that was the captain. She then asked me if I'd like to be her daughter, and of course, I said *yes*! I love her so much. She is my father's little Pillut. Since you are Mother's second, does that mean you are my father too?"

Was there hope in her voice? "Would you like that?"

She pauses and stares at me as if weighing my worth, then smiles brightly and wraps her little arms around my neck, "*Yes! I would love it*!" she practically screams in my ear.

I hear chuckling behind me, "Leena, I have told you it is not polite to scream in people's ears."

She looks at me contritely and says, "I'm sorry. I was just excited."

"It is ok little one. I do not mind." She hugs me again and sits on my lap in the middle of the hallway. She looks sad and stares at her hands, "Are you going to help first father to find Mother? I miss her so much." A tear streaks down her cheek.

I wipe the tear and tilt her face, so she looks at me, "I will rip apart this galaxy until I find her?"

She stares again, then smiles, "Are you coming to live in our quarters? I want to show you my room. I love it. Father made it for me. You should live with us so we can be together until Mother comes home."

She is looking at me with such hope in her eyes I give in. I'm not sure I could say no to this little female, "Alright, I will live with you and Ronin. We are all now family." She wraps her arms around my neck for another hug, then trots off to—I am not sure where.

Ronin squats down next to me, "And that was our little whirl-wind. She is like a little storm that blows through, chaos filled with joy and love. Here let me help you up." He sticks out his hand and pulls me up.

"Is she safe running around the ship?" Already concerned for her.

Ronin chuckles, "Oh yes, every crew member would die for that little female. She has us all wrapped around her little finger. Besides, Sia keeps track of her and keeps her out of the danger-ous areas of the ship."

I stand there staring after her for a while and come to a real-ization. I turn to Ronin, "I think it's time I stopped wallowing in my self-pity and start helping to find our mate."

Ronin gets an emotional look on his face, "It is about time, brother. I need you."

Ronin

It has been two day cycles since Dax met our little Leena, and the difference is significant. She has brought him out of his depression with her effervescent personality and love. He follows her around for a couple of hours every morning, just listens and plays with her.

She loves the attention. It shouldn't surprise me she has had this effect on him. When we were younger, it was Dax who played with the younger children around us. He would see them and have to play with them for a while, so much so that all my sib-lings' children would scream and laugh when he would show up at the residence. I knew he would be a fantastic father. It is why it hurt so much when they declared him unfit; it meant he would never be a father, and I knew how much that meant to him.

Now he has Leena, and light has returned to his eyes. I still feel the dissonance within him, but it has reduced. He is slowly healing. I need him now more than ever, and I wish Aanon were still with us. He was our rock; he balanced us and calmed the anger in Dax. I miss him.

"You ready to get started?" I ask him as he chuckles at something Leena said. When he turns to me, he is smiling, and it is something I was not sure I would see again.

"Let's. We need to find her."

Dax

We walk to the conference room, and Ronin calls the crew to join us. They all filter in, and the last two are the Nlyaxian warriors. I fought all these people in my anger at June's loss. Since I know, they all consider her family, even the Ferin. Unlike most beings in the galaxy, the Ferin do not scare me. Yes, they are fearsome warriors but never have I encountered a Ferin who was openly hostile or doing something vile. When I have seen them, they were always defending someone who could not protect themselves. Always. So whatever the rumors that swirl about them, I knew it all to be wrong. They are good people, and good in this galaxy is rare. She was the only one who refused to engage with me on the dock. I am not sure why.

"I would like to say something if that is alright, Ronin?" I ask.

"Of course."

"I want to apologize for fighting with you all on the station dock. There are no excuses for my behavior, but I had just found June, and before I even got to talk to her in person, they stole her from me. I know how much you care for my Mate. Thank you, and please, again, forgive me."

It is the Ferin, Elana, I think, who walks to me and responds. She lays a hand on my chest. "There is nothing to forgive. Losing June has hit us all very hard, but as her mate and a mate with Kokoro, it would have been much more painful, and I am it still is. It is why I refused to fight with you on the docks. I could see your pain, and it would have been unfair of me to kill you." She winks at me, then sits down.

The one called Doraj chuckles, "It is forgiven, my friend, but I look forward to a sparring match so we can even some scores. Your punches rang my bell, as June would say."

"Ekim, I am sorry I blamed you for her loss. It was not your fault."

"I appreciate that, Dax, but it still feels like my fault. I should have kept a better eye on her…"

Ronin interrupts, "No, Ekim. June and I both let ourselves get very distracted by the prospect of seeing Dax. We made many mistakes, but no one is truly to blame except the Cruxlin."

"And the Lutetian, since the Cruxlin works exclusively for them now," I mention.

"*What?*" Ronin almost yells.

Confused, "Yes, they are wholly contracted to the Lutetian. Did you not know this?"

"No! What else do you know?"

They all stare at me now with a singular focus. It makes me uncomfortable. Ronin notices this, "It is alright, Dax. Tell us what you know."

I nod, "The Cruxlin are currently acting as the Lutetian muscle since the Lutetian run the slave trade now." Several gasps in shock. "From the information I have got over the years, the Lutetian took over the trade about a year after Nlyax fell. Since then, they have been secretly pulling the strings letting the Cruxlin take the blame for most of it. The galactic council has been silent for the last four years. There are rumors saying they have wiped the council out. It's that, or they are pretending it is not happening because they do nothing about the Cruxlin stealing beings from any type of world, so they have gone unchecked for a long time."

It is silent for a while as everyone contemplates what I have said. Elana is the first to speak, "I believe the rumors about the Galactic Council are true. The Ferin have not heard from our representative for over three years. We have assumed him dead because he must check in monthly with our planetary council."

Ronin growls, "How is it possible that the Lutetian survived the destruction of their planet!"

"But their planet was not destroyed," Ronin glances at me, confused. "The surface was destroyed. If you've ever been in a Lutetian ship, you would know this; They keep it very dark... almost cave-like." I can see Ronin trying to work out where I am going with this, "Do you remember when we started the orbital survey of their planet for our bombardment strategy just before they set off their weapons?" He nods. "The survey noted many..."

"*Caves*!" Ronin interrupts before I finish.

"Yes, caves. What if the surface was more for the show? What if they lived *beneath* the surface?"

Ronin thinks about this for a few minutes, "It means that if they lived in cave systems underground that the destruction of the surface was to convince us of their demise. Fuck!" He jumps up and starts stalking the room. I have known Ronin for many years. I know this behavior is not genuine anger; it is how he works out frustration and thinks.

After a few more minutes of stalking, "That gives us options for plans. First, we need to find that ship and see if she is still on it. If she is not, then we need to go to their homeworld and see if there is any evidence that they are still using it as a base."

"We will also need to 'convince' some high-ranking Cruxlin of the need to divulge information, and we will most likely have to act on some of the information we get from them," I say to him.

"Good. Good... I think we should take the Cruxlin ship. It could be valuable in the future. Though we do not have enough people to crew it."

The one called Lessur speaks up, "Actually, we do. Some inhabitants of Haven have been pilots, navigators, and even captains of ships before. They have already expressed an interest in becoming part of our crew."

Ronin is quiet for a long time this time, "I hate to break up this crew. You are all my family, but Lessur could Captain the ship with Ekim as his second. We can flush out their ranks and backfill them with inhabitants of Haven. Thoughts?" Like he can read my thoughts, he says to me, "I will explain about Haven to you when we are done here, alright?"

I nod.

Ekim is the first to speak, "While I dislike the idea of being separated from this crew, I see the need. We could cover a lot more leads if there are two ships and two crews looking for her."

Lessur nods in agreement, "I do not like it either, but I believe it necessary and advantageous as well. We need to find her as quickly as possible. Who knows what..." He stops before he finishes his statement. No one wants to think about what they could be doing to her, but if the Lutetian have her, then I know, and it scares me to death. I am praying to the Goddess that Cruxlin still has her.

Ronin is staring at the display showing the Lutetian homeworld. "It is decided. We continue to pursue the Cruxlin ship. When we catch it, we attack and take the ship. We convince," he says with a smirk toward me, "high-ranking Cruxlin to divulge information and clear the ship. At that point, we will need to review the information we have and decide if we are going to Haven to gather crew or pursue June's location from the information we gathered." Everyone nods.

"Sia, how long till we catch the Cruxlin ship?"

"Four day cycles." She responds. "Assuming they stay in their current location."

He nods, and I can feel his sadness. "We regroup for planning in three cycles." Everyone filters out of the conference room. It's just him and I now.

I walk over and place a hand on his shoulder, "Ronin, I feel your sadness, but the time for that is over. We need your anger, your fury, if we are going to succeed at this."

He wraps me in a firm embrace and growls, "You are right. Thank you. It's been simmering, and it's time to let it out." When he pulls back, he is in full battle fury. "Let's go train."

"Excellent." I release mine. It is always there battling for dominance. I let go and feel my eyes go black.

Ronin

Dax and I enter the training room, and battle fury still consumes us. I stride to the ring and turn, ready to begin, but he is not behind me. He has stopped and is staring at the weapons and training equipment she gifted me. My fury cools but does not release me. I walk back to him and wait for him to speak.

"This is hers?" He asks quietly.

"Yes. She built this wall and the training equipment as a gift. It is all from her homeworld."

He looks at the weapons wall and then back at me with a smirk, "You were probably acting like a child seeing that wall."

I give him a huge smile, "*Yes*! I still feel like a little boy when I see it. She is slowly teaching me how to properly use each."

"Wait. She knows all these?"

I cannot help the chuckle that escapes, "Yes, she is a master of all. Our mate is a formidable warrior. I have yet to win a match against her." The look he gives me was worth telling him that. He even dropped out of his battle fury. He looks dumbfounded.

I bark out a laugh, "Yes, yes, yes. Our mate can plant my ass on the mat... a lot."

He starts genuinely laughing, and it is good to see, even though it is at my expense. "Yes, Yes, ha ha, old male. Let's train because I bet I can still plant your ass on the mat!" I like to tease him about being a few months older than me.

That shuts him up and brings back the battle fury. He smiles, "We shall see."

We square up at the mat. I decide to use one of June's tactics against my oldest friend. I will only use my old combat methods until I can gauge where his skills are now. He is larger than I remember. He has always been taller than me, but his muscle mass is much larger than it used to be. He removes his shirt, and I note the patchwork of scars crisscrossing his torso. My fury ramps up, but I execute some quick mental exercises to bring me back to calm.

I decide to use a second of our mate's tactics. In her match against Elana, she did not know her prowess in battle, so she came out with dominance as her focus. I do not know what Dax has been through, so dominance will be my focus.

I did not hear Doraj come in, but he asks, "Need a governor?"

"Yes." We say in unison.

"Set," he yells. "Go!"

This Dax differs from the one I have been battling since he came on the ship. He is focused, and he is powerful. His punches and kicks are almost twice what they were before, but he still has the same tells. Dax pulls his shoulders before his punches, and his hips turn when he is readying a kick. Good. Doraj calls the first round, and we return to our corners. Neither is particularly winded.

"Set" Doraj yells. "Go!"

We come out again, but this time I add June's lessons to the mix. By the end of this round, I have three points. Though his ass has not landed on the mat, his skill has improved dramatically. He can use what he knows of my fighting style against me to a point, but the new skills I have frustrates him. Emotion is terrible in any battle. It compromises your focus. By the end of the third round, I have five points, and he has an impressive two. It is remarkable because he rarely got one point on me in a match, and this time he got two. He has improved. When Doraj calls the last match, Dax is on the floor smiling, and I am bent over him, trying to catch my breath, grinning as well.

"*Ha*! I got *two* points!" He laughs.

I chuckle in return, "Yes, you have improved, my brother."

"Those new moves you used look eerily similar to how our mate fights." He says as he gets up from the mat.

"That is because she is the one who taught them to me."

"I wish I could have seen her plant your big ass on the mat," he says, laughing.

I tackle him to the ground, and we wrestle like we used to. Afterward, we are laying on the mat. Dax is resting his head on my stomach. "I cannot find her, Ronin. I have been looking for her, but she does not come. I thought maybe she would find me, but nothing."

"You mean in your dreams?"

"Yes. I know you do not believe…"

I interrupt him before he gets any further, "Dax, I believe your dreams, past and present, are very real. I also believe I understand how the Lutetian tormented you far longer than any of the rest of our soldiers." At his confused glance up at me, I explain. "June told me about the dream where the Lutetian were torturing you. Dax, I do not believe you are the only one. I think you were the unfortunate one who remembered the entire ordeal."

He sits up and turns to me, shocked, "What do you mean I was not the only one?"

"During the Lutetian Wars, I was sporadically getting reports of soldiers waking with horrible wounds, wounds they did not go to bed with. I did not put it together until June told me the details of your shared dream."

He lays back down on my stomach, and I wait for him to process what I have told him. Dax is an internal thinker, and he goes quiet until he has fully processed the information given to him. "How many? How many reports did you see?"

"I cannot be sure but I think around twenty-five." I feel him flinch at this information like it hurt him. I cannot handle his pain, so I run my hand over his hair. I feel him relax after a minute or two.

"Ronin, I did not know this until this very minute, but I took comfort from the fact that they could only do this to me. Now they even take that away. They have been torturing our people for decades. This time, Ronin, we do not rest until they are all dead. I was already hunting them, looking for their leader so I could kill them for what they did to Nlyax, but now nothing but annihilation is all that they deserve."

Ronin

I am shaking with fury. I have held my anger and grief at bay for too long. They tortured Dax for years, and now other of my people suffered at their hands. They destroyed my people, and now they have my Mate! I cannot contain the pure rage that explodes forth with this information. My roar rattles the walls and weapons. I stride to the wall and start punching it with my fists. I need blood and battle, but I cannot here, so I bloody my fists. I beat the wall like it was a Lutetian in front of me. There is blood running down my arms and the wall in front of me. I cannot control my fury.

June

Something calls me. I am stuck in quicksand and feel like I will never get free. I feel it again. Great pain and anger. It's Ronin, my

Mate. I must get to him because he needs me. I can lift my arms so I can bring them closer and touch my Kokoro. I feel him and Dax. Dax is worried for him too. He is so angry and sad. Something has brought forward his pain and anger from when his planet and his people died. My poor Ronin. I send all the love I can through the link then I am pulled back into the quicksand.

Ronin

I am furiously hitting the wall then I feel her and freeze. "Dax," I whisper.

I feel his hand on my shoulder, "I feel her too. She is very weak, but she fights for you, Ronin. She feels your pain and seeks to comfort you."

I fall to my knees and rest my forehead against the wall. "Dax, I could never grieve for my people or my family. I could barely think about you and Aanon without my battle fury forcing its dominance. I am sorry I did not look for you."

Dax

I am in shock. Ronin is always so reserved, and so controlled. Did he apologize? I sit against the wall beside him, "Ronin, how would you have known I was alive? Did you know I was off-planet because I was still angry with your mother? That I did not want to witness the transfer of the Matriarchy? Did you develop the ability to detect my presence? No? Then stop it. You and your Mate are the leaders of our people. It does not matter if it is a small group or a planet. We need you both. Ronin, I know what it is like not to be able to control the fury that simmers within us all. Please be the person you are naturally not like me." I glance and smirk at him, "We only can handle one of me."

He turns and sits against the wall with me, "My brother, the fury you battle every minute of every day... you do not give your-self the credit you deserve. I do not believe even I could control a battle fury that strong."

"I always have felt it. Did you know that? Most probably assume it developed after my captivity, but no. From the first time, it exploded from my mind it has been this strong."

"What was the first event to trigger it?" he asks curiously.

"It was the first time I met June. It was in a dream, and she was so scared. When I felt her fear, it exploded from me with such force. My need to protect her drove me. I found her huddled against a cliff face, a crima beast getting ready to rip her apart. The roar that came from me has never been as fierce as that one since."

"She could not have been hurt, though, right? It was a dream."

"I am no longer so sure. I now believe it cannot hurt you in a dream of your own creation. However, if it is someone else's creation, I believe many terrible things can happen to you."

We are quiet in our own thoughts for a while, "Ronin, let us go to the infirmary and have Nalax fix you up. I believe you have suffered enough." He nods and takes my arm for help to rise.

We walk silently to the infirmary. When we get there Nalax seems angry at us both because of his injuries. I even hear her mumble 'males' under her breath. It makes me chuckle because it shows her level of affection for Ronin. "What are you laughing about? Get over here and sit down so I can fix your dumb ass as well!" I hurry over and sit down. I glance over at Ronin in a bit of shock.

He whispers, "She has picked up some of our Mate's colloquialisms."

Nalax's shoulders sag, and she whispers, "I miss her."

"We do, too," I say to no one in particular.

Nalax has patched us up, and we decide to head back to our quarters. It is almost time for dinner, and I would like to read to Leena. She is so behind in her schooling. I have decided I will help her catch up. We walk into the room, and it's the first time I have seen it. I am shocked.

Ronin sees it and gives me a questioning look.

"I do not understand. This looks nothing like the room in her nightmare."

His face hardens a fraction, "No. Sia and I gutted and rebuilt this room. Nothing about it is the same."

I bow my head, "Very good, my Prime. I am sure our Mate appreciated that." He relaxes and nods.

Leena is not back yet, so I decided to ask a question that has been bothering me, "Did he suffer? I need to know he suffered."

He sighs, "I wish I could tell you he suffered by my hand, but our Mate is a warrior. She killed him, cut off his cock, and fed it to him while his heart still beat."

I cannot help the bark of a shocked laugh that comes out, "Good. Not quite long enough by my standards but I like her brand of justice." I am quiet for a bit then say, "I saw him attacking her, taunting her in her nightmare. She was terrified of him."

Ronin nods, "She has had problems sleeping ever since. I can stop it if I can catch the fearful looks and twitching while she sleeps, but when I do not, she wakes screaming in fear. It is very hard to know that he invades her dreams. Maybe with you here now, you can help stop them?"

I nod, "I can help but stop them altogether, no. She must face and defeat them, or she will never be free of them." He nods as if he knew this to be the case.

"Dax, have you defeated yours?" I think for a while because I am not sure how to answer that question.

"Yes, and no. I do not believe I defeated them; I could not. I had no control over when the Lutetian could pull me into a nightmare to torture me. Before the fall of Nlyax, they were constantly trying to get information out of me which I never gave them, no matter how much pain they inflicted on me. After the fall, they still pulled me in and taunted and tortured me for fun. Sometimes the wounds would persist after I woke, and sometimes they would not. Most of the time, they left some just as a reminder that it was real. After some time, I resigned to the half-life of being tortured in my sleep. Does it bother me they still can? Yes. Do I have nightmares about them? No, not really."

"You said you have been looking for her in your dreams?"

"Yes. I can feel her. I know she is there; I just cannot reach her. I was worried it was my inadequacies, not that they sedated her or something, until she reached out this day cycle. I could feel her struggling to come out of sleep before she even touched the Kokoro. When she touched it, I felt her join us, bringing us together, and her concern for you."

Ronin has been quiet for a long time. I get up and start fixing dinner for us. When he speaks, he sounds despondent. "I wish I could say I regret my actions, but now we know they have her sedated and *alive*." He gives me a sad smile, "The first time I 'lose my shit,' as she would say, and it almost felt like a reward because I could feel her again."

"I will not lie. It was good to feel her. Now I need to see her."

At that moment, our little Leena comes sprinting toward me and launches into my arms. With a huge smile, she practically yells, "*You are here! Come see my room!*" We go to her room, and she tells me all about her room and all the things in it. She is such an amazing child. I try to listen to all the information she is giving me, but she speaks so fast.

"... I was so glad when First Father remodeled all the rooms and made me a room. There is no way I could stay in his room anymore."

I freeze, "Leena, what do you mean to stay in 'his' room?"

She give me a sad look, "I was a slave in these quarters for a long time. When Mother came, she helped me, protected me." Tears slip down her cheeks. I pick her up and hold her. My battle fury is out, but since there is no enemy I can keep control. She rests her head against my shoulder, and I can feel her breath on my neck. She whispers, "He used me to make her stop fighting him. He used me against her." My control snaps, and my roar is the ferocity as when I first found June. I hug her to me. I will protect her. I back into a corner. No one will hurt her.

Ronin

When I hear Dax's battle roar, I launch myself toward the door then stop. If he has lost control, my entering the room may make it worse. I know he would not harm her, so the only thing that could have happened is Leena said something about her past. I touch the Kokoro on my arm and feel his anger and distress. His desire to protect Leena at all costs. I try to funnel calm through the link, and I can tell it helps a bit. I send him memories of us playing as children, of Aanon, and of my memories of June. This works. I think he is calm enough. I walk into her room, and he is against the far corner of the room, holding Leena to his chest. Leena is stroking his face. I can hear her calmly saying, "It's ok. It's ok."

"Dax, she is safe. We have her, and nothing will happen to her."

He growls, "Bad things already happened to her! How do you know they won't happen again?"

Then my little miracle female grabs his face and turns it to her, "Father, bad things happen to everyone. What matters is how you grow from them."

He stares at her, then relaxes the rest of the way out of his battle fury. "How are you such a wise little one?"

She smiles, "Mother taught me."

Dax glances at me with a smirk, and I can tell we are both thinking the same thing, 'of course she did.' "You alright, my brother? Because I think our evening meal is getting cold." He hops up with a shocked look, still holding Leena, and dashes into the other room. Leena is giggling the whole way. I follow at a more leisurely pace.

We sit and eat our meal, and Leena while I tell Dax about Haven.

We eat and Dax sits there staring at our Kokoro. "I..." he looks up at me, "our mate has *spoken* to the Goddess?" At my nod he continues, "And Haven was her idea. You all go around the galaxy saving beings in bondage?" I nod again. He returns to staring at his Kokoro. "I am not worthy of such a mate." His sadness and grief beat at me.

"That is not yours to decide." I am a little angry. "The *Goddess* deemed you worthy, are you saying SHE is wrong about you?" In things like this, I know he would never question the Goddess.

"Ronin, you know I would never question the Goddess. I have felt connected to Her almost since birth but..."

I jump up and start stalking the room, interrupting before he can finish, "*No.* She gave you a mate and then marked you both with a symbol that hasn't been seen for centuries. She has deemed you worthy!" When I look at him, he is smirking at me. "What?"

"I forgot how agitated you get when someone slights your loved ones. You are my Triad, and I am eternally grateful to Her for that. Our Triad is everything to me." He chuckles, "I think Leena is going to fall asleep into her food."

Her head bobs back up. "No, I'm not," then back down again.

"Go put her down and I will clean up. And Dax, one of the most joyous days of my life was when I found out you were still alive."

Dax

Two days go by, and we are now in the conference room start-ing the plan of attack for the Cruxlin ship we have been tracking. Ronin starts the meeting once everyone arrives. "Sia, can you pull up the plans for the Cruxlin ship on the display? Please."

"Completed," Sia responds a little terse.

"Sia? Is everything alright?" Nalax asks.

Sia pauses briefly, "I am agitated or maybe worried about June. The longer they hold her, the less likely we are to find her. I keep running through scenarios, and I like the ending of none of them... Sorry for that outburst."

Did the AI of the ship we are on really just say she was 'wor-ried' for my mate? Doraj sees my shocked confusion and chuck-les, "Yes, your mate has the unique ability to assist a ship AI to become sentient."

"It's ok, Sia, we are all on edge. On the display is a title II class Cruxlin transport ship. While it is not a warship, it has defenses. The crew complement is 42, so far from the range of impossible to take. We have me, Doraj, Dax, Ekim, Lessur, and Elana, all of which are superior warriors. I think the surprise is key, but we have no way of getting into that ship without alerting them to our presence."

Sia speaks up, "I may have a solution for that problem. I found plans for technology, in the Haven planetary systems, that creates a field that reflects the visual field aspects back at the direction in which they came. They also have the unique by-product of long and short-range sensor waves being diffracted once they hit the field."

Everyone needs clarification on the jargon. I pose the following question, "Sia... did you just tell us you have a way to hide us from vision AND sensors?"

Doraj excitedly adds, "Yes that is what she's saying! Sia showed me the plans a few days ago but we did not want to get anyone's hopes up until we had a chance to test it."

Sia takes over, "We tested successfully yesterday. We cloaked a small cargo container in the docking bay. Doraj could not detect it visually, and it disappeared from my internal sensors completely but there is a small catch. We can only replicate enough parts to cloak one transport. We can probably cloak the face of the ship so we cloak most of the ship but we do not have the time to do both."

Ronin is excited but is trying to hide it, he strides back and forth across the room looking for holes in the plan he has already formulated in his head. I sit back and wait for him to finish. The male is a genius at everything to do with war and tactics. He is the only reason we got to the point of being able to destroy the Lutetian. Many times the elder warriors questioned his tactics, and they were always wrong to do so. Did we lose many warriors? Yes, but we also won every single battle. Prior to Ronin, it was one-to-one, they would win one then we would win one. We were not getting anywhere. Ronin changed all that. So I have complete faith in the male that stands before me now. Where he directs, I follow.

Without touching my Kokoro he feels my pride in him. He glances at me and sends me warmth, caring, and gratitude then bows his head a bit. I look around the room at Ronin's family, at my family and I am proud of all of them. I glance again at Doraj and notice the bottom of a silver Kokoro sticking out from under his shirt sleeve on his lower left arm. "Doraj congratulations!"

He looks at me confused. "About what?"

"The Kokoro for you and your mate."

He looks at his right arm, "No left bottom. Did you not know?" Doraj looks at his left arm and looks at me confused, "I see nothing."

"Impossible. It's as clear as day!" Now I am a bit confused. Nalax is there, "Nalax, let me see your left lower arm. Please." She lifts her hand, and I see hers clearly as well. "You do not see this one either?"

Doraj is getting frustrated, "This is not funny."

"I am not joking. I do not understand what is happening."

It's Elana who speaks up this time, "I believe I can help." She walks over and stares at me for a bit then nods and looks at Doraj and Nalax's arms. "Can you describe them to us, please?"

I nod, "Silver is like ours, but the design is different. Instead of a split circle, they are intertwined halves. Each half has curled tendrils that reach into the other. The design in one is of a flower, it has six flat pointed petals and four leaves attached to its stem." There are tears running down Nalax's face. "The other half is... gears, wheels, and what looks like an electrical current." I look back at them both, but they are not looking at me. They are looking at each other. I look to Elana, "Why can I only see it?"

She gives me a soft smile, "Back when the Kokoro was more common there were special seers. They could see the designs of the Kokoro before they manifested. They could tell if they were truly committed to each other because they could see if a Kokoro would manifest when they completed their vow to the Goddess. These seers were called The Devoted. They were revered because there is only ever one living."

Shocked, I sit back down, "I do not understand."

"Devoted are chosen by the Goddess. She talks through you. You are special to Her."

"It is true I have always followed the Goddess... I have always felt close to her but," I look nervously at Elana and Ronin, "I have been very angry with her for a long time."

Ronin is the one to respond, "You do not think She understands your anger. Your trials have been great, but I told you, you are special. I have always known it."

I look at Elana, who has a serene smile, "What does this mean? What do I need to do?"

"I do not know, but I know She will show you the way when you are ready. For now," she pulls out a small book from her pocket, "take this. It is what the Ferin study specifically regarding the Kokoro, and the ceremonies associated with them. Read it. She works in strange ways. I grabbed that book today feeling like I needed it for some reason, now I know why." She then returns to her seat.

"I ask you all as a courtesy to me, to not call me the Devoted until I am ready." They all nod.

Ronin comes to my rescue, "How about we return to the mission for now? So we can cloak a transport and eventually we will be able to cloak the ship. That is fantastic news. It gives us an extremely large advantage. We will need to hold that advantage as long as we can so I would ask that we not reveal we have this tech unless absolutely necessary." Everyone nods in agreement.

"Good. Now top priority for Doraj, Sia, and whoever can help them is to get the cloak tech functioning on the transport and as much of the ship as possible." They both nod.

I raise my hand, "I can help. I am pretty good at engineering."

Doraj smiles, "I was hoping you would volunteer."

"Good. So the bridge of this ship is here, and it is where the Cruxlin leadership will be. They are well known for how many high-ranking officers that stay on the bridge at all times. Highly inefficient but works well for us. Sia, when we attacked that first slave outpost you could take over the systems on the Cruxlin ship without them knowing?"

"Yes, I believe so. I can get in through most of the non-critical systems, like cleaning bots or infirmary systems. They are inherently flawed from a security perspective. From there I can easily infiltrate critical systems. What are you thinking Ronin?"

"I think we will do the same thing as you did when we took over this ship. Once we start our offensive, you cut off all communications to the bridge and lock it down. You lock down as many of the combatants as you can in various areas of the ship then we take the ship and clean the ship at the pace we can handle. Thoughts?"

Doraj is the first to voice his thoughts, "That is a good plan but I think we need Sia to find captives, prisoners, and slaves quickly as well so they do not get the opportunity to kill them."

"Agreed. They will if given the opportunity. We should split into teams once we have taken the bridge. Find and liberate the captives and slaves. They will also have beacons on their ship we will need to disable. I would like to state for the record I am very good at getting information out of the vile Cruxlin. I would like to head the interrogation."

"Agreed Dax. You can lead that but I want to be there as well and Elana would be an asset in this as well if she is willing?" Looking at Elana.

"Typically, Ferin try to stay away from that sort of business, but we are at war. I will assist." She looks very determined. I wonder what her capabilities will be. She glances at me and I bow my head to her, "I welcome your assistance." She smiles at me in appreciation.

Ronin grabs our attention again, "So once the ship is clear of most of the Cruxlin and the beacons are destroyed, where do we move the ships to conduct the interrogation?"

Lessur speaks up, "I think there is a black hole in this system. I can work with Sia to find a distance where there is a minor risk but no sensors will be able to see either ship?"

"Good Lessur," Sia says, "That will work well. I can calculate where the optimum safe position would be between the accretion disc and the innermost stable orbit."

"Are there any other things we need to consider?" Ronin asks. "Good. If you think of anything, please do not hesitate to comm or message me. Everyone get some rest. Tomorrow morning we start work on the transport."

CHAPTER

4

Ronin

We are on the transport readying for takeoff. I am looking at the ship that took my mate. Both Dax and I are already in battle fury, we cannot fight it on this. Our instincts are too strong for protecting our mates. We reviewed the plan again late yesterday so everyone has their parts in the operation down.

Sia comes over the comms in the transport, "All cloaking tech is operational and stable. I can no longer detect the transport. I will track your progress from your comm chips. You are ready to launch."

"Doraj, let's go." The shuttle lifts from the floor and heads out the bay doors, starting our trek to the enemy ship. As we get closer, it comes into clear view. Dax stands behind Doraj staring out the window. I can feel his anger, he needs this as much as I do. I need to kill those responsible for taking her. We will have vengeance today. He looks over at me and nods. He knows I need this as well.

Doraj breaks the silence, "Sia, we are in position."

"Acknowledged. Beginning my takeover of ship systems." After a minute, "Take over complete. It was easier than I anticipated. Fools. Opening bay door without fields in place. This will take care of all hostiles within the bay and surrounding hallways." We see the doors opening and the atmosphere vents into space, after a few seconds we see bodies joining the debris. As soon as the door is wide enough, we enter the bay and land, magnetizing the landing gear so it does not blow us into space either.

"No life signs in the bay or surrounding areas. Closing doors."

"Thank you, Sia."

"Bay is repressurized."

"Time to exact my vengeance," I say to no one in particular.

We are in military formation. I am in front, Doraj and Dax flanking me. Behind them are Ekim and Lessur with Elana bringing up the rear. The ship is dirty and cluttered. Fighting would be challenging with Cruxlin if they were decent in combat but they are no better than average.

Sia gives us information as we proceed.

"Seven killed in the bay depressurization."

"Twenty locked down in rooms throughout the ship."

"Ten locked on the bridge with no knowledge of the incursion."

"Five en route to the bay to investigate bulkhead closing then opening to the bay. Contact in twelve seconds."

We stop at a corner and wait for them to arrive. We can hear them now. Just before they round the corner Dax and I attack. The others stay back. It is worth the shocked look on their faces. They are all dead before they even get a shot off. My axe is purple with their blood but my fury is not satisfied. It needs more.

We kill two more soldiers on our way to the bridge. I check around the corner and six stands milling around the bridge door. I turn to Dax with an excited look I whisper, "I have a new skill to show you! There are six milling around the bridge door. I will take out as many as I can with these," I hold up our Mate's throwing daggers, "And you run in and finish the rest."

He smirks, "You will not hit me in the ass with any of those for the arrow incident, are you?"

It is tough for me not to laugh out loud. Instead, I give a mock insulted look, "I would never! On the count of three." On count, I jump to the opposite hallway wall and start releasing blades. I get four before Dax gets close enough to kill the other two.

As I walk up, he turns with a mock pout, "No fair, I only got two, and you got four." One soldier groans, and he smiles and kills him. "There! Now we are even."

As I walk up, he turns with a mock pout, "No fair, I only got two, and you got four." One of the soldiers' groans, and he smiles and kills him. "There! Now we are even."

Now I do laugh. "God I missed this, Dax."

He smiles genuinely at me, "Me too."

Doraj breaks in with disgust, "If you two are done with the love fest can we break into the bridge and do some killing, please? You two have monopolized all the killing." He grumps.

Chuckling, "Ok, ok, Doraj, how about you three lead us in on this one?"

He gets an excited look, "*Excellent!*"

"Just remember to leave a few of the officers alive. Disarm or wound them do not kill them. The rest I do not care about." Dax and I step back and let them ready for the foray onto the bridge."

I tap my ear three times, "OK Sia, on three count..."

Sia counts down and the doors open, we are all focused now and rush the bridge. All combatants are down and only one shot got off. Dax is winged by one shot but it is a minor wound.

June

I am awakened by pain. I fight to regain some level of consciousness. I know the pain is not mine; it is one of my mates' and I panic. I touch my arm. They are fighting someone and looking for me. Dax is hurt, so I send my worry across the link seeking his well-being.

Dax

Everyone is dead except two officers and they are now tied up. Suddenly I feel her. She is panicking. I realize she fears for me; she felt when I the blaster hit my arm and woke in fear for me. I am humbled by my Mate. I look at Ronin and we touch our Kokoro at the same time. I send love and reassurance to her. I am fine; it is just a flesh wound. We are coming for you. I need you, little one. I feel her love for us; it is overwhelming. She falls back under the control of the sedation and is gone. My hand drops from the Kokoro and my head falls to my chest as I try to control my emotions. I feel Ronin's hand on my shoulder and he rests his forehead against mine. "We will find her."

When we pull apart and look at the others Elana has an excited look on her face and her hand covers her mouth. "What is it, Elana?"

Her eyes are teary, "When she connects to you I can see the link... and where it goes."

Ronin asks before I can, "What do you mean? You know where she is?"

"No, I see a filament connected to you both. She is in that direction," she says as she points toward the display in front of the bridge. I close my eyes. It is something. It will help us find her.

I feel Ronin's determination ramp up and we both turn to the prisoners kneeling bound and gagged on the floor. Two are shaking with fear and the other has a look of fury on his face. I stroll over to him and squat down beside him. I point to Ronin, "Do you know who that is?" I do not wait for a response, "That is the last surviving heir of the Nlyaxian royal family." I dislike the calculating look that briefly flashes across his face but I continue, "You stole his Mate who happens is also mine. You should definitely fear him, he is very scary but me, you, and your little minions should be terrified by me. I have survived solar cycles of Lutetian torture. *Solar cycles.* Those Lutetian really have perfected the art." My look becomes extremely menacing, "I plan to use them all on you and that's before I let you speak." He now has the proper amount of fear in his eyes and the others have pissed themselves.

I stand and say to Ronin without looking away from them, "We should find somewhere else to do this. It will be very messy."

Ronin chuckles without genuine mirth, "I know the perfect place. Doraj and team, start cleaning the rest of the ship. Dax, Elana, and I have work to do. Sia, please move both ships to a safe location."

We take the officers to a storage room on the same floor as the bridge so we are not far if something happens. I pick one who looks the weakest of the officers and ties him to the chair I have prepared. He is weeping at this point but I do not care. It's time to start.

After forty minutes, the first is dead. He died of shock. Some species' biologies cannot handle the stress levels of torture, apparently, Cruxlin is one of those species. I walk to the Captain and remove his gag, "So do you have anything you would like to share before we start on your other officer?"

"Kill him too. I do not care; I am giving you no information!" He yells. Good. That is precisely what I was hoping he would do. I put his gag back on. The look on the other's face is fear mixed with fury now. I move him to the chair and remove his gag, "You treacherous filth!" He screams, then looks at me, "What do you want to know?" Excellent.

"Where did you take the human female?"

He gives me a confused look, "We have not had any human females for about fourteen day cycles on this ship." I glance back at Ronin. He nods. He is not lying.

"What about Torgu?"

"We stole a Torgu from the station and delivered it here to the Lutetian. The handoff was about four day cycles ago."

"Do you know their plans for the Torgu?"

"They never tell us their plans for anything. They are secretive and have killed crew for asking in the past."

Again I glance at Ronin. Nod.

Hmmm. "How many human females have you stolen from their homeworld?"

"Our quota is five thousand. We have delivered four thousand one hundred females. We are hoping our next run will net us the last of the Lutetian requirements." He glances at his leader who is furious at this moment.

"Go ahead. He can do nothing to you."

I hear Elana whisper something to Ronin and feel his surprise through the link.

"They intend on continuing the theft of human females once they meet the Lutetian quota. They got a high credit amount for one sold to a Nlyaxian a while back." Ronin growls at this. The Cruxlin pales. "I had nothing to do with that. I have been lobbying the Cruxlin council to cut ties with the Lutetian. They are a treacherous species who will turn on us as soon as we have outlived our usefulness." He is not wrong about that.

He then says something surprising, "I have actually been lobbying the council to get out of the slave trade altogether. There are too many risks and it is an abhorrent practice. That is why they have demoted me, twice."

I turn to Ronin, and to my shock, he nods.

I turn back, and the Cruxlin looks directly into my eyes, "Most people do not know this, but we enslave a majority of our own people on our homeworld. Most hate our current leadership and military."

"Are you one of those?"

"Yes." He looks at Ronin and Elana. Ronin replies, "You do not lie. Why are you in the military then?"

"I was young and idealistic. I thought I could affect change from within. I am a fool. I know my life is forfeit but I will tell you everything you need to know."

I stand and walk to Ronin and Elana. I am not worried about them hearing because Cruxlin have notoriously bad hearing. "Well?"

Elana speaks first, "His expalita is clean." I nod. I have heard of the Ferin's abilities.

Ronin adds, "He has not lied once."

Elana asks, "Can I ask him a few questions?" I nod.

She walks to him and stares for several minutes, "What are your thoughts on the Goddess?"

Again he looks nervously at the Captain then back to Elana, "It means death for me to say this but there is a large population among the slaves that follow the Goddess's teachings. I also follow Her teachings." The Captain screams and sputters through his gag. I walk over and knock him out.

Elana continues, "And what about her teachings called to you?"

"Compassion," is all he says.

Elana turns to Ronin and me, "I believe we should release him and allow him to help us."

To my shock, I say, "I agree. Ronin?"

He nods. We all turn back to a very confused Cruxlin. "What is your name?"

Still confused, "Please call me Sirk. What is happening? Wait! You are the pirates that have been attacking slave routes and stealing slaves?"

"Freeing slaves." Ronin corrects.

"If I join you will you commit to freeing the people of my world when you are able?" He has such a look of hope on his face.

We all smile at him, and Ronin says, "Yes. I think we can commit to that. Dax, cut him free, please."

"Do crazy things like this happen all the time on this crew?" I ask Ronin.

He chuckles, "Yes. Yes, I am afraid they do."

"Are there any other members of this crew like you?" Elana asks him.

Sirk sadly shakes his head, "Unfortunately, I have yet to meet a single like-minded Cruxlin in the military, though I thought there would be."

"You will not automatically be a member of the crew. Like everyone else you will need to prove yourself." Ronin says to him.

Sirk smirks, "How about this for a start? I can show you the location of all the Lutetian outposts known to the Cruxlin."

"Wouldn't all of those be in the ship's systems?"

Sia comes over the comms, "As a matter of fact they are not."

Shocked, Sirk asks, "Who is that? But she is correct. We keep none of the locations in the ship computers per the Lutetian requirement for this exact scenario."

Ronin smiles and slaps Sirk on the shoulder, "Then that information is definitely a start in the right direction. Elana, will you take Sirk to the infirmary and get him patched up please?" She nods and leads him out.

I tap my comm three times, "Team, we have a new Cruxlin recruit named Sirk. Please do not shoot him."

Doraj responds, "Uh what?"

Chuckling, "I know sounds crazy right? We will explain later."

Still confused, he replies, "Ok... I guess."

I look at the captain who came back around at some point. He is laying on the floor glaring at us. "What do we do with him then?"

"Hmmm. I did not get to interrogate anyone." He says in mock disappointment. Fear reappears on the captain's face. Chuckling he says, "No. Let us just space him. He is not worth our time." He sputters behind his gag again.

Elana comes over the coms, "Ronin, you need to come to the infirmary now."

I look to Ronin. He pulls a blaster and shoots the captain then runs out of the room for the infirmary.

As we enter, Ronin asks, "What is it, Elana?"

She steps out of our line of sight and in an infirmary pod is a Nlyaxian with bandages wrapped around his head. Ronin roars at the sight of him and launches himself at the Nlyaxian. I have never seen him so angry and out of control.

Ronin

Sitruc lies comfortably in a med pod. He lies comfortably while they have stolen my Mate from me. Sitruc is mine. I land on the pod with my feet on either side of his head. "Sitruc, what happened to your face?" I say it with such malice I know he will not mistake it for actual concern. The stench of urine hits my nose. "Did you piss yourself, Sitruc? Are you scared because you know *who I am*?" I cannot help but scream the last part.

"Y-y-your mate did this to me. She took my eyes!"

I laugh, "You fucking idiot. Did you think to take advantage of my warrior mate?"

"Ronin," Dax calls to get my attention. I look back at him, and he signals to me to look at something further down the bed. Sitruc is trying to hide something on his arm. I jump down from the bed and walk around to the other side, staring at the spot on his arm. I grab the arm he is trying to hide and pull it free. What I see there cools my fury then it amplifies it a hundred times worse than it was. On his arm is a patch of skin that is not his and it has gold shirka dots on it.

Both Dax and I let out a concussive roar that rattles the walls in the infirmary. I grab him by the hair and pull him from the bed. I walk back to the room we were just in while he cries as I drag him behind me. Dax and Doraj follow me into the room and we close the door.

As I get ready to rip the first limb from his body Dax says, "Ronin we need information first." I give him a menacing growl. "*Ronin*! Think of June." That reprimand is able to bring me out of my battle fury enough that logic returns. I close my eyes in an attempt to regain focus.

"Thank you, Dax. Information is needed." On the trip from the infirmary, Sitruc's bandages fell off to reveal he still has one functioning eye, but the other is completely gone, just a socket in where it's supposed to be. Now I need to test if I can still detect lies from him.

"Sitruc, you will answer my question or I will torture you slowly before I kill you. Do you understand?"

"I understand."

"Good. Whose skin have they grafted to your arm?"

He pauses. "*Whose skin?*" I roar at him.

"It is Kaxlin's skin."

"What was your intent in having it grafted to your body?"

He cries again, "He was my friend. I wanted a piece of him."

Got him. I can detect his lies. I smile, "Do you think I cannot detect your lies because one eye is gone, and the other is damaged? Lie to me again and I remove part of a limb. Now tell me the truth." His blubbering sickens me. I can hardly believe he is the same species as me.

"I thought I could control your mate's shirka if I had it grafted to me."

Growling, I ask, "And what were you planning to do with that control?"

"I wanted to fuck her."

Dax loses control. He is on top of Sitruc pummeling him. I have to pull him off because we have got no factual information from him. "*Dax! June!*" He quiets and regains control but still is deep in battle fury. I put my forehead to his. "We need information." He nods.

I return to Sitruc and return him to his knees.

"Where is my mate?"

"I do not know."

"*Where is my mate?*"

Blubbering, "I do not know. They only mentioned getting to the outpost."

He does not lie. "Who are you working for?"

"Lutetian."

Dax speaks again, "You fucking traitor!"

"Why do they want her?"

"They don't."

I need some clarification. Dax says, "Who do they want?"

"Ronin."

Dax

When he says Ronin's name I have to fight my battle fury for a while before I am calm enough to look at him again without killing him.

"Why do they want him?"

"I do not know."

I scream, "*Why do they want him?*"

"I do not know."

Ronin interrupts me. "He tells the truth."

I look at Ronin and whisper, "They cannot have you."

He puts his forehead to mine again, "And they will not." I try to relax but cannot. They have my Mate and now I find out they want my best friend, the prime of my Triad, no.

Doraj asks, "They sent you after June to draw out Ronin?"

"Yes. They know she is his mate. That he would come for her if we took her."

Doraj continues, "How do they know she is his?"

"I told them. I knew Ronin would never take a female by force so when I saw them together in his bunk I knew what she was to him."

"How do they communicate with you?" He asks.

"I have a subspace communicator they gave me. It's in my quarters."

"What do you know about the Lutetian that we do not?" Interesting question from Doraj. Now I am curious.

"They do not have a governing body or even a military hierarchy. They have one Queen. I have not met her but the Lutetian fear her. They shake in fear even when they just hear her voice."

"How is that possible? How does she communicate and direct all the Lutetian?"

"I am not sure but I can tell you the Lutetian I have interacted with seem like a different being sometimes. One minute they are almost single-mindedly on their task, the next they speak like a master tactician."

Ronin paces slowly for a few minutes, then turns to Doraj and me, "Is it possible there is only a Queen? We always believed there was a military hierarchy because their tactics are advanced. If so, how does she do it? Can she control them via her mind? Across the vastness of space? It is almost too hard to believe."

"Not that hard though, if they can pull me into their mind traps wherever I am? No, I think it's believable."

I look to Sitruc, "You have never seen her?"

He shakes his head, "I never wanted to. The way the Lutetian behave when they hear her made me very wary." He gets a strange look, "She mentioned once she had allies but... I do not think she trusts them because she said something like she 'needs her army to ensure they comply.' I do not think she was really talking to me, she was furious when she found out you were alive at first."

"Anything else?" I ask him.

He thinks for a minute then shakes his head.

I had not heard Elana come in, but she steps forward, "He has no other useful information. Let me take it from here. Do not sully your expalita with his blood."

He looks for Ronin even though he cannot see, "Ronin please I answered your questions, a clean, quick death."

Ronin looks at Elana and nods, "So be it."

He sighs in relief. I am not sure I agree he deserves a quick death but hopefully the information he gave us will give us some advantage.

Five hours later the ship has been cleared of all enemies and we are gathered on the bridge with Nalax on the display. She is unhappy about our decision regarding Sirk but she will adjust. Once she hears what we have, she will change her mind.

"Sia, are there any remaining beacons or signals coming off this ship?"

"No, Ronin. The ship is not broadcasting."

"Good. I do not believe we have enough information to pursue any angles. Sirk I would like you to spend as much time as possible giving Sia all the information you have on the Lutetian installations." He nods. "I believe our best option right now is to return to Haven and staff crew positions on both ships. Thoughts?"

Dax growls, "I am sorry. I am frustrated."

"I know Dax, so am I but I hope that the information Sirk will give us and the information we received from Sitruc will give us the intel we need to make logical choices of where she may be."

He nods, still not happy, but I can tell he agrees.

"No one else? Good. Sia when it's safe pull us from the accretion disc then we'll get everyone to the appropriate ships and start back to Haven."

Dax

We landed at Haven about ten day cycles ago. The planet is beautiful, but I hated seeing it for the first time without June. I understand why she chose this home. It is the perfect location. I wonder if she realizes its similarities to our valley. The grass is different but the river and the falls are there, the distance tree lines. It is perfect. I am sitting on the veranda trying to relax enough where I can sleep. The longer I am away from her the harder it gets for me to sleep. I shut my eyes and listen to the falls in the distance.

I am in our valley. It is almost a disappointment to me to be here because I know she is not. I feel her stronger this time but something is off. There is something that doesn't belong here. I walk in the direction I feel her, and in the distance I see something laying by the river. Is it... I run as fast as I can. It is her. She looks like she fell where she lies. I stop at her side and drop to my knees. She looks blankly at the sky. I gently pick her up and cradle her in my arms.

"June, my Mate. Please look at me. June." I am begging her to respond.

Her eyes blink once then focus on my face. A small smile spreads across her face. "Is it you?"

Her eyes blink once then begin to focus on my face. A small smile spreads across her face. "Is it you?"

"Yes, little one it is me."

"You look different... less sad."

"Because of you, I am less sad but more worried," I smirk at her.

She chuckles, "Yeah sorry about that I was distracted and not paying attention to my surroundings. This is my fault."

"No, little one. Not yours or mine. The blame lies with the Lutetian."

She shivers at their mention.

"How long have you been out of sedation?"

"I'm not completely sure. It feels like a long time but in reality, it's probably been two, maybe three days. I can't really tell the passage of time where they have me." She raises her hand to trace the ridges on my cheek. Her touch is so light. Her fingers move to my neck then she is pulling me to her. I kiss gently but it is not enough for her. She pulls her naked body against mine and deepens the kiss. I cannot resist her. It has been so long and I have been so worried for her. She sits up and moves to lie back in the grass. "You are so beautiful my mate."

"Dax, I need you."

I could never deny her. I can smell her desire for me. I settle myself between her legs because I know we both need this now. I slowly push into her. She is so tight; I feel her body stretching to accommodate my size. Her moans are like music to me. When I am fully seated, I look into her eyes and feel her surrounding my cock and surrounding me with love in our minds. I groan and pull back and push slowly in. The sensations she creates along my cock are exquisite.

I can no longer hold back. I thrust into her faster and faster, blindly driving us to the edge. When her sex locks down on my cock as her orgasm hits, my sprili unfurl and drives her pleasure higher. I can no longer hold my own, and as mine hits and releases my seed, she screams my name as the sprili vibrate.

I collapse trying to keep as much of my weight off her as I can. I roll so she lies on top of me. We lay in silence for a bit but then I have to ask, "June, why did they wake you?" She sits up pulling my cock further into her body and rises then pushes down. I groan and grab her hips, "June. Please."

She sighs and lays back down on my chest. "I'm sorry. I don't want to have this conversation."

"June what is it?"

"I'm not sure where to start. They have been torturing me the last few days." Growl. "I know please Dax, I need you to listen." She lifts her face from my chest and grabs both sides of my face. "You must not come for me. It's what they..." She gives a blood-curdling scream and disappears.

I come awake screaming as well because I could feel her pain.

Ronin is up with knives in hand looking for an enemy. He shakes off the sleep and realizes something happened.

"What? What happened? Did you see her?"

Still breathing heavily I nod, "She is awake. Ronin they are torturing her."

He looks lost not knowing what to do. He roars his frustration and then sits naked on the floor of the veranda. Looking at the floor, "I have never felt so helpless in my life as I do right now."

"She said she does not want us to come for her."

Anger flares on his face then he stops, "What did she say exactly?"

"'You must not come for me. It's what they...' then she screamed and disappeared."

He stands and stalks around the veranda. "She knows they are after me. She is trying to protect us from it." After a few minutes, he stops and looks at me. "She is awake?" I nod. He touches the Kokoro on his arm and nods for me to do the same. I close my eyes and focus on June. I reach for her and find a wall. I touch it with my mind. My eyes snap open, "She blocks us!"

His anger flares again, "She tries to protect us from it, from knowing what she suffers. No! Help me break it. She may be with them but she is not alone, and this is currently our only way to help her!"

We both refocus on getting through the barrier she has created. She may have been strong enough to keep one of us out but there is no way she can keep us both out. I feel the barrier weakening and giving way. We both gasp at the level of pain she endures. "Ronin we can take the burden of her pain but do not take it all or they will know." We both start shouldering a portion of her pain. I feel her relax into allowing us to help her. I then feel her gratitude and sorrow for blocking us. I let my love for her rush out to wash over her and Ronin does the same. After a few hours, I feel them heal her. Once they are done, they put her back under sedation and I relax. I open my eyes and Ronin has passed out on the floor. I stand and pick him up.

As I lay him down in bed he wakes. "What happened??"

"They healed her and put her back under sedation. Sleep, Ronin." He nods and falls asleep immediately. I stand and walk back outside. He is not accustomed as I am to the pain of their torture. I am glad they did not do their worst to her. I hope it stays that way.

Now the worst is over. I focus on the dream. They sedated her, I would think I could get to her mind. She controlled the dreams. I need information... I walk into the living room and tap my ear once, "Sia, do you have a minute?"

She chuckles, "I do not sleep, Dax. You can call anytime."

I chuckle as well, "Oh yeah. I have some questions you may have the answer for."

"I will try."

"Does any other species besides humans and me have dreams?"

"Let me have a look." After about ninety seconds, "Yes three other species from the database have dreams including the species that built Haven."

"Good. Do any of them report the ability to control the dreams?"

"The species database only records the species abilities to have them not much beyond that. The species who build Haven, their database is vast. It will take me several days to go through it looking for more references to dreams and dreaming. Would you like me to do that?"

"Yes please, Sia. I need answers I'm not sure anyone can give me."

"I will let you know when my analysis is complete."

"Thank you."

I am tired now from taking as much as possible from her. I walk in and lay down next to Ronin; he rolls and wraps an arm over my chest. He always was a cuddler.

Ronin calls a crew meeting first thing. We are waiting in the conference room at the community center for everyone to arrive. He paces slowly back and forth across the room. He worries me. The penalty of being the child of a royal family is the inherent responsibility. He believes everything is his to bear.

"I feel your worry, Dax. I am fine."

"Ronin, I know you are fine. My worry for you is because you try to shoulder all the weight, all the responsibility, all the blame." I say that with a little more frustration than I mean to. "I just mean, you are no longer alone. I am here for you. The burden is not yours alone. Allow me to help."

He walks to me and at first; I think he is angry with me but he grabs my neck and put his forehead to mine, closing his eyes.

"Forgive me. Sometimes I forget. I know you are here for me Dax and you cannot know how much it means to me that you are."

I smirk. "I think I do."

He chuckles, "Yes you probably do. I am sorry, my brother. I will try to share the burden. It is sometimes difficult for me."

Doraj comes into the room laughing, "Difficult my friend? It is extremely hard for you." He gets serious and says, "You have many who wish to lighten your burden. We are all here for you." They clasp arms.

Elana chuckles, "You three are going to make me cry."

We all laugh at that.

"Alright, enough fun at Ronin's expense, even if it is hilarious." It is good to see him laughing and interacting with friends. Before the fall, Ronin only talked and interacted socially with Aanon and I. He had withdrawn from everyone else. Professionally he was still the High Commander, but that was nearly his only inter-action. His break with his mother seriously affected him.

"Alright, Dax and I do not want to hide anything from our family, so we have something to tell you." He looks at me.

"Last night June was out from under sedation. I found her in our dream valley. She tried to tell me to not look for her, that it's what they want." They all look angry or confused. "They then pulled her from the dream screaming in pain. They are torturing her. Through the Kokoro, we could shoulder some of her pain. After several hours they healed her and put her back under sedation."

Silence fills the room. Looking at the beings my Mate calls family, I see battle fury, tears, and anger. But what I see in them the most, is determination. Good, because we are going to need that.

"I know that hearing this is hard. Now we need a plan and we need to find her." The tears are gone and in their place is the conviction we need.

Ronin takes over, "Doraj, we have both ships crewed and all new members vetted?"

"Yes. We have filled all necessary positions. All have started combat training but most already have some sort of training. The number of volunteers was surprising. We have more than enough for full compliments in both ships without Haven suffering the loss."

"Ronin, I need to bring something up that I am not sure you will like." He nods for me to continue, "Right now I am slated to be on the same ship as you," I see his anger flare. He knows where I am going with this, "Ronin, one of us should be on each ship in case the other finds her." He thinks through what I am saying and his anger deflates.

"I agree but I hate the idea of separating."

"I do too but I would hate even more if one of us wasn't there for her when she is found." He nods.

"Ok, that is settled. On the Emancipation are Doraj, Nalax, Sirk, and myself. On the... hmmm what do we call the newest ship in our fleet?" He asks everyone.

Nalax softly says, "Liberation because we will liberate my sister." I nod at her. I like it.

"Liberation it is. On the Liberation will be Ekim, Lessur, Dax, and Elana. We have already assigned those who volunteered to each ship."

"Ronin," Sia says hesitating, "I would like to help the system on the Liberation to become sentient. So they have an AI like me to help them."

Ronin is quiet while he considers, but I have questions, "Sia, how similar will this AI be to you? I have the utmost trust in you, but a new AI makes me nervous."

"I understand Dax. I have built a plan to teach the new AI. It will have all my memories of interactions with other species. I believe it will develop as I have."

"I have the same concerns, but I trust Sia. She would never endanger the mission to save June. If she thinks this will help, then I will let her try." Ronin surprises me with this statement, but I am good with his decision.

"Thank you, Ronin. I will start immediately."

"Lessur your crew is set." Ronin's statement surprises Lessur but I am not.

"What's wrong, Lessur?" I ask him.

"Well, I just thought that since you were a ranking officer…"

"While that is true I have been through things that would make it difficult at times to lead. You are the right choice."

"Thank you both for your trust in me. I will not let you down."

"We know," I say to him. Ronin gives me a look of pride.

Ronin, always on task says, "On to the details of the information gathered. Sirk, can you review what we discussed please?"

"Of course. Thank you. Sia, can you bring up the map we built please?" A map comes up on the big display. It shows a wide swath of this sector and an adjoining sector of the galaxy. There are eight red dots spread across both sectors. "This map shows all the rendezvous points or planetary bodies where the Cruxlin have met with the Lutetian for supplies or stock transfer," Nalax growls. "Sorry, sorry, I mean slave transfer. Please forgive me."

Nalax relaxes but only slightly. Ronin interrupts, "It's fine but let us not use that language again please."

"Yes, sir." Sirk looks very nervous now.

I walk over and put my hand on his shoulder, "It is fine. We all have pasts and some things we are not proud of. You are helping us a great deal, and I appreciate it."

He looks at me in appreciation, "Thank you, Dax."

"So the red points with yellow circles around them are points in space where we met their ships so I highly doubt she is there. If we remove those we have three Lutetian bases left. This one close to the Vanin Nebulae is no more than a warehouse for goods, so

I think we can safely assume she is also not there. That leaves these two known bases. One is the original Lutetian homeworld, and the other is basically a very large asteroid that orbits a large gas giant. These both look uninhabited but they are definitely not. Both have at least two hundred Lutetian on them. They also have some of their genetically manipulated soldiers, but the number of those is interestingly low."

Ronin sits forward, "Why do you think that?"

"The Cruxlin dealt a lot with the Lutetian even before the wars. In those times their bases had thousands of mutated soldiers. On the last several trips we had to the asteroid installation I actually got to go down to the base. There was only a handful in any one location, even in the docking bay where there is the largest risk for the incursion."

"Did you even get to go down to the Homeworld base?"

Shaking his head, "No. No one is ever allowed to go down onto their homeworld. To do so is death. We had an incompetent Captain who was insulted he could not meet with the Lutetian leadership. He took a shuttle down with his staff. With no warning, they shot it out of the sky."

"Are there weapons on the surface?" I ask, surprised. That would give away their position relatively quickly.

He shakes his head again, "No. There is no clear landing area or buildings, no weapons platforms, for all intents and purposes it looks like an abandoned dead planet. The shot that destroyed the transport came from a rock face that only contains caves."

Ronin and I glance at each other. This nearly confirms what we suspect. "What?" Doraj asks seeing the exchange.

Ronin steps forward from the wall he was leaning against, "Dax and I suspect the Lutetian outmaneuvered us when they set off the weapons that destroyed their world. We believe they actually live in the caves and tunnels under the surface of their world so when they set off the weapons..."

Doraj finishes, "They were safely alive under the surface. Those vile bastards."

"At that point, we had severely depleted their numbers, especially their mutated soldiers. The war ended almost nine years ago so I do not understand why their mutated soldier population would not be at higher levels. They have had the time and virtually no oversight or outside control. Why do they not have more?" I ask.

Ronin paces, and mumbles, "Why wouldn't they? Why stop producing mutated soldiers? Have they stopped? If they have not, where are they?" He paces for a few more minutes then stops and looks at me. "The only reason they would stop producing mutated soldiers would be if they had another source for soldiers but who? Sirk, have you seen any other type of soldier in your dealings with the Lutetian?"

He shakes his head.

Ronin sighs, "I do not think we are to find an answer to this yet but we need to soon. I do not want to go into these bases blind."

"We may have to." I have to tell him what he does not want to hear because I will go in to find her even if we do not know. He knows this, he knows me. "How does the information the traitor gave us change our tact, if at all?"

Sirk asks, "What traitor? What info did they give?"

Ronin thinks for a while, "So we now know they have a Queen and no other leadership which means if we kill her army will have no orders. They will descend into chaos."

"Yes, but she has allies though we do not know who, their numbers, or their military might. That is a pretty sizeable gap in our information." I am concerned a great deal by this information.

Ronin looks to Elana, "Do you or could your people know who these allies could be?"

She shakes her head, "I do not but I can reach out to the council to see if they have any ideas."

Ronin nods but I can tell he is still worried about this information. An unknown foe is never something you want to deal with. He paces for a while.

"So none of that information really changes anything," I state, frustrated, "We have to find her and ensure they do not get their hands on Ronin. I do not care what her plan is right now."

Ronin gives me a sad look, "But we must. If she is rebuilding her army and has allies, she has plans and we need to understand those."

I nod, "I understand Ronin but we cannot leave her with them even a second longer than we have to. They are barbaric and have no compassion."

"I know that!" He says hotly. He closes his eyes, "I know that Dax and I agree." He rubs his face in frustration, "I agree but I will not rush in unprepared like I did at the station."

I understand now. He still blames himself. "Alright, Ronin. Let us prepare."

He nods in thanks, "Good. So we have two bases, one a black hole of information, the other barely any information. Neither is good but one is worse. We no longer need to go to the Lutetian world to figure out if they are still there, we know they are. The biggest problem with this location is we do not know the number of enemies on that base or if it's just a decoy. We know they defend it. On the asteroid, we have more information. We know it has a Lutetian population and a small contingent of mutated soldiers. We do not know if June is at either base. She could be at neither."

I decide to add, "We have advantages. One, we now have cloaking tech for transports and the Emancipation. Two, we know from a tactical perspective we are better than the Lutetian except for when the Queen is directing her people. Three, if June connects to us Elana can see the thread of the connection. None of these are insignificant in their own right but together they are a substantial advantage for us."

Doraj says, "With the unknowns, I cannot say I think it is a good idea to split the ships."

Ronin is pacing again, "Logically I agree with you Doraj but I am having a difficult time. The idea of not using the two ships as a way to cover more space to find her is creating great conflict in me. My logical mind agrees. We should attack one because we do not know the number of enemies at either base but if we attack one and not the other she will know we are coming."

Elana interrupts, "But that is what she wants, right? She wants Ronin to come for June. We know it. Let us use that against her."

Ronin's face lightens dramatically, "Elana, I am so glad you became friends with our Mate!"

She smiles and briefly nods to him.

"Elana is absolutely correct. She expects me to be looking for June. She wants me to find her so she can capture me for what we do not know but we can use that information against her."

Everyone chats with one another. I am angry and worried about what he is coming up with.

"I feel your anger, Dax. I will not proceed with any plan without your support. Alright?"

I am relieved a bit by his words but I am still worried, "Ronin, you should let me go in your place." I immediately feel his anger spike and know I made a mistake.

"*What* because I am more important than you?! *No! No* Dax! I will not lose you again..." then he almost whispers, "I will not." It is then I truly see the damage losing Aanon, and I has done to him, and now he has also lost our Mate.

"Alright, Ronin. I understand but know this; we are equally important. We go in together." He looks at me as if weighing something in his mind, then nods.

Ronin

Dax is wrong. There is nothing more important than my Triad and my Mate. I would give my life for them. I will respect his wishes but if it comes down to me or them, there is no question, not for me.

"So what are you thinking for your plan?" Doraj asks.

"Hmmm. I need to walk through them. The Queen wants me to find her, correct?" He nods. "So how does she do that without giving herself away?"

Everyone is quiet, Nalax speaks quietly, "She sends a Nlyaxian traitor to do it, in the hopes we catch him and he tells us something that will help us. So what did he tell us that would help us find her?"

Dax snaps his fingers, "In the beginning, he said they referred to the outpost. That has to be the asteroid, they would not call their homeworld an outpost."

"Good, good." I murmur, "Now would she risk keeping June at the outpost she is drawing me to?"

"Yes. I think she will assume she has to," Elana says.

"Why is that?" I ask.

"Yes." Dax says, "Think about it, everyone knows Nlyaxian Mate lore. We do not hide it. She will believe you will be able to feel if she is not there."

"Dax we will be able to tell if she is there or not." He gives me a confused look.

"How do you think we knew you were on the station?"

He gets a shocked look, "But... I just thought it was a coincidence. Luck... I do not know. But you knew?"

I nod, "It was the reason we were both so distracted. We did not think you were there, we knew it."

Elana murmurs, "So she will assume we will know or not if June is there so she will have to keep her at the outpost." She looks at me, "Which means she will need an army there to protect her."

"Maybe." I pace, "If the Lutetian have proven anything to me it is their or I guess her arrogance. She will think it is just me and my crew of pirates... maybe she will believe a large contingent is unnecessary."

Dax and Doraj both shake their heads. Dax is the one to voice their concern, "That is a pretty large gamble Ronin. If she puts a large contingent, then we are captured."

Sirk looks like he has something to say. I nod to him, "The outpost, if it is the asteroid, is easier than the homeworld base."

"Why is that?" Elana asks.

"I already told you we have been allowed to the surface of that base many times. We use the Liberation. There are many ways to mask biosignatures so you all look like Cruxlin to their sensors."

Nalax adds, "We already have several disguises that we could reconfigure to be Cruxlin."

"None of us would pass as Cruxlin even with disguises. We are too big."

Doraj sees it before I do, "No! No Nalax I will not allow you to go onto that base!"

She lifts a delicate eyebrow at him, "*Allow* me Doraj. We shall speak in the hall." He is sputtering mad but follows Nalax into the hallway.

Elana looks back at me, "It is not a bad idea. Sirk, Nalax, and I go down to the base. Nalax and I disguised as Cruxlin. Sirk is Cruxlin so he will blend our little party well. The rest of you can be on the shuttle disguised as the mutated soldiers and at some point sneak off the shuttle and make your way to June."

"I will not go against Doraj's wishes." Elana's eyes have a fire behind them.

"It is not Doraj's decision," she says with more than a bit of venom. I am ready to yell at her when Doraj interrupts, "She is right." He has a determined look, "If I try to force my will on my Mate, I am no better than they are."

I open my mouth but before I can speak Dax interrupts, "They are right Ronin? It is part of the Goddess's teachings."

I chuckle, "Yes I agree. I let my emotions get the better of me. Forgive me Nalax, Elana." They both nod. I look to Dax, "I was getting there."

He barks a laugh, "Sorry Ronin but sometimes you are very stubborn." Everyone laughs, and I act offended but cannot keep it up and laugh with them.

"Alright so now we need to start the proper planning for this operation but rest for tonight. We will regroup in the morning. I want to launch the day after."

____

June

I am dreaming but I am not in Dax's valley. I am also not on Earth in a dream of my making. The Lutetian cannot torture me in my dreams, oh they've tried, and I have killed every one of them. It's actually why they physically tortured me. Someone was very upset that I killed several of their dream torturers.

But this place is different, it feels different. It looks very similar to Dax's valley but where the valley was wild and free, this is quiet and quaint. There is a house in the distance. The surrounding land grows in rows like a farm on Earth.

Surprisingly I am clothed. I wear my favorite sundress from Earth. It's short, only reaching my mid-thighs, has spaghetti straps, and a pretty floral print. I wear my favorite purple Chuck's. The best shoes on planet Earth. All in all, a pleasant dream which differs from my dreams since they took me from Earth.

I start slowly wandering down the road I stand on toward the house. I've decided this will be my time to relax and enjoy the sun. I walk and lift my face, enjoying the warmth. As I get closer to the house I hear chopping, like someone chopping wood. Let's see who it is.

I wander around the side of the house. I admire it as I go. It's beautiful. It is shaped like a dome. And I see large openings that look to be veranda on the second floor. On the ground level, I see what looks kind of like a garage opening but with no door to close. The structure is a light purple color that is perfectly accented to the grass. I giggle a bit because it is too perfect.

When I come around the corner I stop in my tracks. Chopping wood is the biggest Nlyaxian I have ever seen. He is barely putting any effort into chopping wood larger than five feet across. He is slightly different color than the Nlyaxians I have seen. He is a much lighter green, like the color of spring grass at my house when I was younger. He is not wearing a shirt so I see all his muscles and contours. He is magnificent. The pants he wears are like the ones Ronin wears, Nlyaxian military issue and I must say his ass is fine in them as well.

As I am admiring the stranger's ass, of course, this is when he turns and see exactly what I am admiring. I feel my face flush. When he speaks his voice is pure bass, "And who have we here?" Oh my Goddess, that voice alone makes me wet.

He arches his brow waiting for my response, shit, "June. My name is June."

"June is a beautiful name, but it is not Nlyaxian and neither are you. What species are you?"

"I am from a planet called Earth. My species is called Human." I smile at him. I cannot help it, he is beautiful. He returns my smile and I swear my heart nearly stops.

"Would you like some refreshments? It is a warm day."

"Sure. I'd like that."

"Come, you can sit on my porch in the shade." He leads me inside his home and onto the veranda I saw earlier. I sit in a chair that is

too big for me but I don't mind. He comes back with glasses on a tray and the drinks sound a lot like tea. I love it.

"This is your farm?"

"Yes, it belonged to my family." He gets a sad look and I cannot stand it on his face.

"What do you grow?"

He tells me all the things he grows. It is all some kind of produce. "I can sustain myself here without ever leaving. It is a peaceful place for me." He gives me a sexy smirk, "That is until you showed up." Who boy! This male seems to be my fixation already.

"Sorry, I didn't mean to disturb you." I start to get up but he lays a hand on my arm to stop me. His touch sends electricity up my arm. He's looking at where his hand touches my arm and whispers, "What are you?"

His eyes dart to mine, "Please stay." All I can do is nod because I do not trust my voice. He moves his hand but instead of taking it away, he moves it to cup my cheek. I need his touch it comforts me. I close my eyes at the soft touch.

I open my eyes. This is a dream. I stand and walk over to him. He sits on a chair with no arms. I straddle his legs and sit on his lap, his cock rests at my clit. We both close our eyes at the sensation. When I open them again, he has a conflicted look on his face. I lift my hands and trace the ridges on his face with my fingers. His eyes close.

I realize I need to stop I am not sure he wants this. I pull my fingers back, "Forgive me. I did not ask permission." He grabs my hips so I cannot move and puts his forehead to mine.

"Please. Please do not stop. I should not allow it. I am unfit."

My eyes snap open, "Aanon?"

Shock registers on his face.

Pain makes me scream, and I am awake once again with their torturers.

I hear the awful hissing that is the way they laugh. "Sstupid human. You killed the Queensss favorite Ssoul Tormentor."

"I have no idea what you are talking about."

"*You do!*" It seems to yell, but it's not very loud. "You do sstupid. You killed the Ssoul Tormentor of the Nlyaxian. You pulled him out."

I chuckle, "You mean the spider that was torturing Dax?"

"Yess. Dax. You have locked hiss mind. How did you do that? How do you keep usss out of your mind? "

"No clue, and fuck off."

It laughs in its gross hissing way, "Good. Good. Now I get to have fun."

I did not consider it fun, at all. But I walled my mind once again. I cannot let them feel it again. I could feel their pain because of me. I don't want them to come for me. I do not know why they want Ronin but they will not have him if I have anything to do with it.

As it goes about cutting, I try to pull myself away from my body. I still feel it and scream. I think about killing it... slowly. Killing it as I did to the one in Dax's dream. I had control there. Maybe next time, I'll let them in. Perhaps I can control it there and kill them. I just need to figure out how to let them in.

It doubles down on the torture I cannot focus while screaming.

When I wake, I am once again in a cell. It seems they have completely healed the damage wrought by the spider. There is not even a scar. It's the third time they have pulled me out to torture me. I thought Kaxlin was my hell. This is worse, and knowing I am carrying Ronin's child while they do this... it's too much. I cry and cannot stop. I turn to the wall so they cannot see.

I wake, lying in a field of tall purple grass under a massive tree with dark gray bark and purple leaves moving in the breeze. I do not feel like moving. I still feel emotionally drained here.

A large shadow blocks the sun from my face. Aanon. He squats and gathers me into his arms. He walks toward his house in the distance. He is so careful with me. Tears begin to roll down my face. Am I making him up? Ronin said Dax is the only Nlyaxian who dreamt.

But here he is, he feels real, well as real as can be in a dream. I want him to be real. The bass in his voice rumbles through me, "Are you ok little one?"

The concern in his voice starts the tears again. "I'm sorry. I am dealing with a lot. I am not sure I can handle much more."

He sits in a chair on the porch we were on last night and gathers me close. "I am not so sure about that. You seem very strong to me. You look strong enough to handle anything." He rocks the chair.

"I don't feel strong."

"I rarely feel strong." At my shocked look, he chuckles. "I am large but I do not always feel strong. My whole life I saw the way my parents cared for each other. I had fifteen siblings. All I wanted was my own Triad, my own brood of little ones." He gets a tortured look, "they declared me unfit then the males meant for me died."

His sadness is too much for me. I sit up in his lap, "Aanon. Ronin and Dax did not die."

It's his turn for the shock. I pull his face so he is looking at me again. "Ronin is my prime and Dax is my second."

He whispers, "No. It's not possible."

I turn in his lap and grab his face, "It is true. I am the female Dax visited in his dreams as a child. I am the female that Ronin asked to be her prime. You are the last link in my Triad. Please believe me."

He stares at me for a long time and gets a sad look on his face, "I do. I knew in my heart they could not be gone. I would feel it if they were truly gone." He refocuses on my face and lifts his hands to cup it. His thumbs stroke across both cheeks. "I cannot be your third, I am unfit."

June

I am jolted awake by the soldier kicking me in the leg. He is obviously one of the mutated soldiers Ronin was talking about. He is from a nightmare. It looks like it was maybe Nlyaxian but now it is a sickly brownish-green color. It has boney spikes down its arms and is growing from its skull. His eyes are red and his teeth are extremely sharp and pointy. Where it differs most from the Nlyaxians I have seen is his muscles. Its muscle mass is seriously less than any I have seen. It's probably still strong but far less than Ronin or Dax. "Move. Go in front." He points his blaster at the door.

Well, I'm not looking forward to walking around naked again but I have little choice. I walk out of the cell and realize I am not on a ship like I thought. The tunnel walls are dark and smooth but they are rock. So I'm in a cave system of some sort. It directs me through the hallways but we do not leave the floor. He puts me in another cell but this one is different. It's bigger. I look around the room. The sanishower, toilet, and sink are the same, but the bed is bigger. Strange.

I walk the room like I did in the other, to see if there are any weaknesses or something I can use as a weapon. As I am looking around the perimeter of the bed, the door opens again. A Nlyaxian walks in followed by a mutated guard. He is completely naked, and they tied his hands behind his back. He looks pissed.

His eyes register shock then he schools them again. The mutant leaves and we are alone together. I move to the side of the room farthest from him. I hear a little snick and his arms are free. He brings his arms forward and rubs his wrists.

"Mate with her." Comes over the speakers in the room in a hiss. Oh, fuck no. I read myself for a fight. I will die before I allow that to happen again.

The Nlyaxian surprises me, "No."

Interesting. I study him but remain ready to fight. He is slightly shorter than Ronin and not as big but still huge compared to humans. He studies me as well but does not look surprised. "I will not force myself on you."

Like I'm just going to believe him. "Mate with her now!" They say again.

"No."

Angry noises come from the speaker. "Mate her or we kill her!"

He gets a concerned look and glances at me. "They won't kill me. They need me." More angry sounds come over the speaker and I laugh.

"Ssstupid human. You will sssstay in the mating pod until you mate him."

I look at the Nlyaxian, "Looks like we're gonna be roomies."

He smirks, "I will not mate you but you are definitely nice to look at." On Earth, that statement would have made me super self-conscious but now I just nod in thanks. Trust is earned here so my readiness is still high.

He walks to the opposite wall and sits down—a good sign. In good faith, maybe a little conversation, "I am June. What is your name?"

"Do you really wish to know?" His entire bearing screams downtrodden. They have almost broken him. I want to know his name.

"Yes, I do."

He looks at me for a minute, "Divad is my name."

"How did you end up here, Divad?"

"I am not really sure. We were all in shock after seeing our homeworld destroyed. I remember something like an electrical shock and I could see it happening to everyone around me. When I woke, I was here alone."

"Where were you when it happened?"

"Nlyaxian military transport ship. We were watching the coronation from orbit and afterward, we were going for training ops on a remote planet."

"I'm sorry you've been here so long." I'm relaxing a bit. I sit against my far wall.

"It seems like a long time, but as far as I can tell, it's been around one hundred eighty day cycles of being in this darkness."

I cannot school my confused look in time. "What?"

Can he handle what I'm about to tell him? "Divad... Nlyax fell over three solar cycles ago."

He closes his eyes and is quiet for a long time. Then he jumps up and starts pacing, highly agitated. I am up with him, trying to keep as much distance between us as possible. Good job, June. Give a spiraling giant more bad news after he was told to rape you. Smart.

He stops, then looks at me. I am not sure what he sees in my face but he moves like he is coming in my direction.

I raise my arms in front of me in a clear signal to stop. "Please do not come closer. I do not want to hurt you."

He stops, shocked, staring at me once again. Not the response I was expecting... arrogance... a laugh... a sneer but shock, not so much. He looks at me and whispers barely audible, "I need to get very close to you so I can talk. I promise not to force myself on you. You are safe."

My logical mind screams 'fuck no' but something is telling me he is not lying. After a few minutes of weighing in my mind, I nod my head slightly.

He slowly walks across the room like he's approaching a wild animal that might attack him, which is close to the truth. He is very close now. I could touch him right now if I felt inclined to do it, which I definitely do not.

"I need to hold you," he whispers.

I cannot stop the growl. "Please." He begs. Ugh. I nod.

He steps forward quickly and wraps his arms around me.

"Who are you? Who is your Triad?" He must feel my shock, "The mark on your arm. I recognize at least one of those symbols."

Weighing the pros and cons of telling him, I decide there is no actual issue with telling him. "My prime is Ronin. My second is Dax, and my third will be Aanon." I'm not sure why I told him of Aanon, but I guess I need him to understand my Triad is complete.

He's shaking. What is going on?

"Forgive me for touching you. I just do not want to give them any additional information they do not have. How did you get here? Why do they have you?"

"I was ambushed at a supply station and brought here, but it's not me they are really after; it's Ronin," I pause. I need to tell someone. I need to. "And the child I carry."

His body is extremely rigid now. "You carry his child?"

A tear gets loose, "Yes."

"Do not fear my Queen. I will do everything in my power to keep you safe." Uh, I'm sorry; what now? "They must never find out your status as Ronin's mate. Do they know of the child?"

I am still reeling. "They know about the baby. They are the ones who told me, but I am not your Queen."

He chuckles quietly, "He did not tell you? Sounds like Ronin. He sometimes forgets that not everyone knows what he knows. Ronin's mother was the Matriarch of our people."

I sway a bit, and he steadies me. "No. I'm not Nlyaxian. I can't be your Queen."

"I will admit it's a little unorthodox, but Ronin is the last of his line. You have already proven you can conceive a Nlyaxian child, you are our Queen."

"That son of a... why didn't he tell me this OR Dax?!" I am keeping it at a whisper, but it is very hard. I am angry. I feel like they kept something from me.

"I do not know, my Queen..."

"Stop calling me that. Call me June."

"I cannot do that, my..." he stops when he sees the fury in my eyes. "Ok... ok. I will call you June for now."

I guess that will do. "Do you know where we are?" I ask him hopefully. He shakes his head. Shit.

"Am I the first male they have put you with?" I nod. "Do you know why they are putting you with males?"

I shake my head. "It has to have something to do with the child, though because they said it's entered some kind of stasis."

He gets a faraway look then looks back at me, "I am a medical officer. There are journals that state Nlyaxian embryos go into stasis until all three of the triad impregnate their mate."

"Are you telling me that all Nlyaxian females have triplets?" Sway. "I feel sick."

"Do you need something? I can get you water?"

"No, no. It's fine." I press a finger to the bridge of my nose. "It's just a lot of shocks to my system, which was already screwed up because of the torture. I will be fine." When I look up, I see two black eyes. Well shit.

"Divad, I need you to be calm. You cannot lose your shit right now. I need you to be logical." He closes his eyes and takes some deep breaths. When he opens them again, he is back to normal. "Good. Is this the first time they've put you in with a female?" Nod. Hmmm. "Are there any blind spots for the cameras in here?" He nods. "So we sit here to test their threat? What does that get us?"

"Nothing but we cannot, I will not... with you. Your Triad would kill me. Slowly. As they should."

I smile, "No, we are definitely not having sex, but with the blind spot in the room, we could make them believe we did. Though I am not sure, we could be convincing." This feels wrong, even if it were to be fake.

"They know nothing of sex between Nlyaxians or Humans, so I'm not sure it will take much to make them believe."

I shake my head, "No, no, no, I changed my mind. I can't, no I can't."

"June it's ok. I understand. The mate bond is deep. So that means we wait to see what they do." I'm still hyperventilating a little. I run through some of my mental exercises and feel much better.

"Sit down here or on the bed. Please." His concern is authentic, and I appreciate it. With all I've been through with both Ronin and Dax, I cannot even pretend. "Do not worry, my... June. We will figure this out."

"I am tired." I am just wiped out. I want Ronin, Dax, or Aanon. I need my mates. I don't care about anything right now. I lay down and wrap the blanket around me. I am asleep quickly.

I wake, and I am laying next to Aanon. He has his arms around me. I cannot help the tears that fall. He gathers me close.

"Shh, little one. You are here with me now. Safe." I wrap my arms around him. I feel like he'll disappear if I let him. He pulls back a bit and looks down at me with concern written on his face. I cannot take it, grab both sides of his face and pull myself up to his face and kiss him gently. The confusion on his face is sexy, I'm not sure how he pulls it off, but he does.

I run my tongue along the seam of his lips, and he opens. I deepen the kiss, trying to show him how much I need him. I need him as my mate; I need him in my Triad, and I need him inside me.

He rolls on top. He has clothes on. I do not. He deepens the kiss again. My mates are very fast learners when it comes to kissing. He kisses along my chin and feathers them along my neck. I cannot stop the moan that escapes, "Aanon."

He moves lower, feathering more over my collarbone. He moves lower, "June, your body calls to me." Moan. He moves to my breasts. When he sucks a nipple in his mouth, I arch my back and moan. "You are so perfect, June."

"Aanon, please." He moves further down and settles his shoulders between my legs. He wraps his arms around the bottom of my legs. His tongue explores my folds. I push my fingers into his hair. When it dives deep into my pussy, I can only gasp and arch my back.

It comes back out and starts a slow journey toward the apex of my slit. "Aanon, please..." When he finds my clit my moans triple in volume. He circles, circles, and then flicks the hard nub. "Aanon!" He understands my need he becomes solely focused on that spot. The sensations he pulls from me are driving me to the brink, so when he latches on to my clit and sucks, I come undone, screaming his name. He is up at my face and dives into a deep kiss. When he breaks it, he puts his forehead to mine.

"*June. You are amazing. I wish you were real. I wish this place was real. I would spend my days between your legs, making you scream my name.*"

I cannot help it, I cry again. "*I am real.*" *I pull myself from the dream because I cannot take it.*

June

I open my eyes. The sadness I feel is like a tidal wave I cannot avoid. I hear the door open and I hear the puff of a hypo dart then Divad falls to the floor. I feel a mutant grab my arm. I don't fight it. He pulls me from the room.

The first place they take me looks like a lab. They lock me to a standing table. It slowly lays me back. When I'm laying flat, arms come out of the ceiling and start rotating about me but seem to focus on my abdomen. After a few minutes, I hear angry hissing but I'm not sure I care. The table stands back up and the mutant is back unlocking me from the table. He grabs my arm again, and we go to the torture room.

Something snaps in my, 'what *the fuck are you doing June? You are not this person.' It*'s time to snap out of this shit. Today I let them in my mind. When they're in... they die.

I am tied to the wall. I continue to project the mentally broken female persona. Every time I have been in this room the first thing they do is test my mental defenses, so I hope they do the same this time.

Two Lutetian enter the room once I am tied up. That's new. I am hoping they are doubling down on their attempts to get in because it will make them believe the sudden ability to get in.

I feel them; they are testing my walls again. They aren't trying yet so I don't want to give myself away, but I put a minuscule crack in my wall hoping they find it. I feel them testing my defenses and strengthening their pushes.

One of them is approaching the crack. It brushes over the crack and keeps going. Shit. It stops and comes back to the spot. I feel its excitement. Its attack on my mental defense gets much stronger but honestly, I am not impressed. I let it get further and further through the wall. I feel the other one join the attack.

Still not impressed. If I hadn't given them the ability to get in, they never would have. I let them further through the crack faster; then let a whole crumble open. Come get me mother fuckers.

I put myself in the same position as they have me outside. I hear hissing before they appear. They are very proud of themselves. "Ssstupid human. You are not ssstrong enough to keep usss out." The other one is trying to root around in my memories. Nope. I pull it into my room. The first turns to it, "What are you doing? You are sssupossed to be gathering information."

"My turn."

They both turn to look at me and see something very different. I am now clothed, my Katana are on my back, and the look on my face is fury. I feel them try to take control, but they are far from strong enough to do that. I feel their fear when they realize I have set a trap for them. They try to leave. "Tsk, tsk, tsk. You are mine now."

Their only option now is attack, but this is my world, my mind. They both look like they're gearing up to spit at me, so I put

Hannibal Lecter masks on them except with no holes. They are also now locked in place. The fear is rolling off them in waves.

I laugh, "Did you honestly believe you could crack my mind? No. This is what I wanted. So now it's time for questions. Do you think your torture was bad? Mine is going to be infinitely worse. Now let's see who gets to go first... eenie, meanie, minie, moe." I point to the first that came in.

I change the mask so there is a hole where its mouth is but it's covered with a fine mesh so none of its spit can get out. "I will never give you anything."

Chuckling, "We shall see. Did you read any of the information about my world?"

It looks uncomfortably at the other. "No! We do not care about your world."

"Are your people that stupid? Knowing your enemy should be a tenet. Tsk. tsk. tsk. So let me give you a lesson. I promise to be brief." I wander the room close to them. "On my world, we have a high diversity of life. Humans only make up .01% of the biomass on our planet. We have over four hundred thousand plant species, and there are over two million animal species," shock registers on the second one's face, good.

"But the truly shocking number is insects. We have over a million different types of insects. Gross I hate them. Though the one I think you'll be most interested in is the one I hate the most, the arachnid species. Does that translate properly? From the look on your faces, it looks like it does but just in case... what we call arachnids look very much like you. Arachnids on my world have eight legs, their bodies are divided into two sections, the cephalothorax in front and the abdomen behind." They are shaking. They dislike the information I am giving them.

"Now, you might hope or think these arachnids on my world are apex predators?" The first actually gets an excited look. I chuckle, "But alas, no. They are far from the apex. As a matter of fact, most

people kill them when they see them. Would you like to see one? Yes, I think you do." I lift my hand and produce a tarantula. I cannot help the revulsion I feel for it.

"Now, since meeting y'all I have a new appreciation for the arachnids at home. I think I may even like them now because they generally leave us alone and eat insects. I haven't really given them enough credit. But because so many people hate spiders on my planet we have many, many ways to kill them." The tarantula disappears from my hand.

I feel their panic and fear. I walk over to the first Lutetian, "Now are you sure you don't want to cooperate with me?"

It looks at me for a long time shaking then says, "You are going to kill me anyway."

"True. Very true but I can do it quickly and painlessly or I can make it extremely unpleasant. The choice is yours. But let's be abundantly clear, I really hope you choose the slow and painful way because I need to get some vengeance on what y'all have been doing to me."

"I do not fear you." It says as it shakes.

Laughing, "Oh I think you do, but so be it. Slow and painful it is. So let's get started but first you," I point to the second one then point to the wall, it lifts and slams to the wall, several chains criss-cross its body holding it to the wall. "Can't put my focus on this one if I have to focus on you as well."

As I turn back to the first, I realize my display ratcheted up its fear by quite a bit. Chuckling, "What's wrong? Not so sure you gave the right answer before?"

It looks over at the one on the wall and whispers, "Kill her, and I will talk." Vile fucking shit.

"Hmmm, I think I should talk to her first, don't you?" It hisses and carries on so I close off the mask so I don't have to hear it.

Let's see what this one says. I open her mask as I did the other and ask, "Do you want to answer my questions?"

Shaking it responds, "Yess. She is the Queenss master Sssoul Tormentor, but ssshe is only that becaussse you killed her favorite."

She is different somehow. I wall off the other. "Your words are safe now. I feel you wish to tell me something. You are different." Shock comes over her face.

She nods.

"You are different or do you want to tell me something?"

"Both." She whispers. I see a symbol on her neck. It is silver. I recognize the symbol. It is a flame.

"How are you different?"

"The queensss of my sspeciesss are vile. They kill their off-ssspring like they do not matter, all the time." Her eyes dart around, "I was told by a sssilver Nlyaxian that I was to wait for a red-haired human and help her. That ssshe would help me free my people from them."

Whoa. I would not believe her except for the symbol on her neck that isn't there when others of her species are around. "And have you decided to follow the Goddess?"

She gets a little pale for a spider, "Th...that was the Goddess?" I nod. A film closes over her eyes. "Yesss. I want to." The symbol on her neck fares. "You must understand, our God is a ssspiteful, maniacal, sssadist. He visitsss the Annod Amirp, doesss awful thingsss to them."

"I believe you. What is your name?"

"We do not get namesss. We recognize each other through the vibration we make asss we walk."

I give her a lopsided smile, "Well that won't work for me. How about... Neith?" The ancient Egyptians had the goddess Neith. She was associated with a spider as the "spinner" and "weaver" of destiny. I think its fitting.

"I like it," she says. I nod at her.

"I would like to give you something from the Goddess." She looks unsure but nods. She's brave, I like her. I walk close to her as I release her restraints and mask. She lands on her feet... legs... whatever. I walk closer and press my finger to her forehead and push all the teachings of the Goddess into her mind.

She gasps, "I do not underssstand. Gods are not like that."

"Gods are not, but this Goddess is."

"Thank you. What ssshould I call you?"

"Call me June. Now is there any information I can get from her that I cannot get from you?"

"Nothing."

"Good. Would you like a chance at her before I kill her?"

She thinks for a long time, "May I jussst ssstand bessside you? I might sssay sssomething, I do not know."

"That is completely acceptable."

I turn back to the first, remove the wall, and open the mask a little, "Well too late. Neith here is now my friend so I do not need you anymore." Fury registers on her face. I see her lash out with her mind. I grab the filament before it can reach Neith. "Tsk tsk tsk. I allow no one to hurt my friends."

She changes again, instead of fear, she is absolutely terrified of me. The reaction confuses me and I look at Neith. She has a look of awe on her face. "What the hell is going on? Why is she suddenly terrified of me?"

"We have never sssseen anyone with thisss type ability. Ever. Not even the queensss can do what you just did." She looks back at the first with almost a triumphant look, "Ssshe will free us from our oppressorsss but you, you sssadistic... Ssspider! You will be dead and never hurt another!" With that statement she lashes out and severs her head from her shoulders. She gets a shocked scared look on her face, "I am sssso sssorry forgive me. I did not..."

I cut her off, "It's ok. I understand the healing effect of vengeance."

She gives me a strange look, "You are sssso different from usss. We have alwaysss been told how evil and vile everyone is who is not

Lutetian. It isss illuminating to find out it wasss usss that are evil and vile." She says the last part sadly.

"Neith look at me." She looks up, "You are not evil or vile, and now that I know you I am guessing your people are not either. Beings that enjoy inflicting pain and suffering on others are vile and evil. You have helped me when I needed it most. Thank you."

She smiles with all her sharp pointy teeth and I barely notice. I am so universally cosmopolitan. Lol. I crack myself up.

CHAPTER

10

JUNE

June

I let the cell background fade away and a little shaded grove appears in its place. Two big comfy chairs sit in the shade. Hmmm, "Neith, I have a chair for you but I'm not sure it will be comfortable for you."

"It doesss look comfortable. It will be fine. Thank you." She has a bit of a confused look on her face.

I put out my arm for her to sit, "What is it?"

"It isss jussst ssstrange for me. I have never had anyone care for my comfort before."

That makes me sad for her, "I am sorry for that Neith. Ok to business, so I'm guessing we are going to need multiple sessions for me to get all the information I need so let me ask a couple of questions so we can ensure no one finds out about us. Ok," She nods.

"Good. How long do these torture sessions usually run?"

"We are sssuposssed to go until we get the information the Queen wantsss. If we last too long ssshe'll insssert herself into our minds and punisssh usss."

"Hmmm well, that's not good. We need to ensure she doesn't do that to you. It's too much of a risk and needless to say I do not want her to hurt you. What information does she think she can get from me?"

"We are sssupposed to get Nlyaxian mating habitsss, gessssstation, and anything relating to offssspring. Ssshe wantsss to know how many Nlyaxianssss travel with the prince. Sssshe is concerned by the chaos he has created with the ssslave ssupply chain."

So many questions, "How long before we need to exit so she doesn't get angry or curious?"

"I think we sshould be ssafe for another ten minutesss or ssso."

Hmmm. "Ok, I need to feed you some information so she will be happy with you and hopefully not mad about the other one."

"Ssshe will not care about the other. Ssshe will view her as a failure and therefore not worthy."

"Well, I guess that's good. Ok, I, unfortunately, do not know about Nlyaxian gestation but I can give you human information?"

"No. We have that information already." She gives me an uncomfortable look, "The human'sss provided all that."

Grrrr. "Fucking hell. I want to love my planet, but they make it very hard sometimes."

"I can relate." She can and I appreciate her saying that. "Ok, she already has human information. She already knows Nlyaxians have Triads?" Neith nods. Shit. "I can actually get some information if you put me back with the Nlyaxian you had me with before all of this but what do I give you now... tell her that we have four ships we use to liberate slaves."

She gives me a quizzical look, "Liberate?"

"Yes, we free the slaves and find them safe haven."

"You do what? If you want her to believe it you will need to sssay you sssell them if you do."

"We do free them and find them a safe place to live." She looks dumbfounded. "What?"

"It jussst I have never heard of sssuch a thing. It is inconceivable."

"There is good in this galaxy Neith and you are part of that. I am glad you are and I was not lying when I said you are now my friend. So I need you to be very careful. Guard your mind. Please." Neith makes a strange whispered keening sound. "Neith, are you ok?"

She takes a few seconds to gather herself, "I am sssorry. I have never had sssomeone care about my well-being. It isss over-whelming."

I get up and walk over to squat in front of her, "Well you have me now." She just nods, unable to speak. "Will the four ships be enough information for now?"

She nods, "Ssshe will be happy about getting the information but not happy about the information itssself. Which ssshould be perfect becaussse getting all ssshe wanted would give usss away."

I stand, "Ok so I need wounds so it's believable." She is up shaking her head.

"No no no I cannot. I will not."

I stop her pacing, "It's ok. I can do this part myself."

I close my eyes, think of the wounds on Dax, and add them to myself. It is excruciating but necessary.

I open my eyes and stagger a little, Neith catches me and I can feel her worry. "They'll heal me now, right?" She nods.

With a worried face, the last thing she says is, "We need to talk about your abilities next time."

I am awake and the pain is excruciating. Neith is there. She yells for the guards. She points to the dead Lutetian, "Take out that garbage then take the human to the healersss. I want her ready for another sssesssion tomorrow."

To play the game, I moan, which isn't all that hard to pretend pain, "No, please. No more."

Neith laughs, "Hiss hiss hiss, human we are jussst getting ssstarted."

When the mutant comes back he puts me over his shoulder and walks to the infirmary or healers whatever they call them. It puts me down roughly on the table.

One of the Lutetians hisses in anger, "Careful you idiot. The Queen would be furiousss if ssomething happened to the embryo."

I am now wishing I was unconscious. You would think that being healed wouldn't hurt but I have found out it is extremely painful. The Lutetian does not bother to put me under and I can hear it laughing as it heals me and sees my pain.

Once they are done, I take a second to breathe and relax. My muscles are tired from the constant strain from the healing. The Lutetian calls a mutant to take me back. He picks me up and puts me over his shoulder. When we get back to the cell, three more meet him and all are armed. Strange but I do not have the energy to do anything. The two with the blasters open the door and point their weapons into the room. I hear growling, they step into the room followed by the one carrying me. The volume of the growling amplifies. The mutant carrying me drops me to the floor and they practically run out of the room.

As the door closes the growling stops and I am picked up by Divad, "My Q... my June. Forgive me, I have failed at protecting you." He lays me in the bed and covers me with the blanket.

"Divad, come lay down with me." I feel the bed sink in front of me and he gathers me in his arms. "Many good things happened on my trip. I will tell you but I really need rest. Divad, thank you for being my friend."

"I am glad I can be here for you. You know you remind me of my oldest sister. She was a lot like you. Strong, determined, a genius, and stubborn." We laugh. "I am sure she would have liked you."

"I would have liked her too." I yawn and fall asleep as soon as my eyes close.

When I open my eyes I know where I am. I am in Aanon's dream. It makes me a little sad. I didn't react great to his statement but I was tired and emotionally drained. I am not sure I want to see him yet. I am not ready to validate my existence.

I can see his house in the distance, the sun is starting to set behind it. Maybe I'm being a coward, maybe I'm scared he will reject me and I'm pretty sure I can't handle that.

I turn to look at what else is part of his dream. It really is beautiful. I close my eyes and raise my face to the last of the sun. When I open them again Aanon is there standing in front of me looking... worried.

"Hello, Aanon."

He steps forward and he is now very much in my space. I cannot help it when, when he steps close I can smell him, I can feel him, and my desire for him spikes. He smells the air and he now knows the effect he has on me. When he opens his eyes again his pupils are wide and he refocuses on me.

"Please forgive me. I did not mean to upset you. It is hard for me to understand how you are here. I can feel you are my mate, but I cannot do anything because I am unfit."

Hmmm. I have an idea on how to address this, "Aanon, can I ask you a few questions?" He nods. "Do you believe me when I say I am Ronin's mate?"

"I want to believe it."

I pull the sleeve on my shirt up to show him the Kokoro. His eyes go wide and he whispers, "Impossible. The Kokoro has not been seen for millennia."

"The Goddess has blessed my Triad. You see Ronin's crest?" He nods, "And Dax's?" Nod. "And you see one is empty?" He nods again. He looks at me, "And what does it mean that I am Ronin's mate?"

He gets a confused look and then his eyes lose focus as he thinks. I let him work through it, and after a few minutes, he gets a shocked look and takes a knee. Right conclusion, wrong action. I grab his arm, "Aanon please stand up." He does it slowly. "Ok now, if that is true does it matter if someone who is no longer around named you 'unfit'?"

He once again gets a faraway look, his eyes going side to side. I don't even see his decision, one minute I am watching him think it through the next I am in his arms and he is making it impossible for me to think. He is kissing me deeply and slowly, the fire in my core is growing by the second.

I wrap my legs around his waist and can feel his rock-hard cock rub against my clit. I moan at the sensation. He lays us in the grass, his hips settle and he rubs his cock again harder against it. He breaks the kiss and sits back on his heels. "This is my dream?" I nod. He gets the sexiest look on his face and suddenly my clothes are gone. I moan at the sudden chill against my nipples and sex. The next blink and he is now naked. He is perfect.

"You are so beautiful, my Mate. Goddess, thank you for bringing me the joy of a Triad," he settles once again between my legs, "Thank you for the gifts of her mind," steamy kiss and line up, "for her caring and compassion," rub cock up and down, "and for her body which I will worship as long as I live."

He starts pushing into me, and he is as large as Dax. The stretch as he pushes in is not altogether comfortable, but it sets a fire as it goes. I feel every bump and ridge on his cock. His ridges differ from the others, more pronounced, and more prominent. By the time he is fully seated, I am on fire, moaning, "Aanon, oh god, please."

He lowers himself to his elbows, he closes his eyes, "By the Goddess you are so tight, are you ok?"

I can't help the yell, "Fuck Aanon please now." He pulls nearly all the way out, his ridges vibrate his cock as he moves. They are driving my pleasure so high. He is solely focused on my pleasure, every move, every thrust, everything he does is to drive me higher.

His thrusts are powerful and are moving faster and faster. My climax is barreling at me. His thrusts are now fast, but he is focused on my face. My climax hits, "Aanon!!" I scream. I feel my pussy lock-down on his cock. He slows and moans, his focus and control is gone. He is pounding in and out of my sex. I feel his sprili come out and start massaging. I scream as my second climax hits. I feel his cock throb, he roars then I feel his release hit my walls. His sprili vibrates and another climax hits. "Aanon!"

He keeps his weight off of me when he collapses. He rolls me on top; I love being sprawled on my mates' chests. I look at my arm and my last section is filled. It looks like his farm. I love it. He sees it and lifts his arm and his is there too but it's very light I can't help wondering why that is. He smiles, "I never thought I would have a Mate."

I sit up and push my body further onto his. He groans and rubs his hands up and down my thighs. "Aanon, you are worthy of a mate." I raise up on his cock and slowly lower. His hands move to my breasts and run over my nipples. I cannot contain the moan that escapes. "Aanon. I forgot to ask." I smile. "Will you be the third in my Triad?"

He laughs loudly and with his deep bassy laugh, I can feel rumble up through his cock making me moan. "You are mine and I am yours." He sits up, "I will spend my life protecting you, providing anything you need, and making you scream in pleasure on my cock." I stand up and take a few steps back. His eyes don't leave me. I turn and look over my shoulder then slowly go down to my knees.

I bend at the waist and put my hands on the ground. A growl starts behind me, goosebumps explode across my skin and a moan escapes. I look back over my shoulder and he is on his knees staring at me, growling. I barely see him move but he is now wrapped around me, his cock now pushing into my folds.

He takes his time pushing in, drawing out our pleasure. He pulls me up, so my back is touching his front, "I am going to take you hard and fast now, mate." I clench my pussy, trying to get him moving. He growls again, and it rumbles up his cock. I moan, "Please, Aanon."

He pushes me back down so my face rests in the grass. He run his hands over my ass, "Your ass is magnificent."

"Aanon!"

He chuckles and starts a punishing pace. The noises coming from me drive us both higher. His prominent ridges drive me fast to climax. I scream as my climax hits, and his hit as well. He roars as his seed sprays my walls, and his sprili vibrates. I cry out as they send me deeper into my orgasm.

Aanon collapses beside me. I curl into his side and he wraps his arm around me. I know this is a dream, his dream. Will he even remember me when he wakes? Dax is the only known Nlyaxian that has remembered anything from dreams.

His deep rumbling voice startles me a bit, "I can feel your worry, little one. What is wrong?"

I don't speak for a few minutes, "Aanon, you know this is a dream right?"

"I do. I wish it was not."

"Me too," I whisper. "Aanon, do you have any idea where you are?"

"I do not."

"What's the last thing you remember?"

He is quiet for a minute. "It was the day of the coronation of the new Queen. Ronin's eldest sister. I found out he would not be there. I was shocked and disappointed. Our Matriarchy is the cornerstone of our society, I could not believe he would not attend. Then I found out that Dax would not be there either. The two males I care for most in the galaxy decided to ignore our people and our culture. I was angry at them both."

He pauses to get his emotions under control, "So there was only one thing for me to do, find them and bring them back to Nlyax to apologize to the new Queen." He chuckles, "I am not sure why I thought I could get to them but I was angry and not thinking clearly. I thought maybe Dax would be on the military transport heading out for operations. So I took a transport to find him. I was a ranking officer, so I headed straight for the bridge to track him from there.”

“When I got there, everyone was staring in shock at the screen. When I looked at it I did not understand what I was seeing. On it was asteroids and a debris field where my home world should be. We all stood there in shock, I do not know for how long. Suddenly I felt the fire of electric shock, then I was here. How long has it been?”

He feels my hesitation, “It is ok my mate. I can take it. How long? A month?”

“No. Aanon, it's been over three years.” He freezes.

“That is not possible. I have not been here that long.”

“I’m sorry Aanon. I really am.” I roll so I am on his chest again. “Listen to me. Aanon, look at me. Yes, you have been here a long time but we will find you. Ronin, Dax, and I will find you. We are liberating slaves across the sector and giving them safe haven. We will find you.”

He cups my face and starts tracing the contours. “You are the most amazing mate. I could not ask for a more perfect female. Even if you do not,” he stops me from interrupting, “no, listen. Even if you do not, I am happy with what we have had.”

“Aanon, I need you to believe in me, believe in us. We will not rest until you are with us.” He gives me a gentle smile and then kisses me tenderly.

I wake to Divad pushing me to eat. “You are losing weight. The child may not be growing in your womb but you still have to sustain it which means you must keep yourself healthy. Eat, please.”

“Yes ok. I understand.” I grump at him which he chuckles at. I look at my arm and my stomach drops. Aanon’s mark is no longer there. Am I making him up in my head? No he is real but where is his mark? I glance at Divad, “How long did I sleep?”

"Several hours. You moaned a couple times, I almost woke you but you calmed. So you said good things happened while they had you, what happened?"

Well, I'm glad he breezed over the moaning in my sleep I feel a slight blush at the mention. We are under the covers to talk, "Yes. They took me to the torture room again." He growls, "No just listen. So they are constantly trying to get into my mind before they resort to physical torture." He looks confused. "Sorry, sorry *so* the Lutetian can enter and control the mind. They torture in the dream and in Nlyaxians case, they do not remember the torture but the Lutetian can leave evidence on the body of the torture."

"Outside of the dream?"

"Yes."

I wait for him to work through the information, "During the Lutetian wars, soldiers would wake with horrible wounds. Are you saying the Lutetian tortured those soldiers in their dreams?"

I nod and wait.

"Nlyaxian's don't dream so they do not remember." He gets a shocked look on his face, "Dax, he remembered. He tried to tell us." His shoulders slump, "I am disappointed we discounted him."

"You shouldn't be. He is one male of all Nlyaxians. It was something I would have not believed either. Do not be too hard on yourself. They cannot get into my mind, and I have rescued Dax in the past from what he called 'Mind Traps.' This time though I let them in. In the physical world, I have no control. In my mind I am in complete control, at least that is what I hoped."

"That is a big assumption."

"Realistically, if it hadn't been true, then it's torture in my mind or in reality so either way, it was going to be terrible. In my mind, I had the chance. And my gamble paid off, once they were in they were mine. They could control nothing. One died, but the other was a follower of the Goddess."

I see his doubt, "I know it is hard to believe, but in my mind, she had the mark of the Goddess in silver on her neck."

The shock on his face is almost comical. "But... you can see marks from the Goddess?"

I lift my arm, "What do you think this is?" He looks at it. I cannot read his face, "This is a Kokoro. It is an ancient gift from Her to the people of this galaxy. If you and your mate are followers of her teaching and committed to one another, it will display on the left arm."

He continues to start at my arm, "I am a believer of science, this is a lot for me to take in."

I smile, "It was a lot for me as well. The people of my world use religion as a weapon when this showed up on my arm, well let's just say I freaked out a bit. She told me what they mean and I appreciate it and the gift."

He is now looking at me with a bit of fear, "What's wrong?"

"You spoke with Her?"

"I did." I don't see a point in hiding it from him.

"Who are you?"

"I am her Chosen Warrior. I will do everything in my power to give the people of this galaxy safety and peace."

"I... You are so much more important than just our Queen. The Goddess is fundamental to our beliefs. We were turning away from those teachings. I do not know where to go with this information."

"We expect nothing of you. If you decide to follow the teachings, so be it, if not that is your choice."

He nods. "The Lutetian with Her marking, how do you know it is not a trick?"

"I know. Her name is Neith. She didn't hurt me once. Even when I needed wounds to trick the rest of the Lutetian, so they did not find her out. She will pull me for another round tomorrow or maybe today to talk more. I need information before we can make our move."

"I have a hard time trusting a Lutetian, but I trust in you. I dislike that you have to go through the wounds for information."

"So I need help from you. I need information I can feed to her so they do not get suspicious. They want what seems like trivial information but I'd like your opinion on why they want it. They want information on Nlyaxian biology like gestation, breeding habits, young growth patterns... any idea why they would want any of that?"

He goes quiet. His eyes flick back and forth as he thinks. He is silent for a while. When his eyes flick back to mine, I am pretty sure I will not like his theory.

"One thing the Lutetian do when they take a planet is taking a portion of the population to convert into their army."

"You're talking about the mutants?"

He nods, "Yes, they genetically alter them. It is an excruciating, barbaric process, and the subject's mind is damaged. Something irreversibly damaged all we have captured in the mind and body. The facts you've given me, combined with what I have witnessed and the fact they are trying to force us to breed, lead me to a disturbing hypothesis. They are trying to use Nlyaxians as their new army, but they could not use those who have grown up as part of our culture. We would die before allowing such a thing, but... offspring would give them a breeding army, and they would control their upbringing."

I launch out of bed because now I am going to be sick. I throw up and when I am done, I rinse my mouth and turn to see him close and concerned. "I'm ok. Back to bed."

"Are you sure?"

"Yes." Not really but what choice do I have? We are back in bed and under the covers. "So your theory is they want to use my...

baby as their army. They will take them and basically program them to be mindless killers?"

"That is my theory but we need more information before we know for certain."

"I wish I could say that I do not believe they are capable, but I do, and it scares me to death. They cannot have my baby!"

"Of course not. We will not allow it. First, you need the information to feed Neith. Nlyaxian gestation is fourteen months. Our young once born reach maturity at seventeen solar cycles. Males start military training at eleven solar cycles and enter active duty at maturity. They do not reach mating age for another five solar cycles. You already know we mate in what we call Triad. Three males to one female. Nlyaxian females carry three babies at a time. Birth weight is on average six pounds. They grow quickly. Children are walking by one solar cycle and being schooled at four solar cycles. Females are our leaders, scientists, and many other vocations. Males are those things as well but not until they complete their mandatory service at thirty-five solar cycles. Most decide to stay in the military but many also decide to take roles outside. What do you hope to learn from Neith?"

"Thank you for the information. I hope to learn many things. First, where are we and can we get away? Second, why do they want Ronin? Third, your theory makes me sure of one thing, you are far from the only Nlyaxian they have, where are the others? And if human females are their 'chosen' breeders for the Nlyaxians where are they?"

He looks at me intensely, "How can you be sure about the males and females?"

"They have been paying the Cruxlin to steal human females from my planet and they have a 'quota'. If I was a gambling woman, I would bet the quota of human females matches or is a third of what they have in Nlyaxian males."

Divad lies on his back staring at nothing. "Do you know what their total quota for human females was?"

"No. I know the quota for the 'batch' they took me in was 250 but I got the distinct impression that it was far from the first or last."

"I am not sure how to feel about this. It wrongly gives me hope for my brothers being alive somewhere," he glances at me, "and about the possibility of a mate."

"It's not wrong to hope some of your people still live, but the women of Earth were stolen. If they want to go back, then they will be given the opportunity to go."

He nods, "I understand."

I chew my lip, "I worry though, my people sold me. My father had a hand in it. I will have to ensure they are safe first." Divad cannot stop the growl that escapes, I wave to him to stop. "I know. My father is an awful person, evil even but I will need to tear down the business they have built selling human women. I need to find them first."

"Do you think they could be here?"

"Maybe but I know Aanon is not here. I'm not sure what that means for the rest."

"I do not understand. How do you know he is not here?"

"When we approached the station Dax was on, I knew he was there. I don't feel that now."

"Dax was conscious though. Aanon is most likely sedated in some form. That could be affecting whatever connects you."

"I hope you are right. We need information so we can get out of here. I will not let them have my baby... the possibility of more Nlyaxians being here gives me an idea though. If we can get out of here and get to wherever they are we can wake them and basically have a small army to take this base. The biggest problem is we do not know how large this base is and how many of the enemy resides here."

"Well, I hope you can get information from your new friend. The longer we are here the more aggressive they will get about breeding you. They may even put other Nlyaxians in here. Most would never but there are less honorable males that would have no problem doing it."

I snort, "I'd love to see them try. I will have no problem killing males like that. I will not put up with it."

"You're a warrior. I do not know your skill but I do not want you to get hurt or the babe."

"I am a warrior, they will underestimate me and it will be their mistake."

At that moment, I hear the puff of a tranq gun. Divad growls briefly then he's out. They ripped the sheet off—time to play the role. I scream and scramble back to the wall. There are three mutants; one stalks over and grabs my arm to haul me out of the room.

They take me on the same trip, to the infirmary first to check on my baby than to the torture room. I'm relieved to see Neith there. I'm not sure how I know it's her but I do. They take me to the wall and tie me to it. I make sounds of distress as they do so.

Neith screams, "Get out!" They scramble from the room. She closes her eyes and I feel her wait for me to let her in.

We are in my glade again except instead of seeing Neith I see a small human woman. "Neith, what are you doing?"

She gets a shy look, "I know our appearance makes you uncomfortable, so I thought this would be better for you."

I walk to her and grab her hands, "Neith, I want nothing more or less than who you are. You are my friend, and I want to see you." She nods and fades back to her Lutetian form. I smile, "Much better. The way people look does not make them ugly, who they are, does. You are beautiful."

I can feel her emotion. She whispers, "Thank you."

"Now come sit and tell me what happened when you left last time."

We sit. "I was immediately called to what we call the echo chamber, it amplifiesss our mindsss ssignals so ssshe can better communicate with usss. Sssomething changed with my abilitiesss, I am not sssure if it was you or the information you pusshed into me about the Goddesss but I could wall off the memoriesss of our dissscussion and create fake onesss for her to sssee. I could never hide information from her before but I can now and it wasss easy. She watched the fake memories and was angry you could kill the other with your mind, but happy I wasss able to control you and get information from you."

"That's good news. What about the information on the ships?"

"I told her about the ssships asss planned. I could feel ssshe was unhappy about the number of ssshipsss but I alssso felt her feelingsss of sssuperiority because ssshe knew."

"Did she push you to get more information?"

"Yesss. Ssshe wasss unhappy that I did not get Nlyaxian breeding information. Ssshe punished me." Before I can express my concern she reaches out to touch my arm. "I am ok June. Even the pain isss not asss bad."

She nods again trying to get me to understand, "Ok. Well, I have more information I can give you to feed her about that but before we go over that I want to understand why she needs this. Is she planning on using human-Nlyaxian hybrids for her new army?" Neith's shocked look tells me we are right and my stomach drops. "How can that be a viable solution for her? That is a long time to wait for an army."

"We are a long-lived sspeciesss. Queen'ssss in particular can live for sssseveral hundred yearsss. Our longest lived queen was almosssst nine-hundred cyclesss old."

Fuck. "I really hate this news... Are there humans and Nlyaxians here that she's tried this with already?" Neith nods. I become still, "How many?"

She looks uncomfortable, "There are twenty-four hundred Nlyaxian maless and eight-hundred human femalesss on this bassse. There are more at the other basssesss but I do not know the numbersss."

I get up and start pacing; I need to work out energy even though I'm not even sure that works since we are in my mind. "Have they force-bred human women?" I am nearly shaking with anger. I look at her and realize I am scaring her. I try to calm myself but it is hard. "Neith, I am sorry. Please understand I am definitely not angry with you. Ok?"

She nods and relaxes a bit, "Yes. They are trying to force Nlyaxian'sss to breed human women, but it has yet to work. Mossst malesss refussse. The few that are willing to have not sssuccessfully fertilized an embryo. Yoursss is the only known hybrid in existence and it is in sstasisss so ssshe is desssperate to fertilize two more eggss so ssshe can understand why you are different and ssstart to create more."

"The male in the breeding pod with me?" I can barely stand to ask but I need to know.

"This is hisss firsst time out of a ssstasisss pod."

Thank Goddess. "What happened when they refused?"

"Ssshe killed the firssst few malesss but then put them back into sstasisss until ssshe can find a way to control them."

"What happened to the ones who were willing and how many... how many were willing?"

"Four. They are still in the breeding pods... with the females."

The scream that rips from my throat is one of pain, anger, and frustration. I am breathing hard and my focus is broken.

I feel Neith touch my shoulder, and she turns me to look at her. "I feel your anger and frussstration. We will free them and they may have their revenge. I will help you."

The compassion in her cools my anger, and I can calm myself and refocus. I close my eyes, "Thank you Neith." Once I have gathered myself I open my eyes and look at her, "Now I need details about this hell hole. Where are we? How many Lutetian are here and how many mutants?"

"Thisss place is called the Outposst. It is a large assteroid in a ssstable orbit around a planet. The bassse itself is inside the body. We have dug cavesss and cavernss to sssuit our purpossse. The sstassiss podsss are in level fifty-sssix through sssseventy. The Lutetian population is forty. The Mutantss, as you call them isss ninety-five." She sees my surprise, "We have very few ssoldiersss. This basse usssed to have over three-thousand ssoldiersss. Thiss iss why ssshe is desssperate for a new army."

"And she is not here?" Neith shakes her head. I pace again but slowly. "Are we on the same level as the breeding pod I am in?" She nods. "What level are we on now?"

"Thirty-sssix."

"I'm assuming there are security measures in place between here and there?" Nod. "Can you get through them?" Head shake. Shit. I pace again. "Do you know if there are any destructive measures in place if the base is taken?"

She gives me a confused look then understanding dawns, "Not that I know of, and it'sss not been done in our passst. Your people would do sssuch a thing?" I nod sadly as I continue to pace. "Ssshe would love an idea like that." She shivers.

"Are there any large transport vessels docked here somewhere?" Neith shakes her head again. I knew that one would be a long shot since it seems Cruxlin handles the large transport work.

I stop and look at Neith, "Our only option is to take the base but to do that I need to get access to the Nlyaxian stasis pods... Who has access?"

She thinks for a minute, "The only onesss with accessss that I am aware of isss medical techniciansss and the sssoldiersss that patrol thossse levelsss."

"What is the security? Badges, bio readers?"

"I guessss you would call them bio, the doors, and lifts are coded to our pheromones which are all unique."

"Can you add yourself to the system?"

"I am not sssure. Let me think about thisss. I might be able to come up with a way."

"Good. Thank you, Neith."

"June..." She gives me a nervous look.

"What is it?"

"I am sssorry. They are going to put one of the other maless in with you today. They are disssappointed the male you have been with has not been... sssuccessful."

A wicked smile blooms on my face, "Excellent."

Confused, "I do not think you underssssstand... one of the malesss that forcesss..."

I interrupt her, "Oh I understand. They're all in for a rude awakening. He will die if he tries to force me."

She shakes her head, "Ok. Time is almost up."

Hmmm. What information do I want to feed the queen bitch? I could lie and say that humans can only get pregnant by their mates but that risks her canning her 'project' out of frustration.

But... "Tell her humans can't get pregnant from rape. They need an emotional bond. Nlyaxian gestation is fourteen months. Their young once born reach maturity at seventeen solar cycles. Males start military training at eleven solar cycles and enter active duty at maturity. They do not reach mating age for another five solar cycles. If she gets angry about the emotional bond, just tell her to put males in that will not force themselves on the female and if they try to protect the female, the bond has started."

She nods a little sad, "I hate giving her any information."

I walk over to her, "It's ok Neith. None of the information should do any damage to what we are trying to do. We will free them." She looks like she's feeling better. "Ok. Now the sucky part. Time for the damage."

Neith gets a disgusted look on her face. "I know I hate it too," I tell her with a smirk.

"Do not do so much damage this time. The Queen commented on my unusual brutality. If you were not with child, I think she would have been happy with it but I could sense her simmering anger."

"I can't say that's disappointing."

I close my eyes and imagine around 10 superficial wounds. None of them are in places that could hinder fighting if they decide not to heal me. I open my eyes still in my mind with Neith. "How's this?"

"I think that isss good."

I nod, "Ok, time to exit."

June

I open my eyes and feel the slight pain from the wounds and let out a fake moan. Neith calls a soldier to take me to the infirmary. It's the Nlyaxian mutated soldier again. As it grabs my arm and pulls me from the room, I see a small silver marking on the side of his neck behind his ear. What the fuck.

Once we are into the hall knowing they have excellent hearing, "Praise to the teachings of the Goddess."

It pauses in the middle of the hall. After a few minutes, it whispers, "Praise Goddess." It's a little slurred but completely understandable. Huh. It shakes its head and starts dragging me again toward the infirmary.

Once again I am naked on the freezing metal exam table. The healing doesn't hurt as much but most of my focus is on the soldier. He is staring at me as well. I try to ensure they do not notice but his entire focus is on me. I'm not sure if this is what he always does or if this is something different. It's then I notice pain in his eyes. I wonder if I can push myself into minds like the Lutetian do. Let's see if I can.

I close my eyes and try to find him in my mind. I take almost a minute to see it, like a bridge of light and fog. I walk towards it, stopping in the middle of the bridge. I feel the chaos on the other side. Pain, fury, confusion, and sadness all jumbled up in a storm in his mind. Something emerges from the storm on the other side. He is Nlyaxian with no mutations. His eyes are black, and he is in battle fury. I can see the things causing him pain in his mind. They swirl in the storm like shards of glass. I focus on the fragments. It is hard and a little painful, but he does not deserve this. I imagine grinding the glass to sand, from sand to powder, from powder to nothing. I couldn't get that many, I destroyed around twenty shards, so hopefully, he is a little better.

I look back to the Nlyaxian, who is no longer in battle fury. He still looks angry, but not as much. I hope I helped a little. I will try to do more next time I see him, but now I'm tired, and that drained me a bit.

I open my eyes and see the soldier looking at me. Do his eyes look clearer? No, I don't think so. He walks toward me and grabs my arm and drags me from the infirmary. I swear his hand isn't as hard on my arm.

We walk back to the breeding pods but we walk past the one I have been in for a while. Well, I guess they are going to test me out on a rapist. Good. I'm tired but not dead or injured so let's do this.

We walk into an empty pod. The soldier stands there with my arm locked in his hand. I look up at him and he glances down at me. He grimaces, "Forgive," let's go, and stalks out.

Once again, there's a massive bed in the pod. I move to the wall opposite the door and wait. It doesn't take long. A different set of soldiers bring in a Nlyaxian, and I can already tell I will hate him. He's not bound, and he's naked. When he sees me, he gets a lecherous smile. "What is this, my ugly friends? You have a new beauty for me to breed?" I contain the growl wanting to escape. Another? You fucker. The soldiers turn and leave without a word.

He doesn't even acknowledge them leaving. "They talk little." He slowly looks me up and down, "Oh I am going to get a lot of enjoyment out of you."

So as much as I want to play the badass here, I need to keep this as brief as possible. While smaller than all my mates, he is still big, if a bit out of shape. I stay quiet and let him think what he wants to think. However, I never break eye contact because I need to see his tells on his attack. I know Nlyaxians have similar weaknesses as humans at the throat, so my goal will be to hopefully collapse his windpipe.

He wanders the room, "I have had many human women. Most did not want my advances until," he turns back toward me and displays his now rock-hard cock, "I pounded my giant cock into them. Then they begged me for more."

I can't help it. I laugh, "They beg for that? I can tell you this. My *Triad's* cocks are all *much* bigger than that."

His cocky attitude falls away to shock then rage. He slips into battle fury but I'm not actually concerned. Everything about him is sloppy. His movements, language, and even personal hygiene are all sloppy and somewhat gross. I see the switch flip in his brain as he strides across the room.

I am ready. As he gets close, I duck under his swing and move around him, so when the momentum of his swing brings him around, it will add to the impact of my strike to his throat. Most people on Earth are aware of the self-defense strike to the throat, but on humans, its purpose is to damage the trachea and the carotid arteries. I cannot be sure that technique will have any effect on a Nlyaxian, so my goal is to collapse his throat. I do not want him to get up.

The timing needs to be perfect. He swings with the momentum of his punch. I come up and strike him with a fist in his throat as hard as I can. I feel cartilage crush inward, more than I expected. I move out of his reach but he just stands there shocked. I can tell he cannot draw a breath, blood dribbles from his mouth. Bloody foam forms at his lips. He collapses to the floor on his back. I walk over and stand near his head. "You are an embarrassment to your species. Nlyaxians follow the teachings of the Goddess. They respect and cherish *all* females. You will not follow the Goddess into eternity." The panic that comes over his face almost makes me feel sorry for him, almost. When the light goes out of his eyes I relax.

The door opens and soldiers stream in and point weapons at me. I raise my hands and back to the wall. Five soldiers surround me at the wall then I see two Lutetian rush in, one is Neith. I see her eyes search for me and when our eyes lock, I see her relax a bit. The other is furious and screams, "*Kill her*!"

"*Do not*!" Neith yells in a authoritative voice. When she is sure the soldiers are obeying her she looks at the other, "You have sssigned your death. Ssshe will kill you for thisss." To the soldiers she says, "Take her back to the original pod. Ssstand guard outss-side the pod."

The one who grabs my arm is the Nlyaxian mutant. He walks me from the room. As we walk he says in a whisper, "hurt?"

"No."

"Good warrior."

The door opens, and he points the blaster into the pod holding Divad at bay. When I walk in I see him start to go into battle fury. I shake my head at him. He's confused but comes out of it quickly. I hear the door shut behind me. I realize how tired I am but I need to do one more thing. I sit next to the door and patted the floor next to me. Divad sits down beside me and I lay my head on his shoulder, closing my eyes.

Again I go into the soldier's mind and remove the shards. He does not deserve the pain he is in. When I am done, I must have passed out because the next time I open my eyes I am laying in bed. Divad is pacing the room. "Divad."

He rushes over and lies on top of the covers next to me then covers us both with the other blanket. "Are you ok? Your arms had blood on them but I could find no wounds. What happened?"

"A lot. I need you to remain calm." He nods. "I'm not sure where to start but I got a lot of good information from Neith. After meeting with Neith though they put me in another breeding pod and put a different Nlyaxian in with me. Let's just say he was nothing like you or my mates." I can see him fighting his battle rage, "Divad, he was unsuccessful at raping me. He is dead."

He nods, "Good. Why did they put you in with him?"

"Because I don't have a second fertilized egg. There's nothing we can do about that now. Our only option at this point is to take the base." I walk through all the information Neith gave me on the base.

Divad is quiet for a while then asks, "I see what your plan is. You want to get to the Nlyaxians that are in stasis, wake them then take the rest of the base. I understand it's our only option, but it worries me. It puts you at significant risk."

"I understand your worry but I am already at significant risk, but right now so is Ronin. He will find me, if we do not take the base before he gets here we run the risk of them capturing him or worse because he will fight to the death to get to me. I can't allow that to happen."

He gives me a soft smile, "You are a good mate and Queen. I will help you, but I doubt just you, and I can get to the floor the stasis pods are on."

"Neith is working on that for now. Do you think you'll be able to get them out of stasis?"

He nods, "Lutetian do not use technology they create. They steal everything they have so I will bet that the pods they use are models I am familiar with, but even if they are not, I will figure it out rather simply."

"Good. I am not sure we can do anything now until Neith finds a way to get us onto the floors they are on."

Nodding he asks, "Was that male the only Nlyaxian they have that forced himself on females?"

I shake my head, "Sorry Divad but there were four." He growls. "We'll see if they try to put me with one of the others. I'm pretty sure they won't but they may try other ways." I shiver at the thought.

A look of panic comes over his face, "We need to take this base as soon as we can. We cannot allow them to force-breed you. If they tie..."

I hold up my hand not wanting to think about it. It brings up too many painful memories and I am not sure I can live through it again. "I don't want to think about it." I yawn, "I'm still pretty tired, can you stay here while I sleep?" He nods and I close my eyes.

CHAPTER

12

Ronin

We are one day cycle from the Outpost, the ship is in a cooling cycle so I sit staring at a nebula in the distance. I am in the observatory trying to center myself and failing. It reflects my turmoil, I can see the churning of gas in Thackeray globules. I need my mate, the longer I am away from her the more I descend into fury. It is becoming harder and harder to control it and I am beginning to worry I will be a liability to my people.

"Ronin. Are you alright?"

I don't turn to look at Dax, "I honestly do not know. The longer I am away from her the harder it is for me to control it. Am I losing my mind?" I turn to look at him.

He sits beside me looking out into space. He sits for a long time, closes his eyes, and touches his Kokoro. Then I feel the fury he must control is churning and violent. Its strength is something I did not know he battled constantly. He removes his hand, "Your battle is difficult Ronin, but you are so much stronger than me. You can do this. Do you want me to show you how I control it?"

"Yes." Though I am beginning to believe my brother is so much stronger than I even realized.

"Ronin, the first thing you must do is acknowledge that it is not separate from you. It is you. You fight yourself creating an unnecessary battle. We teach our young males incorrectly. We teach them it is not part of us, that it is to be controlled when in reality it is a fundamental piece of who we are. You felt the strength of my fury. Do you honestly think I control it by force?" He looks at me and sees the shock on my face. He chuckles, "Close your eyes. Focus. Dive into your fury, know it, see that it is you."

I do as he says and go into my mind. I'm standing at a wall of dark churning clouds. They have always taught us to force dominance on it. I release my dominance and step into the cloud. I stand within the churning cloud, but to my shock, it is not a whirlwind of fury and emotion. It is calm and quiet. I feel it; my battle fury is not something I must control and dominate. It is like a limb, an extension of me. At that moment, the cloud solidifies into a mirror image of me except with black eyes.

I open my eyes and gasp. Dax chuckles again, "You have done in a few hours what took me years to realize."

"Hours?"

"You have been mentally focused for almost three hours." Again I am shocked. It felt like just a few minutes. "As usual, you are an overachiever."

This time I laugh with him, "I cannot thank you enough my brother. What you have just taught me has helped me in ways I never thought possible." I grab the back of his neck and bring our foreheads together, "Thank you."

"I am here for you." He whispers.

"I thank the Goddess for that daily." We sit for a while longer staring into space. The turmoil in my mind is gone. I still worry for my mate but now I can focus on the tasks at hand. "Time to wrap up our plan."

We stand and head to the conference room. Dax asks Sia to have everyone join us. When we get there, everyone is waiting for us, including the crew of the Liberation, who participate via video. "Everyone, take a seat, please. We are less than a day from the Outpost. Let us review our plan. Sia, please pull up a view of the asteroid." A sizeable irregular body appears on the screen. It orbits a large gas giant. "This is the Outpost. We will cloak the Emancipation when we drop from subspace. The Liberation will continue to the base. Sirk will dress and act as Captain of the vessel. Sirk, have you built our purpose in going to the base?"

Sirk stands so we can see him clearly on the Liberation, "Yes. We go in under orders from the Cruxlin high command. We are here for a tour of the facility. This is a believable reason due to the fact that they have given the Cruxlin the approval for a tour of the base on a somewhat regular basis to keep our leadership happy. We tried to force the same on their homeworld but they refused."

Dax nods, "That will have to be good enough. Now we do not know enemy numbers so Sirk, Elena, and Nalax will go in on the Cruxlin transport ship and Ronin, Doraj, and I will go in on a cloaked Nlyaxian transport right behind them. We will land the transport in a far, unoccupied section of the landing bay. We will be disguised as mutated soldiers and when the opportunity arises, we will exit and start searching the base."

Ronin steps forward, "While we search the base the Liberation team will get their tour of the base. If they see anything that might give us an idea where she is or might be, use your comm to let us know."

Elana speaks up, "Do we know she's there?"

Dax and I nod, "She is definitely closer but we cannot connect with her. She is either sedated still or... or she is blocking us."

Nalax looks at us confused, "Why would she do that?"

Dax paces, "Because she knows we will come for her and she knows they are after Ronin. She will do everything she can to prevent them from achieving their goal which includes trying to prevent us from finding her... or feeling what she is going through."

I cannot help it as I pace with him, "She is headstrong and stubborn but we definitely feel her closer. Nalax and Elana will take explosives with them and placing them in locations around the base so if we need a distraction once we have her we have options."

An unfamiliar male voice speaks up, "There are many flaws in your plan."

Sia speaks before I can ask, "Ronin and crews allow me to introduce Nairb. He is the AI on the Liberation. Nairb, they know there are flaws but we have little choice."

"Of course they do. Forget about the rescue and continue on the mission to liberate slaves."

I cannot contain the growl, "Sia..."

"I agree, Ronin. Nairb we are a family and we *never*, ever leave family in the hands of an enemy."

"Forgive me. I am still learning. I am truly sorry I did not mean to upset anyone."

"It is alright Nairb but remember June is the only reason we are free and Sia is sentient. She is everything to the crews of these vessels. He is right though, we have many gaps in our intelligence on the base. The mission is incredibly risky but we are at our limit of attainable information at this point."

Nairb speaks up, "Not necessarily. When we drop from hyperspace Sia and I can start our attack on the base systems. Lutetian technology is usually stolen from others so we will most likely be able to get in and find where she is on the base. Also, we can attempt to contact her via her comm implant unless it's been discovered and removed. Minimally we can feed information to the teams as we get it."

Doraj smiles, "Good. That is good. Feeding us information will help and if you take over systems even better."

"Yes, our chances definitely go up. Sia, Nairb, the first order of business once you get in is to find her location then we need details on that base, especially troop counts and armaments."

"Understood." Sia chimes.

"Questions?" I ask everyone. "None. Good. Our goal is to get in and out as quickly as possible to limit risk to teams. How much time before we drop from hyperspace?"

"Four hours." As if sensing my surprise Sia adds, "We've been pushing the engines to get here as quickly as possible."

I nod. Everyone wants her back as fast as possible. "Ok, everyone takes time to prepare for the mission we are almost ready to get our family back."

The four hours go by quickly. We are all on our respective bridges dressed and ready for this. Ronin and I stand on the Emancipation bridge as we drop from hyperspace.

Sia comes over the comms, "Out of hyperspace and we are cloaked."

Ronin and I stare at the screen. We cannot see the station yet but she is definitely there. I touch my Kokoro and still cannot reach her. I give a frustrated sigh, "I still cannot get to her, but she is definitely here." Ronin nods.

He looks at me, "We get her back today."

June

They wake Divad and I from sleep as three mutants barge into the pod. They hit him with a tranquilizer and grab me. Strange. Usually, it's just my Nlyaxian soldier, but he's not even here. They don't take me to the infirmary either we are headed straight to the torture room. Neith must have something important.

We enter the room and my stomach drops. It's not Neith. Some other Lutetian stands in the center of the room with a maniacal smile on her face. Not good but I will just kill her when she enters my mind so I relax. The three mutants tie me to the wall as usual but they also tie my ankles and do not leave. They line the far wall by the door. This situation is starting out very different and I do not like it.

"Human," the Lutetian said with a hissing voice, "They have been too easssy on you, and I plan to remedy that."

"The Queen ordered you to do this?"

"No, no, no." It backhands me hard enough to break my lip. "You do not talk unless it isss to ansssswer my quessstionsss." It starts to slowly wander the room. "However, I will ansssswer your quessstion. No, the Queen did not order thisss, but when I get all the information ssshe needsss from you ssshe will reward me."

We'll see about that.

"Now I will sssset sssome… expectationsss. You do not anssswer and I cut. You talk without a quesssstion, I cut. You give me bad looksss, I cut. Do you undersssstand?"

I nod. She lashes out and cuts a deep gash across my shoulder.

"I dislike the attitude." It hisses a laugh. "Torturing isss ssso much fun. Oh I almossst forgot, when I am done…" at that moment a Nlyaxian I haven't seen before walks in the room. He has clothes on but is free. "Thisss Nlyaxian will breed you and sssince you cannot be trusssted to sssubmit, he will do it while you are tied."

She sees the shock on my face and laughs again, "Yessss human, he isss going to have you many, many timesss until you have a second fertilized." She looks back at him, "Would you like to introduce yoursssself?"

He smiles but with no warmth and slowly walks toward me. I cannot stop the reflex to struggle against the bonds. He laughs and leans closely in with his hands resting on both sides of my head. "Hello. I would not have minded having to force you to submit. I rather like the fighters." He removes a hand from the wall and moves it to my breast, gently stroking my nipple until it hardens. Stupid body. He then pinches it so hard I cry out in pain.

"Do you like that? I think you do." His hand wanders lower. He moves his fingers through my slit, luckily I am dry as a bone. I do not get off on pain. "Pitty. Don't worry my cock will make you scream."

"Enough." The Lutetian says. He moves back to the wall with the soldiers. "Time to sssstart."

It feels like it's been hours since she started to ask questions. I worry for the baby. She has hit me several times in the ribs and stomach. I know she's cracked at least one rib. It covered my body in cuts, enough that I'm a little lightheaded. I have given her information but most of it is lies she doesn't seem to be able to tell the difference. I tried to resist at the beginning just because... fuck her, but after a while I just wanted it to stop. She hasn't asked me any questions for several minutes, she just wanders the room.

She then says the words I've been dreading. "Mate her."

"No, I've cooperated." I hate the sound of my panic right now.

She laughs, "I never sssaid thisss wasss not going to happen either way." She looks at him, "Do it."

He chuckles and walks toward me while removing his already hard cock from his pants. "No! I will kill you!" He just continues to laugh.

"Struggle more. It makes me harder." I don't stop because I can't. I can only see Kaxlin walking toward me. My mind is spiraling. He freezes when he is about two feet from me. He's staring above my head. He turns to look at the Lutetian and screams, "*What is that*?" He's pointing above my head.

"What are you talking about?" It asks him.

"The mark on her arm! That is the mark of the royal family! You said they were all dead!"

I'm confused. He has a panicked look on his face now. He put himself back in his pants.

Now the Lutetian is screaming, "I sssaid mate her!!"

He moves fast and takes off its head, and the soldiers attack. As he battles them, I see Divad and Neith come in. Neith comes straight to me and releases the shackles. A blaster goes off, we turn, and the Nlyaxian stands in front of us, looking at me. He whispers, "Please forgive me." He falls to the floor. Divad rushes over since the rest are already dead. He checks him, looks at me, and shakes his head.

"I wish I could say he didn't deserve that, but he did." It's then I notice my Nlyaxian soldier. He looks healthier, his skin is back to a healthier Nlyaxian green. His hair is clean and straight. He still has spikes coming from his skin but his muscles are growing again. He definitely looks more Nlyaxian. It's then I notice he holds my clothes and Katana.

I stagger over to him and grab his arm. A tear falls as I say, "Thank you."

He helps me dress and says, "Thank you."

I nod at him.

"Ok Neith, what's the plan?"

"Follow me. I can get us into the lower levels now."

I pull a Kitana, but Divad says, "June, we need to heal you."

"We don't have time. I will be fine. Neith takes point. Divad follows Neith." I look at the soldier, "What is your name?"

He gets a confused look, "I do not know."

I put my hand on his arm, "It's ok. I will call you Sam. He was my friend and so are you." Sam was my first sensei's name. He nods. "Sam, you take the rear."

We head out. Neith is careful to take us down unused hallways and we duck into rooms when she hears someone coming. The first time we do this she says, "Do not move or ssspeak at all. We can feel the vibrationsss in the floorsss."

We take about ten minutes to reach the lift. Sam steps forward, surprising me. He holds his arm next to the device beside the lift and it opens. We all get on board and Neith presses some buttons I can't read and I feel the lift move. She looks at me, "I could not add myssself to the floor but I can add otherss so I added Sssam so he could get usss to the floorss."

"Genius Neith." She smiles at me. I lean against the wall for support.

Divad looks worried and looks at Neith, "Are there any medical kits or anything on our way or once we are there?"

Neith thinks for a minute, "There should be."

Not completely happy he nods. "Divad. I will be ok. Nothing is life-threatening. Once we take the base you can immediately take me to the infirmary and heal me ok? Just make sure you knock me out because that shit hurts."

Instead of calming him, I can see him fighting his battle fury, "They kept you awake while they healed you? Fucking monsters."

"Please Divad. Calm. You can take care of me as soon as we are safe." He calms himself and nods.

Neith whisper, "There may be a guard on the floor."

"Sam and Divad, can you sweep the floor and eliminate any threats?" They both nod. The lift doors open to another dark hallway. Sam and Divad move out of the lift and go in opposite directions. Neith takes my arms and leads me to a door about thirty feet to the right of the lift. The doors automatically open. Soft lights come on as we enter.

It's a vast cavern. There are rows and rows of black pods. They are stacked ten high. Each has a soft green light that circles each end of the pod. I'm overwhelmed by the number. I walk to the first row. I can see now there is a window you can see into the pods. I look at the one that is slightly below eye level with me. In it sleeps a huge Nlyaxian.

I hear the others join us and turn to look. Both Divad and Sam stare at the space in shock. I start to feel a pull. I turn and walk further into the space.

I try to ignore the pain in my side. About halfway down the aisle, there is a break so you can reach other aisles. I turn because I am drawn to something that way. I walk by five or six aisles before I turn down one. About halfway down I stop and turn toward what is drawing me. I touch the pod and it slides out so I can see it. I can't help the disappointment I feel. It's not Aanon.

I jump when Divad speaks next to me, "His name is Ekul. He is second in command of the Ssadab. They are an elite warriors unit second only to the Queen's guard."

"I was pulled here. Wake him first. I feel the pull again." Sam grabs my arm for support and follows me to the next pod. Again it's not Aanon. I touch the pod so it comes out and head to the next. After about twenty minutes I found every member of the Ssadab. Twenty pods have begun their process to wake their inhabitants. I'm tired. Sam picks me up and takes me over to a wall and sits with me in his arms so I can rest.

"Thanks, Sam." He nods. I decide its time to take care of more of the shards as we wait.

I close my eyes but he shakes me a little to open my eyes. "No. It tires you. When we are safe, not before."

"Are you sure? I don't mind."

He nods his head. "No. My friend. Not right now." I nod too tired to argue.

I must have fallen asleep because I wake to someone holding my arm with my Kokoro. He lets go and bows his head. "Forgive me, my Queen. I needed to see it, to know... that our line continues." He looks up at Sam, "Commander, what are our orders?" Sam gives him a confused look.

"He has been through a lot. He does not remember who he is. For now, his name is Sam, and he is my protector." The Nlyaxian gives me a shocked look but I am too tired to worry about it. "You are second in command of the Ssadab?" He nods. "Did Divad give you any information on our situation?" He shakes his head.

I nod, knowing Divad is busy waking up all the pods I pulled. "We are on a Lutetian base." He gets a shocked look again but I know the reasoning behind this one. "Yes, they are still alive. They took a large contingent of Nlyaxian's prisoners when your world was attacked. You and all those in these pods have been in stasis for three years. The Lutetian Queen plans on breeding these males with females from my homeworld for a new breeding army. We aim to stop that."

He thinks for a long time then asks, "How many enemies are on this base?" Good.

"With the Nlyaxians we are waking we should be able to take the base. They have about forty Lutetian and ninety-five mutated soldiers." He gives me a lopsided smile. "That is a manageable number." He stands abruptly and I realize that Divad and Neith approach. I see him tense but before I can say anything he relaxes and gives me a shocked look. "She has the mark of the Goddess."

It's my turn to be shocked. "You can see it?" He nods. I gently grab Sam's face and turn it. "What about this?"

"Commander... Sam. She marked you."

Sam reaches up and feels behind his ear. Then looks at me with a question on his face. I nod. "It's how I knew I needed to help you." He closes his eyes and reopens them. He is more at peace now than he was before. I smile softly at him.

Divad interrupts the moment, "June, I found something that should heal most of the cuts but if you have any broken bones, we will have to find different instruments."

I nod. "Can it tell if the baby is ok? She punched me several times in the stomach," I put my hands on my abdomen, "I'm worried." I look back up and again I see males fighting battle fury. Ugh. "Calm. Will it?"

Divad closes his eyes to regain his control but the other two are struggling. "Close your eyes and find your calm." They both do as I ask. "Now what is your name?"

When he opens them again, his eyes are back to normal. "My name is Ekul, my Queen. You carry...?"

I finish for him, "Yes, I carry Ronin's child."

"Your mate is Ronin, the High Commander of the Nlyaxian Armies?"

I nod. He closes his eyes again, "I cannot tell you what that will mean to the males we wake. The high commander is highly respected and friends with many of us."

I look back at Divad expectantly, "Unfortunately this device will only be able to heal surface wounds. I am sorry, my Queen. We will need to get you to the infirmary to check." I nod and look at my belly. I hope you are ok little one. "What about broken bones?"

"She broke at least one rib, but that is all I can tell."

"You look pale. I dislike it."

"It will have to wait till we take the base. There is nothing we can do right now. How much longer before we can move out?" Divad heals the cuts he can see.

"The effects of stasis should be worn off within ten minutes or so." I nod. When he is done with the ones, he can see I lift my shirt so he can get the rest. Ekul stands abruptly and turns giving me some modicum of modesty. I appreciate it but at this point, I have been naked so much that I barely notice it anymore.

Once the rest are healed, I feel a little better but not much. I'm worried she did some internal damage. The bruising I saw when I lifted my shirt was shocking.

I look up and notice more males standing guard around me. I pat Sam, "Ok help me up, please." He stands with me in his arms and gently sets me on my feet. Not gonna lie, I am fighting pain still, and it does not bode well.

"Ekul, can you brief your team on what's going on, please." He gives a low whistle and twenty intimidating Nlyaxian males materialize in front of him.

Being around this many Nlyaxian males makes me uncomfortable. I have too much baggage. Sam touches my shoulder, "Alright?"

I give him a nervous smile and nod. "I do not have the best experience with Nlyaxian males besides my mates of course."

He gives me a questioning look. "A story for another time, ok?" He nods.

When Ekul finishes I step forward with Sam and Divad flanking me. "Now you know our current situation. What you do not know is they stole me not because I am your Queen because they do not understand that. No, they took me to draw Ronin here. They need him for some reason and I will *not* allow them to have him." I pause at the look on Ekul's face, "What is it?"

"I know why they want him?" I motion for him to continue. "I can tell you if they had our ruling Triad captive, the males would do just about anything they said to ensure their safety."

"I assumed that was why they wanted him but I doubt you would be willing, at least I hope you would not be willing to do what they want. They want you to take the females of my world by force and impregnate them. They want you to rape females."

I need to see their reaction to this and I am satisfied with what I see. Revulsion, denial, and disgust are all I see written on the faces of these males. Good. I relax a bit.

A male at the back of the group speaks up, "We would die first."

I close my eyes, relieved by his statement. "Thank you for that. I have met Nlyaxian males since they took me from my homeworld that do not have such honor." I open my eyes again and give them a determined look, "So we need to take this base. Ronin and my crew will try to rescue me, and we need this base secure before they get here."

Ekul speaks up, "What about weapons?"

I motion Neith forward, "This is Neith. Yes, she is Lutetian, but she is the reason you are awake right now. She is my friend and blessed by the Goddess. She is under our protection. Understood?"

They all salute. Ok, that's cool. "Neith, are there any weapons storage areas we can get to before we begin?"

"Actually," Neith begins, "I can pull up a map of the base over on a display on the wall, and we can walk through all the information."

Ekul gets a smile on his face, "Excellent."

The males all follow Neith over to the section of the wall that has a screen. Divad and Sam hold me back, "What is it?"

Divad is the first to speak, "Can you feel where your mates are?"

"Yes. They are close."

"Can you reach out to them via the link?" He sees the uncomfortable look that comes over my face. "What is it?"

"I have been blocking them."

Sam asks, "Why?"

"I didn't want them to feel what I was going through. They have both been through too much already. I don't want to cause more pain for them."

Sam looks uncomfortable, "You should not block. They are your mates. I am sure they are distraught."

That is the most I have ever heard him speak at once. It makes me feel more guilty. I drop my chin to my chest. "I'm not sure I could handle their anger with me right now. I may seem strong but they came close to breaking me here."

Sam puts his finger under my chin and lifts, "They are your mates. They are anxious, not angry." I nod. Sam's face is becoming more Nlyaxian with every treatment.

A tear rolls down my face, and I think about the baby my mates do not know exists. I shake my head and back away, "No. No, I can't. Not yet."

I turn and walk to where the others are but not before I hear Divad say, "There must be something else stopping her."

I wish I knew why I feel fear when I think of that wall, but I do. I'm not ready to handle them yet, and I don't want them to feel my pain.

Ronin

Both ships sit orbiting the base, just above where the Liberation was instructed to be. One visible, one not. Dax, Doraj, and I sit in a cloaked transport, waiting for clearance to dock. We sit directly beneath the other transport. We plan to go in as one just in case they can detect two ships entering.

"Sia, how does the attack go on your front?" I ask.

"It has been challenging. An energy field surrounding the base prevents our signal from getting in. We hope that once the transports are through the field, we will be successful."

Doraj asks, "You will use the transports as signal boosters?"

"Essentially, yes. As soon as we have system access, we will start our attack. Sirk has received clearance."

"Ok. Here we go."

We are using magnetic locks to keep us attached to the other transport until we pass through the docking field. Once through, we will release them and find a place to land. I dislike that we have not been able to feel June. I can only pray to the Goddess she is safe.

We pass through the field and release the maglocks. "Sia. Any indication they know we are here."

"No indication. We are starting our systems attack."

Doraj points to an area far from the rest of the transports lining the bay. I nod and he begins his descent. Dax and I lift our hoods and seal the masks. Now there are two mutated soldiers standing behind Doraj. We are bigger than most of the Lutetian soldiers but there is not much we can do about that.

He shuts down all systems except the cloak and pulls his hood up. Dax chuckles, "Goddess, we are hideous."

Doraj snorts, "You are, but I am handsome no matter what."

I chuckle, "Ok, enough. It's time to find our mate."

Dax

Both Ronin and I are on edge because we have yet to reach June. I can feel her; she is very close. I need to find her because I know something is wrong. I haven't told Ronin of my concern, but it has worsened as we got closer. Something is wrong, and she needs us.

We exit the transport on the far side of the ship to minimize someone seeing us materialize from thin air. We all fought in the Lutetian wars, so we all remember how the mutants walked. Their gait is irregular, and we mimic it as best we can as we start across the bay.

In the distance, we can see the other team at the bottom of their ramp talking to a Lutetian. I cannot help the spike of dread at seeing one of them. I quickly push it down and continue forward, flanking Dax and Doraj. As we go behind a transport, I stop them.

I look at the floor. Whispering, "Ronin, she is beneath us." He closes his eyes and when he opens them he nods and turns to continue to the door, we see in the distance. We are almost at the door when alarms begin to sound. Shit. They know.

I look over at the other team, and they are being directed back to their transport. Strange. Once they are back aboard the transport, Nalax comes over the comm, "They don't know about us. The alarm is because they discovered some missing prisoners. I also heard something about an incursion in the lower levels."

Ronin and I look at each other and nod.

"You three with me." A Lutetian yells at us. It's the best way to find June because I'm pretty sure my mate is causing this trouble. We fall in line behind the Lutetian, hoping it takes us straight to the problem.

June

We are all packed in the lift and since I am the only one with weapons; I am at the door with my Katana out and ready. My new friends were extremely unhappy that I was unwilling to give up my Katana. I chuckle internally, remembering that conversation.

Ekul makes a mistake saying, "My Queen, we can be more effective with your swords."

I squint my eyes at him, "Tell you what, if you can take them from me, you can have them. I hear Divad chuckle behind me. He knows. "I am giving you permission."

I see it when he decides because he doesn't want me to go at all. He stalks forward and when he reaches for me I grab his wrist and use his momentum to flip him onto the mat. I almost laugh at the look on his face. I feel one other reach for my Katana. Excellent. Before he can grab them I grab his arm and deposit him on top of Ekul.

Two more land in a pile before Ekul yells, "Enough." He pushes everyone off him and stands. "Point taken, my Queen. You are a warrior in your own right. I dislike the idea of you at risk, but the decision is yours."

Divad walks up, still chuckling, and slaps him on the shoulders, "Do not feel bad, Ekul. Ronin has yet to beat her in the ring."

The shock is back on his face. To me, he says, "Truly?"

I nod.

He lets out a loud laugh, "Oh, Goddess. I cannot wait to see that!"

So we wait in the lift to get to a level that has a weapons locker. The lift stops, and the door opens. On the other side stands three Lutetian, but before they can even get their minds out of the shock of seeing us, their heads are no longer attached to their bodies. We all studied the map, so I take off at a trot with Neith at my side. She stops in front of the door and waves her arm in front of the scanner. The doors open to a large room with many weapons. Everyone filters in, and Neith shuts and locks the door.

All the males are loading up with weapons but most of what is there are blasters and weapons similar to those. I look around when I see something leaning in the corner of a far wall. Run over and slide on my knee to get to them.

It's another set of hand-forged Makoto Katana. The Saya is a genuine buffalo horn on the mouth and ends with genuine sharkskin under red cotton Sageo. The Tsuka (handle) is Rayskin wrapped with Red Japanese cotton Ito with Menuki. They are identical to my own, except mine are wrapped with teal Ito. They are Ahmya's. Tears are streaming down my cheeks.

Sam softly asks, "Who do those belong to?" As if he knows the owner of these is special to me.

"My sister. Her name is Ahmya. If these are here…" My voice is barely a whisper. I close my eyes and hug them to my chest. "I will find you. I promise."

"May I carry them for you?" He asks.

I nod, knowing I cannot if I plan to fight. He takes them gently and slings the harnesses over both shoulders. I open my eyes, and I am once again furious. I need vengeance. I stand and turn to the rest. "It is time. My team will head to the control room the rest of the unit have their missions. No fucking mercy. Kill all Lutetian you come in contact with; Neith is the only Lutetian blessed by the Goddess on this base. If you do not have to, do not kill the soldiers. Their situation is not their fault. If they fight, then lethal force is authorized. Questions?"

Once again, they all salute. We line up at the door, and I yell, "*Move out!*"

My group is Ekul, Divad, Sam, and three others. We are moving fast and killing everything in our path. At some point, the alarms start. "Ok, they know we are coming." I stop the group from rounding the corner. I can sense them. There is a large group of Lutetian waiting for us. Not on my watch. Not my team. I close my eyes and lash out at them with my mind. The Lutetian screams and fall. They are dead. I stagger a bit. That took a lot out of me, but I have things to do. I round the corner with a blaster. The soldiers seem confused. Three of them stand there in shock.

"June?" one of them says.

I... I know that voice. I stumble again, and Sam grabs my arm for support. There is a roar, and two mutants launch themselves at Sam. "*Stop!*" I scream. I can barely keep my eyes open. Everyone freezes. "Ronin? Dax?"

The two mutants remove hoods from their heads to reveal my mates. My beautiful mates. I cry again, but my body can no longer hold up. I collapse. I see their faces go from happy to scared before I descend into darkness.

Dax

The Lutetian are waiting for something in the hallway. There are five of them and three of us. We are all pointing blasters down the hall. After a few minutes, the Lutetian drop their weapons, grab their heads, and begin screaming. It is an awful sound. They collapse dead, bleeding from every hole in their heads. I hear Ronin murmur, "What the hell just happened?"

Then our mate rounds the corner. She looks like a vengeful warrior, angry and dangerous. Goddess, she is beautiful. I cannot stop the word that falls from my lips, "June?" I cannot believe it's her after so long.

She staggers and almost falls but a mutant grabs her arm. I launch across the room, letting my battle roar shake the walls. We are almost to her when she screams, "*Stop*!" Then I noticed the six blasters pointed at me, ready to kill us. But my mind cannot process what I am seeing. Armed Nlyaxian males surround my mate.

I hear her voice and look back at her, "Ronin? Dax?" We have the disguises on. Both Ronin and I remove our hoods. The most beautiful smile blooms across her face, then she collapses. We once again launch ourselves at her. I catch her. "June. Please," I whisper. I look at the group, which is on a knee, saluting Ronin, but he is next to me, looking at our mate. A Nlyaxian comes forward; I recognize him, I think.

"I am a medical officer. Can I look at her?"

I nod, and he looks at Ronin. He is staring at her but not responding. "Ronin." He looks at me, lost, then looks at the medical officer and nods.

He examines her and then looks for someone, "Neith. We need an infirmary now!" It's then a Lutetian step forth. I pull my blaster, pointing it at the Lutetian, but before I can pull the trigger, all the Nlyaxians step in the way. "What are you doing?"

The medical male answers, "She is under June's protection and is blessed by the Goddess. She is the only reason we are free. Her name is Neith."

I am utterly shocked by this. I look down at my unconscious mate, "Neith, can you help her? Please?" She steps around the males protecting her.

"I will do everything in my power."

I stand with June in my arms. The one, I think his name is Ekul speaks to Ronin, "We still need to take the base." I can see his conflict. He needs to be near her, and he needs to make this place safe for her.

"Ronin. I will take her to the infirmary and keep her safe." He looks at me and, after a minute, grabs my neck and puts his head to mine, "Keep you both safe."

The mutant, medical male, and I follow Neith towards the infirmary while Ronin and his new team go to rip apart this base.

"What are your names?"

Neith surprises me by answering, "You know me. I am Neith, a name your mate gave me. The medical officer is Divad. And this," pointing to the mutant, which I realize is a Nlyaxian, "is Sam. She also gave him his name."

We come to a lift and take it to a new floor. We get off when it stops and are met with some resistance, but it is easily ended. We enter a room with two Lutetian in lab garb. They immediately panic, and Sam puts them down.

"Put her over here."

I set her on the table he indicated. He runs tests on the display next to the table. He mumbles, "Damn it. I knew she was worse off than she was letting me know." Instruments lower from the ceiling and begin to move about her.

"Is she going to be ok?" I ask quietly.

"She has internal bleeding. I am healing it now. Neith, how do I synthesize new human blood?"

Neith rushes to a machine, "I can do it."

After a few minutes, she calls to Divad, "It'sss ready."

I realize I am in the way the third time I need to duck out of the way of a medical arm. "Please back up and let me work."

I step back next to Sam. He whispers to me, "She will make it. She is a warrior."

I look at him. I know him. "You are the commander of the Ssadab. Your name is…"

He interrupts me, "Sam. My name is Sam."

"Alright. Sam. You helped June?"

He shakes his head, "No. She saved me. I was lost; she helped me find my way back."

Divad walks over, "She will pull through, but the medical table will work on her for a while. Where is Aanon? I expected him to be with you."

Confused, "Aanon is gone. He died on Nlyax."

Now he looks confused, "I don't understand. June said Ronin, you, and Aanon were her mates."

I cannot comprehend what he says, "She said that?"

He nods.

I freeze, "How many more Nlyaxians are here?"

"There are around twenty-four Nlyaxian males in stasis."

Sam says, "She was disappointed in the room the pods were in. I think she would have found him if he was there."

"Dax, this is not the only base with Nlyaxians in stasis. Neith told us that there are more at other bases."

"I want more than anything to believe he is alive."

Sam finishes my thought, "But you fear finding he is not."

I can only nod.

Neith speaks up from June's side, "I do not think June would say he was her mate if she didn't know it to be true."

"Thank you, all of you, for helping her."

"She is special. You are sure she will be ok?" Neith asks Divad, and he nods. "And the baby?"

My entire body locks up. I look at Divad. He sighs, "This really should come from your mate." I can only growl, "You need to remain calm. Yes, your mate is carrying Ronin's child."

The arms lift into the ceiling signaling the healing cycle is done. I walk to the table and lift her into my arms. She is so perfect. Ronin comes over the comm in my ear, "Are you ok? What's wrong?"

I tap my ear, "Nothing. She had internal bleeding, but Divad repaired all the damage. She is resting. Ronin... she is going to be fine." I cannot tell him yet. When the base is taken, and we are safe, she is safe.

"Dax." I look down, and her eyes are on me. Seeing her in person feels fundamental to my existence.

"Hello, beautiful. You gave us quite a scare."

She looks at her lap, "Sorry, I wasn't paying attention to my surroundings. I have no excuse."

"June, look at me. None of this is your fault. The only ones to blame are the ones that stole you, and they are dead."

Fear registers on her face, "Sitruc..."

I nod. "He is dead as well." She relaxes a bit and raises her hand to caress the ridges on my face. I close my eyes and just enjoy the feeling of her fingers on my skin. I cannot help my body's reaction to her hands on me. "Mate, as much as I love your hands on me, I think you should stop for now because my control is thin."

I open my eyes and see fear cross her face, "Divad! The baby?"

She looks over at the medical officer, but I answer instead. "The baby is fine, my beautiful mate."

She looks back at me, "Are you sure?" I nod. She wraps her arms around my neck and holds me close. "Does Ronin know?" she whispers.

I shake my head, "That is for you to tell." I can feel her shaking, "What is wrong?"

"Will he be upset? Will he want the baby?"

I pull her back to look at her face, shocked by her question, "Why? Why would he not be ecstatic you carry his child?"

She shrugs her shoulders, "Not all human men want to be fathers, and we've never discussed it."

Divad growls in the background. I smooth her hair back, "June, a child to a Nlyaxian, is the highest joy. Only finding our mate ranks higher."

She nods, not looking altogether convinced. "Did we take the base?"

I shake my head. "Ronin took your team to take the base."

She gets off my lap, "Neith, can you tell where we are taking the base?"

Neith looks down at the display in her hand, "Team one is fighting for the control center, teams two and three have secured their goals, and team four is very close to taking the bay."

June looks at me and chuckles at the look on my face, "I have a lot to tell you, but first, we need to assist Ronin. Neith have teams two and three start a sweep of all floors starting at the bottom and work up but tell them to leave prisoners where they are until we can figure out what's going on there." Neith nods and relays her orders.

My mate is a born leader.

June

"Neith, is there a way to flank the enemy team one is fighting?" We are on our way to help Ronin. He may not need our help, but I do not care. I need to see him.

"Not flank, but we can come in from a different hallway and achieve nearly the same goal. I will lead the way." I nod at her. She switches directions a bit, and we go to a lift.

We get to the floor, and I stop the group and look to Neith, "I am worried for your safety. Lutetian are not the best fighters. Sorry, I don't mean to insult you."

She nods, "I understand, but I want to fight for you. I am very good with a blaster, but hand-to-hand is not my strong suit."

"Ok. I'm good with you being with us, but Divad, if we get into close quarters battle, I need you to stay near Neith. Protect our flank." They both nod. "Dax and Sam, you're with me at the front." Both nod. I draw my blasters from my thighs and move out.

We can hear the sounds of blasters. "I'm going to the other side of the hallway. Dax, you're with me. Sam, you'll handle this side. As soon as we are across, start taking out the enemy."

Dax and I leap across the hallway and start firing into the sides of the enemies engaged with Ronin and the team. We are able to take out almost half of the enemy before they return fire. They begin to panic and start firing wildly in both directions. Good. They're off balance and making mistakes.

They're down to five Lutetian and about eight soldiers when they retreat into the control room and close the door. Dax, Sam, and I move to meet Ronin and the team at the door. When I come around the corner, all I can see is him. A tear escapes, and I run toward him and leap into his waiting arm.

He's kissing my face, then his lips lock onto mine, and I get lost in the passion he pours into it. He eventually breaks the kiss and puts his forehead on mine. "Mate."

I put my hands on both sides of his face."I missed you. I'm sorry I wasn't focused on my surroundings."

He shakes his head, "No, June. I should have been there."

My turn to shake my head, "No, Ronin. Definitely not your fault." I notice all of the team around him are on their knee with a salute to the chest. "And I'm mad at you." I give a fake growl. "You don't think it was important to tell me who you are?"

He gets an apologetic look, "Yeah, sorry about that. I did not think it was important at the time." I kiss him again and get down.

I chuckle, "It probably wasn't until I found an entire cavern of Nlyaxian males." He gets a shocked look on his face, "I have a lot to tell you, Ronin, but we need to root out the last of the enemy so we can relax a bit. Neith, is there a way we can override that door?"

Neith steps forward, and I see surprise but not hostility on Ronin's face. He gives me a look that says, 'of course, you made friends with a Lutetian.' I chuckle. "Unfortunately, like most ships, it is almost impossible to get in from the outside."

Sia comes over the speaker, "I believe I can help with that."

"Sia! It is so good to hear your voice!"

"It is good to hear from and see you as well, June. I was distraught. Nairb and I have gained access to the internal systems. The Lutetian made a rather large mistake connecting the control systems in a way that made it easy for us to gain entry. What would you like us to do, Captain?"

I smile and look at Dax and Ronin, "Ready?" They both nod in excitement. I draw my Katana and say, "Open the doors, Sia."

As the doors open, the three of us go in as a unit. We are deadly, and all the enemies in the control room are dead in a matter of minutes. Blood drips from my Katana and Ronin's axe. I spin my blades to remove the blood and return them to where they belong.

I turn to look at the others joining us. I'm confused by the look on their faces. As one, they go to a knee and salute. I whisper to him, "That's going to get old fast." Dax and Divad burst out laughing.

Ronin addresses the issue, "Stand my friends."

I need to tell Ronin before someone else lets its slip, "Ronin, I need to tell you something." I'm nervous and start fussing with the edges of my shirt.

He grabs my hands, "What is it, my mate?"

I cannot handle the worry in his eyes, "I'm pregnant." He gets a confused look on his face.

Divad speaks softly, "He does not know that word."

I close my eyes. Of course, he doesn't, idiot. I open my eyes and say, "I carry your child."

His face goes blank, and he is quiet. The longer he is quiet, the more I panic. "Ronin?"

My voice brings him out of it, and he kneels in front of me. Gently he places his hands on my abdomen. After a few minutes, he wraps his arms around my waist and pulls me close, laying his forehead against my stomach. "I am not sure what I did to deserve this, but thank the Goddess and my mate for this gift."

When he looks up at me, my heart nearly stops. The joy and awe on his face bring tears to my eyes. "Are you happy?" It's a dumb question, but I need to hear him say it.

He kisses me tenderly and pulls back to look into my eyes, "Very, my mate. Very." I pull him in for a hug. I want to hear his heartbeat. There's a small part of me that's worried that this is some sort of dream. I feel Dax join our circle. I angle my head back for him to kiss me. He does it with passion. When he releases the kiss, Ronin does the same. Someone behind us clears their throat.

Ronin pulls back and smiles down at me, "Soon, mate."

Dax adds with heat in his voice, "Very soon."

I cannot stop the small moan, "Not soon enough."

Suddenly we hear a scream, and I turn to see Nalax and Elana racing toward me. I open my arms, and I am now surrounded by my friends. I love them so much. Elana leans back after a few seconds and looks down at my stomach.

She looks back at my face in shock. I nod.

"What?" Nalax asks as she notices our silent communication.

"I carry Ronin's child." I am expecting the scream that comes from Nalax, so I am prepared; the others, not so much. I see a couple of them grimace at the sound. I chuckle.

I then notice the Cruxlin that walked in. The smile falls from my face. I look at Ronin. "This is Sirk. He has joined our cause. His people are in bondage by their own, and he has asked for our help to free them."

I look back to Sirk. "Welcome, Sirk." He bows his head.

"Let me introduce my new friends. Neith has also asked for help to free the oppressed of her people. Ronin, I believe you know Divad already, but he has been my friend since they tried to force him to rape me." Ronin and Dax both growl low and dangerous. Divad pales a bit. "He refused and did everything he could to protect me."

I walk to Sam. "This is Sam. He has been through a great deal and remembers nothing of his past. He has been my protector." Both my mates look at me, shocked. "What?"

Ronin is the first to speak, "By naming him your protector, you have named him commander of the Queen's guard. A great honor."

I don't even need to think about it. I nod. "He is worthy."

Ronin and Dax walk to Sam and put a hand on each shoulder. "Sam, will you give your life for hers?"

I dislike that question, but before I can speak, Divad catches my eye and gives a slight shake of his head. Fine.

Sam looks to me, "Without hesitation."

My mates seem satisfied with his answer and nod. Dax smiles at him, "Sam, you and I were good friends in your past life. I trust you with the life of my mate." Sam nods at Dax.

"Do you both know the warriors?" Speaking of all the new males.

Both nod and smile, "It is good to see so many of our brothers again."

Oh. "Well, they are far from the only ones. We woke all the Ssadab, but there are still around twenty-four hundred Nlyaxian males in stasis in the caverns below us."

Ronin stumbles a bit, and Ekul steadies him with a hand at his elbow. "Impossible."

Ekul answers him, "Yes, old friend. You have been alone far too long. Your people are here." I can feel the deep emotion emanating from Ronin right now.

"There are also eight hundred human females on this base somewhere. Some of them are currently in breeding pods, possibly in horrible situations. We need to go there."

Many of the males in the room growl. "I think it would be best if myself and Nalax be there every time we open a door. The humans that are awake most likely have been through the same trauma as me." I look at Ronin and Dax. They both look very dangerous right now.

"Are you telling us there are Nlyaxian males that raped these females?" Ronin growls most of this question.

"Yes. I killed one of them, and Sam killed another," more growling, "but Neith says there were four, so two are unaccounted for. I need you all to calm yourselves. These women will see you like they see their rapists." That shocks them out of their anger. "I know they will be safe with you all, but I still have a hard time with Nlyaxian males I do not know. I have had months to recover, but it will be very fresh for them. Understood?"

They all nod. Good. I walk over to Ronin and Dax and hug them again. "I am not altogether comfortable with you putting yourself in danger in your condition."

I expected this statement at some point. "I know, Ronin, but I am the Goddess's Chosen Warrior. I have work that needs to be done and will not be prevented from doing so. Besides, the baby is in stasis, and it seems, will remain that way till we find Aanon."

Both of them freeze, "Yes, mates; he is alive and in stasis somewhere. He wasn't on Nlyax when it was attacked." I look at Dax with a smirk. "He was looking for you because he was angry you were not at the coronation. We will find him."

Dax barks a laugh, "That does sound like Aanon."

Ronin is still and whispers, "Are you sure?"

I put my hand over both their hearts and close my eyes. I pull them into my mind and the memory of his dream.

Ronin

I open my eyes, and I am somewhere else, but I recognize it. I look at my mate, "What is this?"

"Ronin, my skill in dreams have developed, but I can give you the details of that later. This," she waves her arms around at our surroundings, "this is where I met Aanon."

"Where?" I whisper.

She leads us toward Aanon's parent's house. I want to see him more than my next breath. We walk around the side of the house, and he is there. "This is a memory. He will not interact with you. It is an echo of him."

Dax whispers, "Aanon. He's alive."

I put my hand on his shoulder, unable to voice anything because my emotion is choking me. Aanon stands straight and turns to look at something next to the house.

We are back in the control room of the base. "Mates. Aanon is alive, and we will find him, but right now, we need to free those on this base."

At that, she turns and walks from the room with Sam and the Ssadab flanking her. Dax and I follow, still in shock. Divad is next to us. "Divad, what did she mean 'the child is in stasis until we find Aanon'?"

He nods, "Nlyaxian females exhibit the same from a biological perspective. The egg, once fertilized, goes into a sort of stasis. It does not restart growth until all the triad fertilize an egg."

"I never knew that."

He nods, "Most don't because usually all the mates are to-gether, so fertilization happens quickly." Makes sense.

"But the baby is healthy?" Dax asks.

"Perfectly healthy. Your offspring is strong, Ronin. Your mate has been through a lot here."

"Neith!" I hear June call the Lutetian. I'm still shocked my mate is friends with a Lutetian. "Neith, the communication device in the control room, does it give her the ability to connect with people here easier?" What is she referring to?

"Yes. We should dismantle it as quickly as possible."

She sees my questioning look. "There is a device in the control room that amplifies the mind so the Queen can communicate more clearly with the Lutetian on base."

I stop. That puts both my mate and my brother at risk. "I will take care of it if Neith could help me?"

Neith nods. Everyone has stopped. June looks worried we just got each other back; the idea of separating is less than pleasant. She turns to Neith, "Can you open a comm to the entire base?"

She nods, "Open."

"Team two, report."

"Sweeps completed," a voice comes over the speakers.

"Report to the control room. My mate is en route to meet you there."

"Understood."

"Please take care, Ronin. There can still be hostiles on this base." I walk to her and give her a kiss filled with the passion I feel for her.

"You as well, we have business to take care of later." I smell her desire in the air and chuckle.

"Go. Ugh, males."

I laugh loudly. "See you shortly, my beautiful mate!"

June

Males. I cannot help the laugh that escapes at his antics. I missed him so much. I hate he is leaving my side, but it needs to be done. I turn and look at the group waiting for my orders.

"Ekul, I don't want to wait to wake the rest of the Nlyaxian in pods, but before we do that, I need to understand if we can support waking that many people. Can you assign some warriors to gather that information? Elana, Doraj, can you help them?" As an afterthought, I add, "Doraj, you lead the effort." He nods.

Dax, Sam, Nalax, Divad, Ekul, and I head down to the level with the breeding pods when they leave.

We walk onto the floor with breeding pods. The torture rooms are also on this floor, but I don't want to think about those. Unfortunately, we have to pass them to get to the pods. "Sia, do you have control of systems on this level?"

"Yes. I have full control. There are no beings outside the pods."

Well, at least there's that. Put on your big girl panties and get moving. I move toward the pods. I have one of my Katana out, and I'm not sure why but it makes me feel better. We pass several closed doors. Ahead on the right, I think, is the room I was in last.

Dax

I am following June when she noticeably slows. I suddenly smell something in the air. Blood. I take the lead and move toward the open door. As I get closer, I realize why my fury is in control. The blood is June's. I glance back at her, and she is pale, staring at the door in front of me. I move to the door, and I see my nightmare, but instead of my blood, it's June's blood that covers the wall and floor.

There's a dead Lutetian, three mutants, and a Nlyaxian on the floor. The Nlyaxian makes my fury uncontrollable. I roar, unable to stop myself. Did he take my mate?!

I feel her arms wrap around my waist. She rests her head against my back. "Dax. I need you." That is all it takes to pull me out of my fury. I turn and wrap my arms around her.

She must know what I am thinking, "He didn't rape me." I pull her tighter against me. It does not make it better because she has now gone through what I have, and I would not want that for anyone, let alone my mate. That fact they did this while she carries a child threatens my control again. "I love you, Dax."

My mate. "Let us leave this room, and there is nothing here." She nods.

I am at her right as we walk further onto the floor, and Sam is at her left. I could not have picked a better protector for June. Sam is only second to Ronin in fighting skills. He came second at the High Commander Trials.

"Sia, open the first pod door, please," June asks.

I am not prepared for the scene as the door opens. A Nlyaxian male is fucking an obviously unresponsive human female. Her skin is dark like our own but a little lighter and more brown tones. Her hair is short with curls on the top. Her hair is dark brown but has purple streaks throughout. The roar that rips from my mate's lips alerts the male to our presence. He turns in surprise and smiles at what he obviously thinks is his rescuers.

June moves like water, and before he is off the bed, his head is separated from his body. Blood splashes the female's face. She blinks. June flicks her blade to clean it and puts it away. She grabs a sheet from the bed and covers the female.

Softly June asks the female, "Can you hear me? What is your name?"

The female blinks a few more times, then refocuses on June's face. "There you are. You are safe now. My name is June."

"Tamara, my friends call me Tami." She whispers. She gets a confused look on her face, "Is this a dream? I know you."

It's June's turn to be confused, "It's definitely not a dream. Can I call you Tami? I'd like to be your friend." Tami nods. June continues, "You look familiar, but I don't think I know you."

The female is becoming more alert and nods, "You're that world champion in martial arts. I follow you and your friend on Insta. I'm an MMA fighter."

June smiles, "Excellent. We need fighters."

Tami notices us in the background, and her face shutters. "They are the good guys. The one that was in here with you was an outlier. They teach the Nlyaxians to respect and protect females. Sia, do you know somewhere we can get her some clothes?"

"Affirmative Captain. Out the door, twenty-two feet to the left, is a synthesizer. I created clothing like you wear. I had to estimate her size."

"Thanks, Sia. Divad, will you get them? The rest of you wait outside the door."

"They follow your orders?" she asks.

"Yes. It's a long story but one I will tell you later, ok?" She nods.

Divad returns with the clothing. "My Queen." Then leaves. Ugh. I pinch the bridge of my nose.

I look at Tami, and she has a smirk on her face, "Long, *long* story, I'm guessing." I bark a laugh.

"You got that right. Do you want me to leave while you change?"

She shakes her head, "I think I would feel better if you stay." I nod and turn so she has a little privacy.

"To bring you up to speed, we are on an enemy base. We have taken the base and killed all the enemies. I was a prisoner here as well. Right now, we are going through the pods to free whoever is in them, unless they are rapists. Then they die."

I'm not sure if it's the way I said it, but Tami quietly says, "It happened to you too."

I nod. "Not here, but I was sold as a sex slave. It took me a while to free myself and kill him, but I still have nightmares. I'm not sure if I will ever be completely free of him."

She sits next to me, "It helps to know you understand me."

I nod, "I get it. I will take time, but it will get better." I stand. "Remember, the beings with me are friends. I am not asking you to be friends with them if you are uncomfortable, but I ask for you to be civil."

She nods, "I will try."

"Divad, Ekul," they both enter the room. "This is Tami. She will stay toward the rear of the group. Protect her but do not touch her, understand?"

They both nod, but Ekul turns to Tami, "We are not like him. I am ashamed that he is the same species as me." She relaxes a fraction and nods at him.

Sam is standing next door. I walk up beside him. "Sia, open the door."

The door opens, and a naked Nlyaxian jumps up and stands in front of a human woman. Both my Katana are out, and Sam is pointing two blasters at him. "If you know what is good for you, you will step away from her."

The male growls at me.

Ekul yells in an authoritative voice, "Stand down now! You speak to your Queen." He gets a confused look, his eyes bouncing from mine to Ekul's. "*Now, warrior!*" That snaps him out of it, and he goes to a knee.

"Forgive me, my Queen."

I can now see the woman standing behind him. "Step to me, please." I hold out my hand. To my surprise, she shakes her head.

"Don't hurt him. He's been protecting me."

"Ok. This is very important. Has he taken you against your will?"

Her eyes go wide in understanding, "He hasn't. Others have, but he has never touched me that way." Divad hands me more clothing. Ekul stops me before I step toward the pair.

"Stand and move to the wall." The male hesitates but does as he is told. Divad takes him some clothes as I step toward the woman. As I get closer, I see she looks in her mid-thirties and beautiful. She has blond hair, but she's tiny. She can't be more than five foot three.

I struggle to keep the anger out of my voice, "What's your name?"

"Heather."

"Good. Nice to meet you. My name is June. My team and I have liberated this base. Right now, we are going through the pods and letting the prisoners free unless they have raped someone. They get special justice."

The girl gets a disgusted look, "Good. They deserve it."

"Do you want us to leave so you can get dressed?"

She nods, "I'd like Neirad to stay." She points to the male, who is now dressed.

"You're sure?"

"Yes."

I nod. "Everyone into the hall."

We wait in the hall for them to join us. They both exit the pod and stand in front of me. I take my measure of this warrior. He doesn't melt under my focus, so at least that is good. "Warrior. You will need to answer questions from my mate before we no longer consider you a threat."

"I can ask him now," Ronin says as he walks up.

Neirad salutes Ronin and bows his head. "Look at me, warrior. Have you taken any female by force?"

"No, sir."

"He tells the truth."

I wrap my arm around his waist, "I'm glad you're here, Ronin." He wraps his arm around me and then kisses my forehead.

"Warrior, I am glad you have stuck to the tenets of our people. There are too many who have not, and they will pay the price with their lives."

We continue opening pods as we go. Most are empty; some have females who we free, dress, and give the information we can for now. Nalax has a way with women. She has a calming effect, and she loves she can help them.

"Ronin, we are missing one rapist. Neith said there were four." I'm agitated, but it's not all because of this.

Ronin grabs my arms, and Dax is beside him, "Mate, what is wrong? We will find him."

I sigh in agitation and glance at Sam. Sam quietly says, "We did not find her, did we?" I shake my head.

"Who?" Dax asks, confused.

My shoulders fall, "The Katana Sam carries are Ahmya's. We found them in the weapons room we stopped in before we started our attack."

Sam speaks up in his quiet way, "She could still be in stasis with the others."

Ronin's head snaps to Sam, "What others?"

"Sorry, Ronin, there's so much information. Along with the twenty-four hundred Nlyaxians in stasis, there are also eight hundred human females in stasis somewhere on this base."

He sees something and gives me a soft smile, "We will find her, June. Finding her weapons just solidifies that fact." He brings his hand to my face and rubs his thumb across my cheek. "You look tired, my mate. You need sleep."

"There is so much to do. She knows we took the base. She will come for it, come for you. We shouldn't stay here long."

He nods, "There is much to do, but for now, you need rest. We can handle the details for a while." I want to fight him on this, but honestly, I am exhausted, so I just nod. "Sia, is there a secure place for June to rest?"

"Hold, please." After a few seconds, "Yes. There are unoccupied quarters on the fifth level. There are no life signs on that level, and the doors and floor can be secured."

"Good. Thank you, Sia."

"Will you both come with me for a little while?" I hate how my voice trembles a bit.

Dax smiles softly, "Of course. We'll both take you and stay till you sleep. One of us will be with you at all times."

"We should probably give all the women quarters on that floor until we figure out what our next steps will be."

Divad says, "We will take care of it, my Queen. You need rest." Ronin and Dax see me give him a dirty look for calling me that again, and both laugh loudly.

Ronin, chuckling, says, "You need to get used to that moniker, my mate. I do not think it will go away. Come." He grabs my hand and pulls me toward the lift. Sam follows as well.

I lay my head on Dax's shoulder. I am more tired than I realized. He picks me up, and I smile at him, "I'm not that tired."

He chuckles, "I know, but I enjoy holding you."

The lift stops, and we exit. "Follow the lights, please," Sia says quietly. We follow, and a door opens as we approach. Ronin, Dax, and I enter the room while Sam takes the station outside the door.

I don't like Sam just standing outside by himself.

Since I'm still in Dax's arms, I close my eyes and find Sam's bridge. I walk to the middle and destroy shards of glass. When I'm done, I can actually see the sky through the churning clouds. Good. It should be done in a few more visits. He doesn't deserve the pain from those.

I open my outside eyes. I'm snuggled between Dax and Ronin. They're both looking down at me with worried looks, "What were you just doing? I could feel the pain in your body."

I'm shocked they could tell I was doing something, not just sleeping. "My abilities have grown since we last were together. I let Lutetian in and could kill them easily. It's where I met Neith and found the Goddess blessed her. I can also now go into the minds of others. Sam is in a great deal of pain. It's like shards of glass flying around in a great storm, cutting and causing chaos. I cannot enter his mind because of it, so I stand on the edge and destroy the shards, so he has some semblance of peace. There are so many; I can only do so many each time I try."

Ronin has a soft smile on his face. "You are amazing, June."

Dax still has a concerned look, "And the pain?"

I nod, "When I grab the shards with my mind, I can feel the pain they cause him. It's terrible he has to go through that."

Dax kisses me lightly on the lips, "Sleep, little one. We will be here for you." I can only nod and close my eyes.

Ronin

I look at Dax, and he has the same concerned look on his face. We both look down at our mate; she is evolving and changing. My feelings for her only grow, but I am worried. What does she need such abilities for? Why does she have them? Will my compassionate mate overextend herself trying to help too many?

Dax and I sleep with her for a while but eventually, I need to get up to take care of the things we need to do on the base. I stare down at them, the two most important beings in the universe. Aanon is alive. Where is he? If he was on this base, I am confident June would have found him, so where?

Shaking my head, I turn; I cannot worry about this now. There is too much to do. I walk to the door and exit the room. When I see Sam, I am shocked. Sam looks almost entirely Nlyaxian again. The only thing that remains from his genetic manipulation is the spikes running down his arms and back. "Sam…"

He nods, "I do not think she understands what she is doing. She aims to remove the pain from my mind but doing so also removes the genetic perversion the Lutetian did to me."

I nod, "She does not. Her aim is focused on removing the pain."

"Your mate, my Queen, is an incredibly special female. Know this; I will kill anything that threatens her or die trying to protect her." He says this with such conviction. I nod. If I had not already determined that, I would be convinced now. This male will put himself between danger and my mate. I could not have chosen a better male.

"Ronin," Sia comes over the internal base communications.

"What is it, Sia?"

"Leena is nearly beside herself to see June."

"Can you put her on, please?"

"*Father, Father,* is she there? Is she ok?" Leena's panicked voice comes over the comms, and her emotion breaks my heart.

"Yes, Leena. She is here, and she is safe. She is resting right now."

"Can I come over and see her? I need to see her, Father."

"Not yet, Leena. Give me a chance to make sure the base is safe enough for you to be here, ok?"

I hear a sniffle, "Ok." then, in nearly a whisper, she says, "I really miss her."

"I know you do. I will bring you over as soon as it is safe."

"Ok. Bye."

A beep sounds when she cuts the comms. My shoulders slump a bit. That little female can make me feel sorry faster than anything. I was almost ready to let her come.

Sam interrupts my thoughts, "It was the right decision. This is no place for a small female child. Is she our Queen's daughter?"

"Yes, and no. Leena was a little stowaway when I took the ship out on its test run. She was a slave on the same ship as June and I. June found and protected her. Leena is now our daughter."

He nods in understanding.

"Keep them safe."

He nods again and returns to a ready position at his post.

I head to the lift, there is a lot of work to do.

"Sia, where is Ekul?"

"Ekul is currently in the command center."

"Let him know I am en route."

"Acknowledged."

When I reach the control room Ekul and several other Nlyaxian turn and salute, it is so strange to see so many of my people. I thought that would never happen again.

"Report."

Ekul steps forward, "All enemy combatants are dead except for the missing Nlyaxian traitor. We have a report on supplies. We have enough on this base to wake all stasis pods and supply a ship for a twenty-two day cycle trip. What are your orders?"

I notice the crew standing off to the side. I see something pass between my team and the Nlyaxians. I need to address this now. "Ekul, have all Nlyaxians meet me in the landing bay." He nods.

I turn to my crew, "Join me in the landing bay, please. Ekim, Lessur, please remain here. We'll need someone on this bridge the entire time we are here. Please pull up the vid of the bay so you can listen in as well, but the majority of what I have to say will be for the 'newly awoken' males." Understanding dawns on both their faces, and they nod.

I look at Doraj, Elana, and Nalax, "You are to flank me, understand? They need to understand that you are my family." They all nod, and we head to the landing bay.

We arrive, and there are twenty-three Nlyaxians standing at attention. Something bothers me about that number. "Divad a moment, please."

He walks to me, and we step into the hallway. My crew is still at my side. "Were you the first to be woke from stasis by my mate?"

He shakes his head. "No, sir. I was in a pod with the Queen."

Hmmm. "How many did you wake from stasis?"

"Twenty."

"Were any other Nlyaxians pulled from these pods?"

"There were two others. The Queen killed one, and the other is the one you determined was not lying about breaking our laws."

"Divad, please have Ekul join us. Stay in the bay and monitor everyone. No one leaves." He gives me a confused look but nods and leaves.

Ekul joins us, "Yes, sir."

"Ekul, there is a Nlyaxian in that group that does not belong." He gives me a questioning look as well, but then it dawns on him. Fury darkens his face.

"Sir, are you saying there is the wrong number of males in that bay?" I nod. "Please allow me to take care of this."

I nod, "But do not kill him immediately."

Ekul turns and strides into the bay, and we follow.

Divad steps back when Ekul steps in front of him. He moves to my side with anger on his face, then whispers, "There is one too many, correct?" I nod.

I see when Ekul finds the male, his muscles tense before he launches himself across the floor. His fist connects with a male in the third row, and he crumples to the floor. He grabs him by the wrist and drags him to my feet.

I am unsure what I expected, fear, sorrow, something other than what I see. On this male's face is pure contempt. Ekul has already removed all his weapons. "Stand up."

He slowly gets to his feet, his eyes never leaving my face. "Do you have something to say?"

With a sneer, "You are not fit to rule our people." Ekul moves to strike him, but I hold him off with a hand. "You sully your bloodline with filth. Did I take the human whores by force? YES! They deserve no better." He is screaming by the end.

"Are you done?" I do not wait for him to answer. I pull my axe.

Ekul steps forward, "Sir, he does not deserve to lose his life by that weapon."

He's right. I pull my blaster and shoot him in the chest. He deserves no better. I step over his body and move to stand in front of the males. "Do any of you share his beliefs?"

"No, sir!" They all answer—no red eyes. I relax a bit.

Time for business, "I know the fall of Nlyax is still fresh in your minds, but for me, it has been three years. This is Doraj, Elana, and Nalax." I point to each as I introduce them. "They have been with us for almost a year, some longer. These beings, including Ekim and Lessur, who remain in the control room, have fought with me. Bled with me. They have had my back and the back of your Queen. *They are my family.* You disrespect them; you disrespect us."

I let that sink in for a few seconds and continue in a calm voice, "The days of old died with our planet, and make no mistake, that is our fault. Our ego and hubris allowed an enemy with vastly inferior numbers to destroy our world. We as a people need to reevaluate ourselves and our priorities. Your Queen sees the needs of many and aims to right what has been done to them. The people of this galaxy are in need, oppressed by an evil force. Our Queen has been named the Chosen Warrior by our Goddess. Tasked with freeing *Her* people, and we will do everything in our power to help her."

They stare in stunned silence. I walk back and forth in front of them, "I know this information is shocking and a lot to digest but digest you must. You are the Ssadab. Elite warriors every, one."

Divad steps forward, looking as if he has something to say. I nod for him to start.

"I have seen this. Our Queen has extraordinary abilities of the mind, and her fighting skills rival our own. She chose you all. She knew nothing of the Ssadab but found each and every one of you spread throughout that cavern. She said she was drawn to you. The Goddess was guiding her to the Ssadab." He steps back.

I nod, "What Divad says does not surprise me? It also drew her to find our second, Dax. Who was held in an underground prison on a slave outpost. Her fighting skills do not rival our own. They are much better. She sparred with Elana, who is a Ferin, and won that match." This statement gets a few gasps and shocked looks. I chuckle, "And I have yet to beat her in the ring, which Dax finds highly entertaining. There is too much information to give at one time, but our Queen, my mate, has a purpose in this universe, and we will do what we can to support her. Does anyone have questions?"

A warrior steps forward, and I motion to him to continue, "Are we meant to be the Queen's guard?"

"You know that will be her decision but know this, I feel war coming, and our Queen is not one to sit out a battle. The Queen's guard today will differ greatly from old. They will be at her side in battle. So they will need to learn new fighting styles and tactics."

He gets an excited look and steps back. "Any others?" When no one steps forward, I continue, "As I said, it is a lot of information to take in at once. When we are more stable with the status of this base and are certain of our next steps, we can meet again for questions you may think of. Divad, build a plan for waking the rest of the warriors. Nalax, I would like you to work with Divad on a plan to wake the human women. You can present the plans to June when she wakes." They both nod.

"Elana, Doraj, and Ekul, I am concerned they found so many warriors willing to go against our ways. Can you three work on a plan to address that risk? I do not want males like that in our army." They all nod. I look at the Ssadab, "I need two volunteers to guard the lift on the Queen's floor." All lift their heads to volunteer. Good. I point at the male who was guarding the female in the pod and another warrior then I send them up to the floor.

"Do any of you have bridge experience?" Three nods. "Head up to the control room. Ekim and Lessur will give you any tasks that need to be completed."

I think for a minute, and I point to eight warriors, "I have an important assignment for you. Find where the human females in stasis are stored, and sweep then patrol the levels. No one enters without express permission from the Queen or me. You can shift each other but four on duty at all times." They nod and leave.

I send the rest to patrol the levels of sleeping Nlyaxians. Probably unnecessary, but I will not risk their lives.

June

My bodily functions wake me. I need to pee. I'm still tired, but I feel better. Dax sleeps beside me. I'd love to stay and stare at his face, but nature calls. Why do I still have clothes on? I hate sleeping in clothes. Before I take care of business, I strip. After I'm done, I wash my hands and head back to bed. I'm pretty sure I could sleep for a while longer.

I get halfway back to the bed and realize Dax is awake, sitting up against the wall. The look he gives me is pure fire—my desire spikes. I haven't been with him outside of a dream, which drives my core to throb.

I walk to him slowly. I cup my breasts and stroke my nipples earning me a growl from the bed. Goosebumps erupt over my body, and I cannot suppress the moan that escapes. Dax continues to growl and holds out his hand for me. "Dax," I whisper and continue my walk to the bed.

When I reach it, I take his hand. He pulls me forward and grabs my waist. He lifts me, then settles me straddling his lap.

His knees are bent, so I relax back against them. I don't break eye contact until I relax my neck, so my face looks at the ceiling. I am breathing heavily in anticipation of what he will do.

He growls again, and I shiver, "My mate, you are magnificent."

"Dax," I moan his name, "touch me." I rock my hips forward and feel his hard cock through the fabric of his pants.

Growl, "Be careful, mate, you play with fire." His fingers are at my collarbones, caressing and wandering slowly to my breast. His hands cup my breast and thrum my nipples with his thumbs. I arch my back and moan at the sensation. One hand continues its journey when his thumb parts my folds, seeking its treasure. I shake with need, "Dax!"

He grabs the back of my neck and pulls me forward for a passionate kiss; when his thumb flicks and circle my clit, I moan into the kiss. He pinches, and I come undone. He continues kissing me as I orgasm. When I come down, he lays me back on the bed, gets up, and undresses.

Unable to help myself, I crawl to the side and stand. When he stands in his naked glory, I guide him to sit. I can tell he does not understand my goal, but he will learn. I sink to my knees between his legs and gently take hold of his beautiful cock. His breath explodes from his lungs, "Mate?"

I hear fabric rip when I put my lips on the tip of his cock. "June..." My name comes out as a moan on his lips. God, I love the taste of his cock. I take it into my mouth and throat as far as I can take it. I moan, sending shockwaves down his shaft. I bob up and down, wholly focused on the pleasure it gives us both. I feel his cock throb in my mouth. "June!" He tries to move me away, but I will not be denied. He roars when his release begins, and I suck it all down, already addicted to his taste.

When I'm done, I look up into his eyes and what I see makes me moan with need. The pure fire in his eyes makes my core clench with need. He lifts me from the floor and puts me in the center of the bed. He stands back and stares. "Dax!"

He climbs on the bed like a predator toward his prey. He pounces and enters me so quickly that I scream. Not in pain, the pleasure is almost too much. His cock stretches me so much. He freezes, but before he can ask if I am ok, I scream, "Dax, fuck me now!"

The small amount of control he had breaks, and he is pounding into me. He makes sure that his base ridges hit my clit on every stroke. I am incensed with pleasure, scratching my nails down his back. My orgasm hits, and my pussy locks down on his cock. He growls and starts pounding into me harder. His sprili release making him growl louder, and my orgasm goes through the roof. As it abates, Dax roars with his release, and the sprili vibrates, kicking off another massive orgasm.

When we come down from the high of our release Dax is collapsed on top of me. He rolls, so I am sprawled on his chest. I cannot stop the moan that escapes from the movement. "Are you ok, June?"

"Are you kidding?" I lift my head so that I can see his face. There is worry there and something else... shame. "Dax. I loved every second of that. Every single second."

He looks at me, unsure, "I lost control. I..."

I interrupt him, "Yes, you did, and I wanted it that way, Dax. You are my mate. I know you struggle with control, but I do not want your control. I want you and only you when we are together."

He relaxes and strokes my face, "I do not deserve you, my mate."

I kiss his chest, "That is not up to you. You do deserve it. You deserve happiness. You deserve love. You deserve super hot sex."

He laughs loudly, and I moan at the sensations it sends up his cock. His eyes go molten again, and rolls me under him. He thrusts into me. He brings his face close to mine and grabs my hair, bringing my head back. He licks my prone neck, "I very much enjoyed your lips on my cock." He pulls out and thrusts back in hard. I moan at what he is doing to my body. "I think you enjoyed having your lips wrapped around my cock." Thrust. "Did you, mate?" Thrust.

"Yes, Dax." Thrust.

"Yes, what, mate?" Thrust.

"I love sucking your cock." Thrust. "I love the taste of your cum." Thrust. Thrust. Thrust.

"Good female. What do you want, my mate?" Thrust.

I look into his eyes, still prone, "Flip me over." His growl vibrates down his cock, and I moan at the sensation.

I'm suddenly on my hands and knees. Dax slams his cock into me and starts a punishing pace. I am mewling and moaning. The sounds coming from me should embarrass me, but I'm not. "Join us, Ronin." I gasp in shock, and my desire spikes. Ronin is naked in front of me. I grab his cock and take him into my mouth.

"June." Ronin moans.

I am bobbing up and down on his cock, and Dax pounds me from behind with his. His sprili unfurl, and I scream with Ronin's cock in my mouth. My pussy locks onto his cock as Ronin's release hits the back of my throat. I am sucking down his cum as Dax roars, and his sprili vibrates. My orgasm exponentially increases as I scream again.

Ronin pulls from my mouth and pulls me into his arms. He's on his knees and grabs my ass. He lifts me, and I wrap my legs around his waist as his cock pushes in, "Ronin." I moan. He gets off the bed and stands. He lifts me and then pushes my hips down onto his cock. I feel Dax at my back. He's kissing my shoulder. I reach back and pull him to my lips for a deep passionate kiss.

I feel Dax at my exit. His arms wrap around me as he pushes. His lubed cock eases the journey, but he is so big. I moan at the sensation. Both my mates are kissing me, stroking me, and trying to ease the invasion. Dax is fully seated. I feel so full. All I can do is moan, "Move."

They move in sync. Pulling out, thrusting in. I cannot think, just feel. I can feel an orgasm already building. The feeling of both of them pounding into me at once is too much. My orgasm crashes into me, and I scream. I feel my body lockdown on both of them. They both moan and release their seed. Their sprili unfurl and immediately vibrate. I scream again as another infinitely more intense orgasm hits.

Ronin

Dax and I stand panting, holding our mate impaled on our cocks. I look at Dax and put my forehead to his. "I told you she was made for a Triad." She moans. We both slowly withdraw from her body. I pick up her legs and carry her to the sanishower. Dax cleans himself when we are done. We lay down in the bed with her snuggly between us. She falls asleep quickly.

"You were right, Ronin. She is perfect. Her body was made for pleasure. Made for our Triad."

She lies back to my front, and I relax. I am tired.

Dax

I wake up a few hours later. I stare at my sleeping mates. Ronin is on his stomach with his arm on her torso, hand cupping her breast. I chuckle; even in his sleep, he reaches for her. I cannot help my sadness that one is missing, but that I now know he lives brings me great joy.

My eyes return to Ronin's hand cupping her breast, and the sight stirs my cock. I move and settle my shoulders between my mate's legs. I lightly run my tongue through her folds. She moans in her sleep. Ronin wakes and lifts his head to look for me. When they find me, I run my tongue through her folds again and firmly run it back and forth across her clit. Desire is now written on his face as well. He licks her nipple and then latches on to it. She gasps awake from our ministrations.

We proceed to make our mate scream our names while she comes undone on our cocks. I will never get enough of her.

June

I stretch like a content cat when I wake, reaching for my mates. Dax and Ronin are gone. I sit up in bed, looking for them. Dax walks from the bathroom, fully clothed. I'm a little disappointed. They may have woken me several times last night, but I am honestly well-rested for the first time in several weeks.

Dax chuckles, "You, my beautiful mate, are made for a Triad." He runs and jumps onto the bed, landing over me. I am laughing with him and then kissing a path up his neck. He growls and gives me a scorching kiss. Damn. He gets up, "*But* we have work to get to!"

Fuck. Nope, not this time. I walk naked into the adjoining room and see him eating something from a plate. He freezes in the middle of shoveling something towards his mouth. I lean against the wall next to the bedroom door. "Dax. I promise fast and hard."

He growls, "Mate, I was told to bring you to the control room."

"Who will know? Dax..." I run my fingers through my folds and find my clit. I moan and close my eyes. Suddenly I'm pinned to the wall, my arms pinned over my head. His growl is constant, and his eyes flicker between black and their normal color. Fuck I love it when he loses control. "Mate. You test my control."

I strain and run my tongue along his jaw, "Fuck your control." That does it. His eyes are black. I hear his pants rip. He grabs my hips, lifts me, and impales me on his cock. "*Yes, Dax*!" He's pounding hard and fast, but it's not enough, "*Deeper! I need you deeper*!"

He gets his arms under my knees and pushes my knees wide. He's now pounding and filling me like I need. My climax hits, and my pussy locks down on his cock. He roars and pounds into me harder. His sprili unfurl, and another climax crashes onto the last, "Dax!" I feel his cock throb, and on the next thrust, he stays locked in as deep as he can. I feel his release splash, and his sprili vibrate, making the last climax crash into me. My pussy locks hard onto his cock and milks it for every drop.

"Mate, your body is made for pleasure." He moves slightly like he's going to pull out. "No! No. Not yet. Your cock is where it belongs."

He trails kisses down my neck and across my shoulder. "Sorry, I don't know what came over me, but my need for you when I woke... it was intense. Is that normal?"

He chuckles, making me moan. He pulls out and pushes slowly back in, causing a riot of aftershocks. "It is normal. When a male first joins a Triad, sexual appetite is elevated. But I have never heard males talk about this much of an elevated appetite."

"Even now, my body's need is ramping up for more. Goddess Dax. More, I need more. It's not normal." He pulls from my body and sets me down. I wish I was joking, but my need is ratcheting up again. I grab my breast and pinch my nipples, groaning. It's then I realize he has striped. "Oh, thank the Goddess." I jump into his arms and kiss him with all the need in my body. He growls and stalks to the shower.

We get in, and he turns it on. The water is cold, but I don't care. He presses me to the wall and sets and punishing pace. He is fast and hard. I am moaning and mewling for more. His climax hits at the same time as mine. He roars, and I scream his name. We are both holding on to each other tightly and panting heavily.

He pulls from my body and sets me on the floor. He grabs the soap and begins washing our bodies. By the time he's done, the need is back, and I moan. I see the worry flash across his face, but he schools it quickly. I step out of the shower, turn, and go down on my hands and knees. I moan his name, "Dax."

He enters me gently, "Dax!"

He starts at a fast pace driving us to the edge quickly. We both climax again, and I collapse to the floor. Dax picks me up and carries me back to the bed. He lays me down, crawls in beside me, and covers us both. He pulls me in close to him. "Sia, ask Ronin to return to our quarters... and tell him to bring Divad."

Dax

Before Ronin and Divad come in, we mate twice more; her need driving us both. I am worried for my mate. I can feel her desire spike, and my body responds in kind. I hear the door, and Ronin bursts into the room. "What's wrong? What's going on?"

June moans, and I feel her need spike. I see his body respond as well. "Ronin, something is wrong. Her need is extremely high, and she is almost solely focused on mating."

He gives me a confused look. "We have mated five times since you left the room." June moans again, and I feel her desire spike higher.

"Dax... Ronin... I need." She is nearly writhing in her need.

I look back to Ronin, and he sees and feels it now. He looks worried. "Divad!" He rushes into the room. "What is wrong with June?" She moans again.

"Her need is great and nearly constant," I tell him.

He gets a focused look, "I need to check her vitals." Both Ronin and I growl. Shocked looks cross both our faces.

"What is going on?!" Ronin nearly screams, shocked by our own reactions to his request.

Divad pulls a device out of his pocket, "Please run this over her whole body slowly."

She is moaning and writhing now. It is driving me crazy. I grab the device and run it over her as slowly as I can manage. I hand it back to him when I'm done.

He seems to go through several screens, then nods and looks at us, "we have not seen it for a very long time, but she is in the mating frenzy. She has one fertilized egg in her body, and it is driving her to complete the process."

Ronin asks the same question I have, "So she will be like this until Dax fertilizes an egg?" He nods. "What about Aanon?"

"He is not here, so she should be fine until you find him. Then I expect this will happen again."

"Ronin!" June screams like she is in pain.

"Get out." Ronin growls, and Divad almost runs from the room.

Over the next twelve hours, Ronin and I take turns satisfying our mate. It is not a hardship, but I am still worried for her. I look at the clock and realize she has been resting for forty-five minutes. Till this point, she has not gone up to twenty-two minutes. I roll over to her, "June, are you ok?"

She moans, "Shit, I feel like I've run several marathons."

I look at Ronin, and he has a shocked look on his face. That was the first complete sentence since before Divad was here. Ronin and I both fall to our backs on the bed in relief. I pop back up immediately. A test! I kiss her on the shoulder. She groans, "Tired."

I smile at Ronin, "You know what this means?"

"Yes, my brother," he says, exhausted, "Congratulations."

One of June's eyes pops open, "What are you congratulating him for?"

I lean down and kiss her stomach right above where my child rests. Both her eyes are now open and looking down at me. Tears spring to her eyes, "Do you mean?"

I sit up and gather her into my arms, "Yes, my mate. Ronin's babe now has someone to talk to." Tears roll down her cheeks, and she puts her hands protectively on her abdomen. I put my hand on hers, and Ronin puts his on top of mine. She kisses us both, and we all lay back down and promptly fall asleep.

June

"Both embryos are in stasis," Divad says happily.

Both... "Divad, am I going to become a sex-starved maniac every time I get pregnant?"

Ronin chuckles, and I give him a *shut-up* look. "June, mating frenzy hasn't been seen for a long time, but I found some information on it in the Emancipations database. I believe this has occurred because you are separated from your mates."

"That makes *no* scientific sense! My body is not Nlyaxian! How would it know to do this? Humans have nothing like this!"

"I believe I can answer that mystery as well. I had Dax run a comprehensive scan on you, and the results were fascinating. Apparently, our seed has the ability to modify the body it enters." He sees the panic on my face and continues quickly, "Minutely, it has made minor modifications to your genetic structure. It's modified code so you can carry a Nlyaxian child, and apparently, this minor adaptation means your body inherits the ability to have fertilized embryos in stasis and mating frenzy."

I am trying to control my panic, but I do not like the idea of modifications to my genetic code. "Are there any other modifications I should know?"

Ronin grabs my hand, "I do not think you should be worried, June."

"Oh no? What if these modifications make me grow horns or a tail? What if they reduce my life expectancy by fifty years? You don't know!"

Now Ronin and Dax look panicked at Divad. "I do not believe that will be the case, but I started mapping a genome from one of the sleeping females so I can more fully understand the implications of these changes. My Queen, you are healthy. The embryos are healthy. That is all we can be sure of right now, and that is good news."

I'm calming down because he has a plan. "How long does that take?"

"Mapping and understanding the full genome structure will take time. I need genetic code from multiple subjects, and then I can ask Sia to help me with the analysis. It could take upwards of ninety-day cycles."

My shoulders slump. That seems like a long time, but then I remember that on earth, it would still be impossible. Humans have mapped around ninety percent of our genome, so look at the positives, June. Your babies are safe and healthy.

"How long can they stay in stasis?" Divad gets an uncomfortable look. "What?" My panic rises again.

"The longest recorded case of a viable birth in Nlyaxian's history is forty-seven day cycles."

Ice forms in my stomach, "How many days have I been gone?"

Dax answers, "Fifty-six day cycles."

"Have Nlyaxian females gone past that and not had viable births?" My voice cracks.

Again Divad gets an uncomfortable look, "For Nlyaxian females, the risk to the embryos and mother rises every day past that. However, as you have pointed out, you are not Nlyaxian, so the risks may not even exist for you."

Ronin's voice growls, "Are you saying the risk to June elevates as well?" Divad nods. I can feel his rising anger and panic. I grab his hand and pull him towards me, where I sit on an infirmary table.

I pull his head down, put my forehead to his, and then pull Dax to join us. "We need to be calm. Our babies will be fine."

"I will not lose you. I cannot." Ronin says in a sad whisper.

I can feel Dax shaking, "Dax..." I make him look at me. "Ronin, you will not lose the babies or me. We need to find Aanon. I just wish we had an idea of where to start our search."

A male voice comes over the internal speakers, "I believe I can help with that."

"Who the fuck was that?"

Dax and Ronin chuckle. Dax answers, "That is Nairb. He is the AI on the Liberation."

Ronin chuckles at the confused look that remains on my face. "Obviously, we neglected to give you information about what happened to us since you were taken, but before we get into that, Nairb, how can you help us find Aanon?"

"When Sia and I started our attack on the base systems, she went for control systems, and I attacked ancillary systems. The ancillary systems were barely a challenge except for one. I found an open communications link. That link went directly into the Lutetian's main data storage on their homeworld." The room explodes with people talking and yelling.

"*Quiet*! I need Nairb to finish. Continue, please?"

There's a brief pause, "Thank you. I knew as soon as they found out we had infiltrated the base, they would cut the link, so I tried to reason what would be most important."

"What did you find?" I ask, hoping against hope.

"I did not find Aanon's specific information. They do not list names in the information they have on subjects, but I found every base that houses Nlyaxian and Human stasis pods."

"How many?" My brain is working overtime.

"Four more bases with twenty-five hundred warriors and three hundred human females each. This base was the biggest."

Ronin poses the following question, "Are either of those the Nlyaxian homeworld?"

"No." Shock is written across his face. He obviously thought it would be.

"Did they know you accessed the files?" I worried she'll move them or destroy them if she knows.

"They do not. I removed all traces of my access as I left their systems."

"Did you get any other information?" I ask.

"I did. As I was leaving, I was able to grab the layout of their operations on the Lutetian homeworld."

"Nairb, while you cannot possibly understand how important this information is to me personally, you put yourself at significant risk. If they had cut that comms link while you were in the system, you would have been trapped or..."

"Died." Sia finishes my statement. She sounds pissed.

"Yes. Remember, you are as important to this crew as anyone else. Be careful and thank you very much."

Again there is a pause, "You are welcome. I am beginning to understand Sia."

Um ok. I look at my mates, "Let's get to work. Sam and Divad with us, please." They nod in response, and we all head out. Our destination is the landing bay, and it's the only place that makes sense because the control room is too small, and I'm not going in a torture room or breeding pod ever again.

As we walk into the room, half the inhabitants turn, salute, and bow. Ugh. Nalax, Elana, Doraj, Ekim, Lessur, Ekul, and two other Nlyaxians I do not know look surprised to see us. "I read the reports from Divad and Nalax on waking the remaining warriors and human females. The plans are solid. I want to start implementation today. The longer we stay here, the greater the risk the Queen will try to take back this base. Since we have no data on her military strength, it is a risk we cannot afford yet. Nalax, I expect the females to be... shocked by their situation." I hear someone snort and notice Tami is in the bay as well. I smile and motion her over.

"Tami, I was wondering if you would help Nalax with the women as they wake. As you know, they will be very disoriented and scared. We just want to educate them on their current situation and safely onto the Emancipation. Once we are all back on the ship, I will meet with them to address questions."

She nods, "Are you taking us home?"

That is not a question I wanted to address yet because I know they will not like my answer. "No. Not yet." I see the fury light her face. "There are many facts you have yet to be given, but the biggest is that they sold us to the Cruxlin. Not stolen or abducted, sold." I say this with a little too much heat. Her fury evaporates and changes to shock. "Sorry. It's still a little raw for me as well."

"I know you and the rest of the women will want to return home, but I need to ensure that you and the rest of them are not just returned to the Cruxlin, and Lutetian first. Can we chat more in a bit?" She nods.

"Ok, back to the topic. I want to wake warriors and humans today. Four more bases have humans and Nlyaxian warriors. We'll have to hit them one at a time and hope we get to all of them before the Queen moves them or worse."

"Mate," Ronin interrupts.

"Yes?"

"We have two ships." He says.

"Well, shit. Maybe you need to walk me through what has happened since I was taken."

About twenty minutes later, we are all sitting on boxes in the landing bay, sorting through the new information. I hop down and pace.

"This is good. We can crew two ships with decent compliments of warriors and attack the bases simultaneously. Load all the pods on the ship and move to the next two and do the same. If we execute this way, we may be able to liberate all the pods from her grasp before she has the opportunity to do anything about it. Ronin, Dax, Thoughts?"

It's Ronin's turn to get up and pace. After a few minutes, he says, "I think it is our only option. Attacking one base at a time virtually guarantees she will have the ability to move one base, possibly two before we can reach them."

Dax adds, "Agreed."

"What about you, Ekul? What gaps do you see?" I ask.

He jerks in surprise, "Well, I definitely agree we have to attack simultaneously. Moving the pods to the ships will eliminate the brief chaos of waking them but do we know the armaments or number of soldiers at each base?"

"Nairb?" I ask.

"Unfortunately, I did not have enough time to look for those details." He responds.

Ekul now paces, "If that is the case, we need to ensure we have enough weapons before we hit them, and honestly, I do not think it would be responsible to take eight hundred human females into a situation this dangerous."

I nod. "Excellent points, Ekul." I think for a few more minutes, weighing my options. "So here are our options, one; we wake them all, split the warriors, and hit the bases. Two, wake a small set of warriors, load all the pods onto the ships, head to Haven, wake them there, load up on credits, head to the station for weapons then attack the bases. As much as I want to load up and hit those bases as fast as possible, I think option two is the right choice. Thoughts?" Everyone nods in agreement—just a little longer, Aanon. We are coming for you.

Divad raises his head, "What is Haven?"

Dax slaps him on the shoulder with a smile, "It's home."

I chuckle, "That it is. Ekul, I will leave it up to you on how many warriors we need to wake up and which ones. Divad, Nalax, and Doraj, please assist."

Suddenly there is a high-pitched squeal behind me, and I instantly turn and sprint to the sound. Leena launches into my arms, laughing and crying. I sit on the floor, holding her to me and rocking. Tears streaming down my face. All her words are gibberish until she calms, "I was...*sniff* so worried about you. I missed *sniff* you so much."

"I know, baby. I'm sorry you were scared for me. I missed you so much and thought about you every day." We sit on the floor for a bit longer. I pull her back to look into her face and wipe her tears.

She glances over my shoulders, and harrumphs, "Ugh, seriously? More males?? Yes, I am a Nlyaxian female!" I bark a laugh and grab Ronin's hand to hoist me up with Leena in my arms.

I'm not setting her down for a bit, and I think my mates understand that. I walk over to the group. "Leena, this is Divad, Ekul, and Sam. Sam is the captain of my guard, so he'll be around a lot." She looks at him and then, to my shock, holds out her arms to him.

Sam looks at me, "It's ok if you're comfortable." He reaches out and takes Leena.

"You will be a great protector." She says, "And I love your spikes." The look of awe on Sam's face is worth it.

"Our little Leena has a way with people," I say to no one in particular. She holds out her arms to Dax, then promptly falls asleep on his shoulder. I chuckle and look at Ronin, "Already wrapped, is he?"

Ronin and Dax both laugh, "Within seconds of meeting her."

I look at Sam, and he is still watching Leena. It is the first time since we've met that he genuinely looks relaxed. "Ok, let's get started. Oh, and Doraj, if there is anything you'd like to strip from this place, feel free."

Dax looks slightly uncomfortable, so I say, "Out with it."

"I think it would be best if you and Leena return to the Emancipation."

I'm gearing up to fight this point when I look around and see they all agree. Divad tips it over the edge, "My Queen, I would like to see you rest a bit more."

"Ugh, fine." I actually am still pretty tired, "Who's taking me, Leena, and Sam back? Tami, do you want to come with us?"

"I should grab the others first. Can someone transport us once I round them up?"

I'm going to like that woman, "We can wait." She jogs off, and I turn to Dax.

He chuckles, "I will take you over. That was easier than I thought it would be."

I slap him on the ass and walk over to Ronin. "Are you sure I can't be of more use over here?"

"I can feel your exhaustion through the link, my mate. Please rest. We will be done and on our way in no time."

I nod, wrap my arms around his neck and give him a steamy kiss. I walk back to Dax and say to Ronin over my shoulder, "Don't take *too* long."

Ronin growls, and I laugh loudly as I enter the transport.

Sam and I sit in the transport, waiting for Dax and the humans. Heather, Tami, and Nalax enter the transport and sit down. Nalax sits beside me and says, "Dax said he will be here in a few minutes."

I nod and look down at my sweet girl. I realize she is staring open-mouthed at Tami. "Leena..." before I can tell her to stop staring, she jumps down and walks to Tami.

She smiles and says, "Hello, lil' mama. What's your name?"

Leena, still open-mouthed, whispers, "Leena... you are beautiful." She climbs into Tami's lap.

She chuckles, "Why thank you, lil' mama. Leena is a beautiful name for a beautiful little girl."

Leena sits quietly, staring, then after a few minutes, "I wish my skin was like yours." She looks confused and looks at me, then back at Tami, "Why are you different from Mother?"

Tami smiles, "Well, humans come in all sorts of sizes and colors. We value our uniqueness. I very much like your skin color as well."

Leena whisper, "I love the purple in your hair. It's my favorite color. The grass on my homeworld was purple." She looks at her lap.

Tami looks at me for more information, "The Nlyaxian home world was destroyed three years ago. Leena lost her family. She was a slave on the ship with me. So now she is a daughter to my Triad."

Leena gets a big smile, "I love them."

Tami looks at Leena with concern, and I can tell Leena is going to have another Auntie already. Tami grabs one of her short purple curls, "You want to know a secret?" She whispers.

Leena nods excitedly.

She whispers, "The purple isn't natural. I dye it that color because it's *my* favorite color too." Leena's eyes get wide, and her head whips around to me with excitement.

I laugh, "We'll see what we can do, baby. I'm sure there has to be a way to change hair color out here."

Leena lets out a loud squeal, and at that moment, Dax steps onto the shuttle and puts on a mock stern look, "Is there a selix on my transport making all that noise?"

Leena gets a fit of giggles, "No, silly. It was me!"

Dax sweeps in and scoops her up, "You are the selix? You do not look like a selix?"

We are all chuckling at the silliness. Dax looks at me, "Ready?" I nod. He kisses me on the head and walks to the front with Leena in his arms. "Ready to drive co-pilot?"

"Yes, sir!" She says in her little voice. Goddess, I love them. I lay my head back for the trip and fall asleep.

Dax

Ronin was right; we were on our way to Haven within six hours. June sleeps with Leena in our quarters, and Sam stands guard outside the door. It makes me feel better he is there, and he is her chosen protector. Sam's name before he lost his memory was Samoht, so actually close to what she named him. He was an amazing warrior, second only to Ronin.

He was a good friend to me before all this. Quick to laugh and joke around, brilliant tactician. I wondered why Ronin did not make him his second in command. He had a temper back then, so maybe that was it, but he did not deserve what they did to him.

My mate still amazes me. Somehow she reverted the genetic changes made to his body—something our scientists could not do. I hear someone talking outside our door. I walk over and open it. Elana is outside smiling at Sam.

"Everything ok?" I ask both.

Elana chuckles, "Yes, fine. I was telling him his expalita is truly beautiful. The colors are so much more vibrant than most. I'm not sure he knows what to do with me."

Sam softly speaks, "I am sorry. I am having a hard time adjusting to speaking with others. I like your feathers."

Elana gives him a soft smile, "You remember nothing of the Ferin, do you?" She asks him. Sam shakes his head. "It is ok, Sam. It will come in time. Give yourself time to heal." She turns to me. "Is June awake?" I shake my head as we hear my mate yell, "Yes!"

I chuckle, "Apparently, she is. Go ahead." Elana hops and gives a little squeak, then trots into the room. I turn back to Sam, "I would like to speak with you about the Queen's Guard if you do not mind, and I am sure Ronin would as well."

"I would!" Ronin says, walking up to us. He looks tired. As if he can hear my thoughts, he says, "I am fine."

I chuckle and look at Sam. "I would actually like to get both of your thoughts." He says.

June and Elana walk from our quarters smiling. She looks at us and says, "I need to work some kinks out of my muscles. Elana and I are going to train."

Ronin is the one to make the mistake, "Is that safe?"

Our mate's demeanor changes dramatically. She is furious, "I carry your children but make no mistake, we are now at war. I will not stand by as people fight my battles for me. Understand?" She is in Ronin's face right now. "Do you want me rusty when I am in battle?"

Ronin sighs, "Forgive me, June. It is hard for us to change our ways and thinking. Of course, I want you at the top of your game when you are on the field of battle."

She smiles and gives him a light kiss on the lips, "Don't worry, mate. Sia has already developed a belt that creates a shield in front of my abdomen. Our babies will be perfectly safe."

Then she walks away and chats with Elana. "Our mate is magnificent when she is angry."

Ronin chuckles, "Wait till you see her fight." He looks at Sam and then me, "Want to watch while we talk?" We both nod.

June

I knew that overprotectiveness would come from my mates, but I guess I just didn't expect it so soon, *and* that was the second time it's come up in as many days. It instantly brought the redhead to the surface, and she wasn't having any of that shit. I do feel a little bad about my reaction. Ronin has never given me any reason to believe he would be unreasonable about this. Shit. I'm an asshole. My shoulders slump.

Elana chuckles, "He will be fine, my friend. You may have overreacted a bit, but there is no reason you cannot train or go into battle. Ferin females do so all the time. We are infinitely more effective on the field when pregnant."

"Thanks, Elana. My people are not so... progressive. Females were only allowed in combat zones in the last ten years or so. We are at war, and our numbers will not allow me to sit it out even if I wanted to. I hate the idea of sitting out when others may die in my place. No. I will go into battle, and we will win. My life is no more important than anyone else."

"I don't know about that last part, my friend," she laughs, "but I will definitely be at your side no matter what."

I loop my arm through Elana's. "You mean the world to me, Elana. Thank you for being my friend."

We walk into the training room, and there are more folks than usual. All three rings have matches going. We move to the side close to the training equipment and start our warmups and stretches. We are getting a lot of curious looks, and I try to tune them out.

After about twenty minutes of warmups, I look at Elana, "Bo's again?"

She smiles, "Let's make it interesting. You choose a training weapon from the wall for the first round, I will choose for the second, and the final round will be the Bo."

I cannot help the huge smile that blooms on my face, "Oh my Goddess, Elana. That is the best idea ever!" I give a little quiet squeal and skip to the wall. Hmmm... what do I choose? What do I choose? Let's start with my favorite. I pull four bokkens (wooden training swords) off the wall, turn and smile at Elana.

She laughs, "Ok, ok. Hmmm," She looks at the wall and pulls four wooden Karambit from the wall.

"Oh, nice choice!" She wants me in close. Excellent. We give each other our weapons, and both grab a Bo. We walk to the ring that just freed up and place our weapons outside the ring. "Lessur!" I call out. "You want to want to govern?"

"*Yes*!" he jumps with his hands in the air. Elana and I chuckle. He trots over. "Lessur, we are using a different weapon in each round. Weapon contact is a point. Each round goes to three points or twenty minutes. No throwing weapons. If you drop, it is out. The highest points, win. Agreed?"

Elana nods, "Agreed."

Lessur interjects, "With the Karambit as one of the weapons, I think we should have a second governor." I nod.

"Nalax! We need a second!" She hoots and runs to the ring. We go over the rules with her, then walk to opposite sides.

"Bokken first?"

"Sounds good." At my surprised look, she smiles, "I've been practicing with your weapons."

"Shit."

She laughs. "Have no fear, my friend. I doubt I am close to your skill."

I snort, "Elana, your ability to control a weapon with no previous training scares me." Now we are both chuckling.

Dax

I am excited to watch my mate in the ring, but worried she is going up against a Ferin. Ferin are known throughout the universe for their skills in battle to where most will never wage war against them or their allies. When the Ferin pulled back their engagement in the universal community all suffered.

Ronin sits on my right, and Sam on my left. We are supposed to talk about the Queen's Guard, but we are all focused on the mat where June and Elana warm up.

Sam surprises me by being the first to break the silence, "You are comfortable with our Queen fighting an Iarumas of the Ferin?"

Both Ronin and I stare at him, and when he doesn't explain, I ask, "What is the Iarumas?"

Sam looks at us, confused, "I am not sure how or why I know this, but the Iarumas of the Ferin are the best of their warriors. There are only ten chosen. If one dies or retires, they choose another to replace them."

Now we stare at him open-mouthed, and Ronin recovers first, "How do you know Elana is one of the Iarumas?"

"The mark on her neck." He says this like everyone should know this information.

Now we both stare at Elana. We have both noticed the design on her neck but never asked if it had meaning, but with the Ferin, we should have known it would.

Ronin has an incredulous look on his face, then shrugs his shoulders, "She has already won a match against Elana."

It's Sam's turn to look shocked at us, "Truly?"

Ronin nods.

We are not discussing the Queen's guard, at least until the match is called.

June holds two of what has to be practice swords. I can see Lessur is getting ready to start the round when my mate executes what has to be part of her warm-up because she is not the type to show off. She swings the swords around her body fast, never once touching the blades or her body. The action is so fast it almost looks like there is a white shield around her.

When she stops the movement, both swords are in front of her, one level with her chest and the other with her waist. The focus in her eyes is hard and calculated. I can almost feel her planning her moves against Elana.

Lessur calls the start. June and Elana are both aggressive and fast. The clack of the wooden swords against one another sounds like the clatter of many wooden cups falling to the floor. The movement of the blades is very difficult to follow. When Lessur calls the first point for June, I do not see the wooden blades connecting against Elana. Many warriors gasp when she gets the point.

Neither slows at all. Occasionally, over the next twenty minutes, they break apart, both panting at the exertion and circling the other then are back at it within fifteen seconds or so. When Lessur calls the round, June has two points, Elana has none, and I have a painfully hard cock. My mate is fantastic!

Ronin chuckles beside me, "Our mate is amazing, is she not?" I nod then I notice he has the same problem as me.

June grabs two more small weapons from the floor. They are talon-like daggers about four inches in length, and the grip has an open circle at the end. I ask Ronin, "What are those? They have to get in close for those?"

"They are called Karambit. Elana chose those most likely for that exact reason. It's what I would have done. Many of June's weapons are arm's length or more, so it's an excellent strategy to bring her in close to try for an advantage."

"But you told me June was a master of all the weapons on that wall, and I have to say our mate likes pointy, sharp objects. I think this may backfire on Elana."

Then I notice the human woman, Tami, standing near the doors watching the match. She seems as into the fight as we are.

"Hmmm," Ronin breaks my thoughts, "You may be right. The last time she fought Elana, she was aggressive and dominant. If she comes out with the same tact, I think it will give us a clue as to what June is thinking, that she needs to dominate. However, if she forces Elana to go on the offensive, make her come at her, then she agrees with you, and she wants Elana to believe she is nervous or unsure about coming in close."

Lessur calls start for round two. June holds back, and the two of them circle. Elana breaks the standoff and attacks swiftly. Again these two females are so fast they are hard to follow. They are both trying to get through the other defenses to draw the wooden Karambit against the other. Suddenly June is in under Elana's defenses, but it allows Elana to get the point; before I know it, June gets two.

I jump up, then quickly sit and look at Sam, "Did she just sacrifice a point to get two?!"

Sam chuckles and nods, "I think she did."

The fight goes on for the entire twenty minutes again. Elana got another point to bring the match to June four, Elana one. When Lessur calls the round, both females bend at the waist, placing their hands on their knees. They are breathing hard, sweating heavily, and have huge smiles on their faces. They are having fun!

I hear my mate say, "Damn it, Elana. This match is a lot harder than the last, but oh my Goddess, am I having fun." She chuckles.

Elana laughs, "I can barely breathe, but I love it!"

They both return to their side of the mat, chuckling. They put down the Karambit and pick up long wooden sticks. How is this a weapon?

Ronin sees my confusion and chuckles, "It is called a Bo, and believe me when I say she, well, both of them, are lethal with it.

She taught me my first weapons lesson with a Bo, which was an education for me."

I bark a laugh, "Did she put you on the mat with it?"

He chuckles, "Several times. This will be the best round. They are incredibly evenly matched with the Bo. All three rounds were with the Bo the last time, and no one got points until the very end."

Lessur calls start for the last round. Both come out aggressive, trying to dominate the fight. If they are as evenly matched with the weapon as Ronin said, then it's their only option.

Their proficiency with this weapon is fantastic.

Ronin

This round goes much like the last match June and Elana had. The fighting is incredibly fast-paced. The cracks of wood on wood echo around the room. No one has won a point yet, and we are about twelve minutes into the round.

Both females' focus is impressive, but I know they are both very aware of their surroundings because even though they have both got very close to the line, neither ever steps over it. It's a mistake a lot of folks make in the ring, not Elana or June. Another thing that impresses me about the two of them is their competitiveness without ego. Both could have enormous egos but neither do, which means they just have fun when they spar. I have seen many, many males get into actual fights when they lose a match, and that behavior has everything to do with ego.

Elana is pushing June back with a highly aggressive tact. To the point, I'm sure she is going to get the point in this round when my mate smiles. She is smiling! Suddenly she executes a flip backward, and when her feet follow her, she catches Elana's Bo with them and rips the Bo from Elana's hands.

Everyone, including Elana, freezes in stunned silence. June lands in a finish pose, her feet spread front to back, and the Bo tucked behind her.

Elana begins to twitter, laughing so hard she falls to the mat. June laughs and lays down beside her. Suddenly the seats around the rings erupt in cheers and the pounding of feet. The warriors are very impressed by the match they just witnessed.

Elana and June flinch and look shocked at the seats, like they forgot they were there. Dax and I jump down and trot over to our mate. She still has a smile on her face.

She chuckles, "I know that move will only work once on you, really like a lot of the 'shock' moves I use, but it was worth the look on your face."

Elana twitters loudly, "Yes, that was very much a shocking move, but it was successful! That was a brilliant match, June! I thought I would have had you with the Karambits but bringing you in close gave me no advantage like I thought it would."

I chime in, "It's what I would have done as well, Elana. I have learned my lesson from you. My mate with sharp, pointy objects is deadly either way." I chuckle.

Dax holds out his hand to help her up, and I help Elana up. "Done for the day?" He asks.

"No, I really should restart training." Nalax and Lessur smile at this statement. She chuckles, "Go get warmed up." They trot off, calling Ekim and Doraj to join them.

Leena streaks into the room but instead of her happy, bubbly self, she looks scared and launches into June's arms. Immediately concerned, June asks, "What is it, baby? What's wrong?" She looks at me, "She's shaking. Leena, look at me. What happened?"

She snuggles in closer, and I hear her say, "One of the males tried to pick me up when I told him 'no.' He chased me. He reminded me of Kaxlin." When she says his name, it is barely audible.

Dax and I are instantly furious, and I tell June, "We will take care of this." She nods. Nalax is back, and she, Elana, and our mate surround Leena with love and concern. I notice Sam and several of the Ssadab surround us and relax a little, but I will find this male. As we walk away from the group, I call out, "Sia, do you know who did this?"

"Yes, Ronin. He has retreated to the common room."

June

We are all gathered around my little Leena. I'm pissed as hell that someone would dare try something like this, but I hide it from her so she can relax. Nalax and Elana both rub her back and arms. They love her as much as I do and hate to see her upset; the contact comforts her, and she stops shaking.

"You ok, baby," I ask her as she sits back in my arms.

She nods, "He scared me, but I'm better now." She is still not smiling, so I know she's still a little upset, but she's trying to be brave.

I see Sam over Nalax's shoulder, and he also looks upset for Leena. It gives me comfort that he is so concerned for her. I know he is my protector, but being mine, means he is also hers. I know he will protect her as well.

Leena also notices her new friend and holds her arms out to him. Sam swoops in and grabs her once he gets a nod from me. I cannot hear what he says to her, but she giggles and shakes her head. I relax a bit more with that beautiful noise.

"Leena, do you want to stay with Sam as I do some training?" She nods and whispers something into his ear. Sam bursts out laughing. Wow. My Leena is a miracle worker. I have never seen Sam smile, and she can get him to smile *and* laugh.

I turn to the training area and stop in stunned silence. "Uh…" All the Ssadab warriors stand ready in rows for training. Doraj, Ekim, and Lessur stand in front of them. They shrug their shoulders like, 'what they want to train too.' "Well, I guess my training ranks have grown a bit." I look at Elana, "Wanna help me?" She bows her head in confirmation.

Dax

As Ronin and I approach the doors to the common room, Sia's voice comes over the comms in our ear, "He is sitting on the couch toward the left of the room."

We stalk into the room and look at the male in question. My anger deflates a bit, but when he sees us fear flashes across his face, then resignation. He stands and goes down to one knee.

Ronin gives a menacing growl, "Do you want to explain why I should not space you now?"

He does not raise his head, "I do not have a good reason. You should."

I can see and feel Ronin gear up for more, but he is too close to this; I put my hand on his shoulder. He looks at me, and I try to convey that I need him to let me try. He is still angry, but he nods. "Please, explain why you did this?"

He flinches like I have struck him. After a few seconds, he looks up at us and begins, "I thought she was my daughter. I wanted to believe she was my little Denci, but she was not. Denci died three years ago. To me, it feels like days." He sighs, "I did not mean to scare her," he gets a confused look on his face, "but when I saw her playing in the hallway, all I could see was her. My little one. I was so happy to see her again." He bows his head and slumps his shoulders, "It was not until she screamed that I snapped out of it and realized what I had done. I am ready for my sentence."

I can feel through the link that Ronin's anger has deflated completely. I look at him, and he nods.

"Please stand and tell us your name," I say to him.

He does so, "I am Nivek."

"Nivek, Ronin, and I forgot that the loss of family and friends would still be very new to those we woke. That grief and loss took us both a long time to get past; would be where they are now." I feel like I am channeling June, but I continue. "What you did was wrong and scared Leena greatly, but if we are being honest with ourselves, we understand. Your 'sentence' for this act is this; help me develop ways to assist those who wake through their grief. Help me help them."

He smirks, "Do you know what my role in our army? I am a mental health physician."

"Then you are the perfect person to help our warriors with their grief. We really understand how this could happen. We suffered the loss of family and friends. It was extremely hard for me to get past it alone."

Ronin interjects, "I think this is a suitable solution, but please refrain from approaching my daughter?"

Nivek nods sadly, "I hope you and the Queen can someday forgive me for my transgression, High Commander."

Ronin sighs, "There is nothing to forgive. As Dax said, I was in a deep depression for a long time after the fall of Nlyax. My mate is the only thing that could bring me out of it after three years. Include Divad in your planning, please."

We nod to Ronin, "Nivek, let's go find Divad and talk." I put my hand on Ronin's shoulder. I can feel his gratitude through the link. I can also feel his guilt, which I imagine is rooted in the fact that he feels like he should have known there would be mental health issues we would have to address with the newly awakened males. "You are not responsible for this, brother, and we will address it now." He nods and smirks at me as I turn to leave.

Ronin

I return to the training room to find my mate not only training the usual suspects but also the entire Ssadab ranks. I cannot help but chuckle as I sit beside Sam and Leena on the mat.

Leena crawls onto my lap, "How are you, my little Leena?"

"I'm good. Sam has been playing with me while we wait for Mother." She whispers enthusiastically, "We will get a treat when we're done!"

Chuckling, "Is that so little whirlwind? And what kind of treat do you want?"

She nearly screams, "ICE CREAM!" she giggles at her outburst. "Mother has put a program in the food synthesizers to make it. It's from her homeworld. *It is so good*!" She promptly yawns after her declaration. I cuddle her, and her eyes eventually close as she falls asleep.

June

It was a great training session. I thought the twenty-ish warriors were going to muddy the waters, but they listened well and followed directions. It was great!

I'm putting away weapons, and when I turn around, a young-looking warrior is bowing behind me. "Oh! Hi. Please stand. Do you have a question?"

He bows again and says, "Yes, my Queen."

Oh, Lawd help me. "No more bowing. What do you need, Maas, right?"

He gets an awed look on his face and nods. I wait for him to tell me what he needs, but I feel like this may take a while. "My Queen, I was wondering if you have made a decision about the Ssadab?"

Uh... "Decision?"

Ronin chuckles as he approaches with Sam holding Leena, "We have not discussed it yet, Maas. The Queen does not have all the details on the Ssadab yet to make an informed decision. She has only named Sam as her protector. We were going to talk to her about it now."

Oooh, he knows it annoys me when he calls me the 'Q' word. I narrow my eyes at him. "I am sorry, Maas, I have not, but once I have the details, I will."

He bows again, "Thank you, Mama." And he's gone. I chuckle and shake my head. I turn once again, narrowed eyes on Ronin, "Call me Queen one more time, Ronin, and I will put you in the ring with me again, and no games after!"

He mock growls and picks me up, so I have to wrap my legs around his waist. He puts his lips next to my ear and whispers, "You like those 'games' as much as I do, Mate."

I chuckle and kiss him lightly and jump down. "You're right," I say cheerily. "So what is this decision I need to make?"

He growls again. I laugh loudly and walk toward the door, "Come on, let's all go to our quarters so we can lie down, Leena. Then you, Sam, and I can talk about whatever this is."

We get to the quarters, and I take Leena to her room to lay her down. As I am walking out, I realize I stink badly. "I'm going to take a real quick shower, and I promise I will be right back."

I am true to my word and am back in the room clean and de-stinkied. "OK. What is this about?"

Ronin, to my surprise, looks at Sam. "As part of the Queen's Guard, which, by naming me your protector, you made me the Captain of the Guard. The Guard are the best of the best. There are no other units better in battle. Second to the Guard is the Ssadab."

"However," Ronin interrupts, "When I took over as High Commander, I mixed the Queen's Guard and the Ssadab. So we have the best in the military and at the Queen's side."

I think I see where this is going, "So the two of you think I should name the Ssadab the Queen's Guard." They nod. "All the Ssadab were in my training this afternoon?" Sam nods.

"Are you sure they would be ok guarding *me*?" I am still having a hard time believing, well, everything.

Sam gets a confused look, "It is the highest honor, and honestly, you are a Battle Queen. Nlyax has not had one of those for many centuries. It will please the warriors who are to be your guard that they get to battle *and* guard the Queen."

I stand and pace the room slowly so I can think. I return to them and sit down. "It would honor me to have the Ssadab as my guard, but I will require them to learn my fighting styles and train with multiple weapons. Oh, and instead of the Queen's Guard, I want to call them the Queen's Ssadab. Elite warriors who have the added duty of my safety." I hate the last sentence to come out. It just feels strange.

Ronin gives me a soft smile, "That is completely acceptable, my Mate, and because you are a Battle Queen, I think Queen's Ssadab is perfect. The rough translation of Ssadab is Master Warriors."

I look at Sam, "So your memories are coming back?"

"I have no memories of me or if I had a family, but I do remember details of things around me. Divad says it may, or it may not return." He doesn't look sad when he says this, but I am sad for him, but I do not show it.

"I would like to take care of more of the pain now, but since you are more... since your mind is clearer, I want to ask permission from now on. You do not have to, but I want to help you, Sam."

He stares at me for a while. I wait patiently for his answer. "Please. The pain is sometimes distracting."

I nod and close my eyes. I find him, and I can tell which bridge is to who. I walk to his bridge, and instead of stopping at the center of the bridge, I cross and stop where the bridge ends.

Sam steps from the churning cloud, "Are you ready?" I ask him. He nods. I look at the angry mass of clouds and can feel the shards of glass. There are fewer than when I started, but there is still a lot.

I grab onto as many as possible with my mind and grind them away as I did before.

I do this several times, and then I notice something large or several large items churning around in the cloud. When I do, I flinch; I thought the small shards hurt. This one is terrible. I decide I will do the same with this as I have done with the others. I start breaking it up into smaller and smaller pieces. This one feels like it's taking me forever. Finally, I am at the point where this piece is dust, and I grind it to nothing.

I think about which I will grab next until Sam lays a hand on my shoulder, "That is enough for now, my friend. Removing that one shard lightened the pain dramatically."

"Ok. I am not done, though."

He chuckles and nods, "I have figured out that when you attack a problem, you never give up, but I can feel you are tired. There will be a next time after you rest."

I nod. I am tired; that big one took a lot. I stop at the bridge's center and look back at the storm. There are now significant gaps in the clouds. Most of the tiny shards are gone but now that I am back where I can see again, I see two more big shards. I will take care of those. I walk back and open my eyes.

Dax is now in the room with Divad. I am wiped out. I lean back against Ronin. He wraps his arms around me and kisses my hair. "You are amazing."

I look at Sam, and he seems nearly healed. The spikes along his arms are still there, but everything else they did to him is gone. He smiles at me. He looks very relaxed. "I will go talk with the Ssadab. What time would you like us in the training room tomorrow?"

"How about 09:30?"

He nods, stands, bows and leaves.

Dax comes over to sit by me and pulls my legs into his lap. He massages my legs. Divad interrupts my thoughts. I almost forgot he was here, "My Queen," I give him a dirty look, "Sorry, June. I was scanning Sam as you healed him, and the data... the data is amazing. You were able to unmake the bonds the Lutetian created to mutate him, *and* you did it with no pain. Amazing."

Dax interrupts him, "Divad, our mate is exhausted. Can we discuss this tomorrow?"

He gets a shocked look and looks around, "Yes, of course, forgive me! See you tomorrow." And he leaves. I chuckle at his abruptness.

"Thanks, Dax. I am exhausted but hungry too."

Ronin picks me up, carries me to the counter, and sets me on it. "Do not move. I will get you something." Dax stands next to me and leans his hip against the counter.

"Your match today... I have never seen anything like it. You and Elana are truly spectacular to watch. Though it's hard to track your weapons... moves... well, I guess everything. You both are so fast in your movements, and the movements themselves flow in ways I have never seen before. It was entertaining to watch."

Ronin chuckles, "He jumped up at one point when you were battling with the Karambit. He thought you lost a point, then realized you sacrificed one point for two."

I laugh with him. "Yeah, I have got Ronin with that as well."

Ronin has a plate in his hand and gives me a fork. I eat every-thing, but not without yawning several times between bites. He grabs the plate, Dax plucks me off the counter and walks to the bedroom.

He sets me down and removes my clothes, "Get into bed, little Pillut." I smile he is now using that endearment as well. I climb into bed and under the covers. He and Ronin climb in shortly behind me. "Sleep, little one. We will be here." I nod and yawn, promptly falling asleep.

I am in Aanon's field. I cannot wait to see him. I wish Ronin and Dax could be here. I freeze. Hmmm, I wonder if I can pull them here.

The Lutetian could do that, and it has to be what I am doing now unconsciously.

I look for Ronin bridge, and it appears. He is on the other side. I motion for him to join me. I do the same for Dax. I see him hesitate, "It's ok, Dax. It's me. Join me."

Ronin and Dax now stand beside me in the field. "What's going on, June?" Ronin asks. "Are you showing us the dream again?"

I shake my head. "This is now. We are dreaming. Aanon is here." Both freeze in disbelief. It's ok. I walk to the house. When we reach it, I knock on the door.

A big bassy voice boom from the house, "Come in, June. I am in the kitchen." I open the door and walk in, with Ronin and Dax following. We enter the kitchen, and Aanon isn't facing us. "I am cooking us some lunch."

I look at Ronin and Dax. Tears stream down my face. Ronin, in nearly a whisper, Ronin says, "I always loved your Bruga Cakes."

Utensils fall to the counter he works at. He doesn't turn around. I walk over to him and touch his shoulder. "Aanon."

"For the first time in my life, I am terrified. What if I turn and he is not there?"

Dax speaks up, "We are here, Aanon." Again he flinches—Dax, not one to be denied, launches across the room and spins Aanon around. I think neither believed it was the other. They wrap each other in an extremely tight hug, like the other will disappear if they let go.

Aanon looks up and sees Ronin. His knees buckle, and they go to the floor. It's Ronin's turn to run across to them. He lands hard on his knees and wraps his arms around both. They've been like this for a while. I hear Aanon say, "I do not want this to be a dream. It is too much."

I walk over and squat in front of them, "Aanon, while this is a dream, we are not. I have the ability to visit dreams and minds. I discovered this just now when I woke in your dream. I can also pull others into dreams. So when I woke into your dream, I decided to pull in Ronin and Dax. You all needed to see each other to know it's real."

Aanon hand disentangles from the pile of males and grabs the back of my neck, pulling me forward into a deep, passionate kiss. Ronin and Dax pull me into the middle of the three of them. I wrap my arms around Aanon, lay my head on his massive chest, and whisper, "We are real."

Aanon chuckles, "I am beginning to believe that, little one."

Ronin snorts, "Do you think your mind could make up a mate like June? She is so different from what I used to imagine for us, but she is perfect."

"No, I do not think I could." He chuckles, "The Goddess is wise."

I pull back from him and grab both sides of his face, "We are coming for you. We have information on where we think you are and are getting ready to come for you."

He gets a concerned look, "June, do not endanger yourself for me." The look he turns on Ronin and Dax is one of anger and confusion. "What are you thinking?"

They both look at me, "He does not know about your skills?" Ronin asks.

"No. It has never been necessary here. He is such a calming presence."

Dax laughs, "You are not wrong there." He looks at Dax, "Let's sit somewhere, and we can explain." We stand and walk to the porch I enjoy so much. I start to sit in a chair when Aanon picks me up and sits down with me in his lap. This puts big smiles on both Ronin and Dax's faces.

"Explain, please." He says to us.

I'm not sure why but it makes me nervous. He is such a gentle male. Will he dislike I am also a warrior?

Aanon lifts my face to him, "What makes you feel this way, little one? No matter what is said, my feelings for you will not change."

Ronin softly asks, "Would you like me to explain?"

I sigh, "No, but feel free to interject information if I leave something out." He nods. I look at Aanon, and he has such a look of love on his face, "Aanon, I am a warrior. Ronin, Dax, and I have been through a lot these past months. Some of it was bad, but finding each other was amazing. Ronin and I were slaves on a ship." I can't help but break eye contact at this point, "I was a sex slave to a horrible Nlyaxian. As punishment, he threw me into the male slave area, where I met Ronin. Eventually, we freed ourselves and decided to free the slave of this galaxy and give them Haven."

Ronin interrupts, "She freed us, and it was her idea to find and free slaves. Our mate is a formidable warrior, even beating me in the ring." I feel Aanon's shock at this.

Dax chuckles, "I even hear she put him on the mat several times. I have not seen it yet but I cannot wait!" I feel Aanon's laughter; it's big and bassy.

Ronin laughs and gets serious again, "She is a Battle Queen, Aanon, and the Chosen Warrior of the Goddess." Aanon freezes and slightly lifts his hands off me like he shouldn't touch me.

It breaks my heart. I whisper, "Please don't treat me differently, Aanon. I'm still me."

His enormous arms wrap around me and pull me close. I wrap my arms around his neck and pull myself, so my face is at his neck. I still cannot look him in the eyes. "June, please look at me." I shake my head. "Forgive my reaction; I was shocked, is all. The teachings of the Goddess are fundamental to who I am. I have read all the texts I can find. Please, my mate."

I pull back and look at him. All I see is his love for me written on his face, with no reservation or regret. I relax a bit, and I feel Dax lay a hand on my back and begin to rub up and down, trying to ease my anxiety. Ronin lays a hand on my leg. I look at him and then look back at Aanon.

"*I am Her Chosen Warrior, and maybe you can help me understand what that means.*"

Aanon smiles, and my heart stops. This male is my kryptonite. I'd give anything to see that smile. He says, "It would be my honor. Now please tell me in great detail about your match with Ronin." We all laugh at that and discuss everything from fighting style to family.

Aanon is laughing once again, and the bassy rumble is affecting me. I am becoming very wet. Suddenly they all stop and turn very steamy looks in my direction. Fuck me.

My clothes disappear, and I gasp. Aanon dives into a passionate kiss. Hands are roaming my body. One set finds my breast, and another set explores my folds. I moan into Aanon's mouth, and he deepens the kiss. I feel someone spread my legs then my fingers change to a tongue that dives deep into my pussy. There's now a mouth sucking my nipple. My body barely knows what to do with the barrage of sensations hitting it. When the tongue in my pussy finds my gspot my body instantly explodes, I arch my back and scream. I hear all three whisper, "Beautiful."

As I'm coming down from it, Aanon stands and walks into the house. I'm laid down in an enormous bed. He stands back, and I now see three Nlyaxian males, dark and beautiful, standing and looking down at me with fire in their eyes. I do not think I deserve these males but thank Goddess; they are mine.

Aanon stands between Ronin and Dax. Almost as one, they bend and crawl into the bed. Ronin settles his hips between my legs, Dax and Aanon settle at my sides. Dax dives into a kiss, Aanon's mouth latches onto my nipple, and Ronin firmly, slowly pushes into my body. His cock is big and stretches me to my limit. I moan into Dax's mouth, and his kiss becomes more passionate.

Annon is licking, nipping, and pinching my nipples. His ministrations are driving me higher. Ronin thrusts in and out the ridges on his cock, vibrating his cock as he moves. My moans are elevating their desire. Ronin increases his speed, and I feel my orgasm building. Aanon pulls back and looks down at Ronin's cock entering and leaving my body. His hand moves to my clit and starts rubbing back and forth. My orgasm explodes, and I scream. Ronin moans as my pussy locks down onto his cock.

His pace increases, and I feel his sprili unfurl. I am screaming again as they drive my orgasm higher. As I am coming down, I feel his cock throb; he roars as his release hits, and the sprili vibrates. The orgasm that hits is so intense the scream is silent. I feel him leave my body, and I'm picked up and put on my hands and knees.

Dax

My mate with her ass in the air is magnificent. She looks back at me and looks into my molten eyes. I thrust into her, and she moans. Ronin settles under her and begins sucking and pinching her breasts. "Aanon! In front!" She screams. He looks confused but is on his knees in front of her, his enormous cock perfectly positioned.

I smile at the sensations her body creates on my cock, and knowing what my brother is about to experience for the first time. Her hand grabs his cock, and when her lips wrap around it, I about lose control right then. Aanon's breath explodes from his mouth. I am thrusting into my mate hard. Feeling her wrapped around my cock while she has her lips wrapped around one of my Triad's cock is too much. I feel my sprili come out, and I roar as my seed hits her walls, and they vibrate. I see and feel her orgasm hit. Aanon roars as he releases down her throat.

I pull from her and wrap my arm around her waist. Standing away from the bed, I motion to Aanon to take her. He wraps her legs around his waist and slowly enters her. They both have their heads thrown back in ecstasy. I nod to Ronin and lie on the bed so I can watch.

June

Aanon is so big that the stretch is not altogether comfortable. He is going so slowly and carefully. Once he has fully seated himself, we both moan.

Ronin is kissing my shoulders and neck. His arm wraps under my arm around me, and his hand locks on my shoulder. His other hand grabs my ass. I feel him pushing in, and I moan his name. Aanon wraps his other arm around the both of us and puts his forehead to mine while I feel Ronin's forehead on the back of my head. I feel so full and feel like I could orgasm by just breathing. They start slowly, alternating their thrusts. I am panting, moaning, and intensely focused on the sensations they are creating in me, but I can take slow no more, "Faster," I whisper.

It breaks the control they were holding. They are still alternating their rhythm but now fast. We hold each other tightly. I feel my orgasm starting when their sprili unfurl, which makes my orgasm crash into me. I am screaming as they moan and release as my body locks onto theirs. When their sprili vibrate, a second orgasm joins the first, sending me to the stars.

When my brain finishes its restart, the three of us are still standing on the floor, I'm still impaled on my mate's cocks, and we are all trying to catch our breath. I lean forward and sprinkle kisses along Aanon's shoulder. I moan as Ronin leaves my body. Aanon walks to the bed, pulls from my body, and lays down on the bed. We are a pile of arms and legs, yet somehow, we are all comfortable and touching the others in some way.

"Aanon, we believe we know where you are, and we are coming for you." I need him to know we are coming for him.

He runs his fingers through my hair, "I believe you, my fire-haired mate." Good. I feel him turn his head to Ronin, "So if you are attacking slavers and coming to get me, you must have a ship?"

"Yes. We have the Nlyaxian ship I was testing when Nlyax fell. I see the anger in your eyes, Aanon," the sadness in his voice makes me turn my head to face him. "I have beat myself up about that for a long time."

I cannot take his guilt. I move so I am lounging half on his chest, "You need to forgive yourself for that, Ronin. Your family wouldn't want this guilt hanging around your neck like a weight." I put my hand on his cheek.

Aanon's bassy voice interrupts, "Forgive me, brother. I feel like it was yesterday, and our mate is correct. Your family, especially your mother, would not want that for you." He pauses, "I talked to her that day." I feel Ronin still with the impact of that statement.

He whispers, "Oh?" He fears what he is about to tell him.

Aanon chuckles, "Your mother always had a way of seeing right through us. She always knew when you two were up to something. That day she saw me in the hallway. I was looking for you both. She asked me to join her in her study. She stood at the window looking out and said, 'You should not be mad at them, Aanon. I have handled things poorly with all of you.' she laughed then said, 'Of my sons, Ronin is the one I am most proud of, the one I knew had a purpose in this universe. I wish he were here so I could tell him that and how much I care for him.' She looked disappointed, Ronin, but it was not in you but in herself."

Strong emotion is bombarding me from all three, but the most from Ronin. It helped heal a piece of him. I cup his face, "Are you ok?" He gives me such a look of peace and love that I pull his face to mine and kiss him gently.

I am feeling a tug. We need to leave, and I do not want to risk anything since I brought Ronin and Dax here. I sit up and look at Aanon, but before I can say anything, he nods and says, "I feel it too. It is time for you to head back."

I imagine clothing back on us all, so we do not get distracted, and Dax groans, "Awe, I hate clothes."

We all chuckle, and I say to Aanon, "Walk with us?"

We are walking the road away from his farm, and I hate it. It is wrong, and he should be with us. Dax hits his hip against me, trying to get me to smile. I do, but it's a little forced. I look past him and notice something in the distance.

I stop and stare, trying to figure out what I am seeing. Ronin steps beside me, "What is it?" He is looking in the same direction as me.

"What is that?" I ask, pointing to the dark clouds in the distance.

"What?" Ronin asks. I look at my mates and all three look confused.

I look back at the clouds. They are too far away, but it seems like a distant storm. "The storm in the distance." They all look concerned for me. "Seriously? You don't see it?" Dax and Ronin shake their heads, but Aanon says, "Oh, that. Yes, I've noticed that as well. I never go there."

I am about to ask more questions when the pull gets much more substantial. I am compelled to draw their mind bridges. "Go. Hurry." They both hug Aanon and trot to their bridge to disappear across it.

I turn to Aanon, but he and his farm are gone. I wake up in my bed with a gasp.

June

The next few days go by, and I am distracted. I can't help but be bothered by how the dream with Aanon ended. I spend an inordinate amount of time in the training room, mostly by myself. I run training sessions and then spend time on the equipment trying to figure out what is setting my alarms off.

Nothing is working, so I sit on the mat after everyone has left the training session that just wrapped up. I need to calm my mind. Meditation is a process. I envision the stress leaving my body through my fingers, and I quiet my mind and picture blackness. I am lying in the water, floating. My mind is at peace.

After some unknown amount of time, I open my eyes to the blackness. Now I am sitting cross-legged on an inky black floor. I feel something disturb the surrounding air, and that is when I feel it. The air feels oppressive, stagnant, and almost evil.

I hear a chuckle. I slowly stand and turn in a circle. I can see nothing but black space. I see nothing. I feel the air move behind me and freeze. I can feel the dangerous situation I am in, but I am not sure how to get out of it. Arms snake around me; I look down and feel nauseous.

The arms belong to someone my brain refuses to acknowledge. Kaxlin cannot be here. I killed him.

"You killed me, but the God I worship, the one true God, he deemed me worthy and brought me back."

"Liar," I whisper.

Whatever it is, it spins me around, and I am face to face with my nightmare, but instead of descending into fear, it has the opposite effect. I immediately go into an aggressive, offensive attack. I intend on killing him again. I land many blows, and he ends up on the floor. I am on his chest, driving multiple blows to his throat. I cave it in on itself. Kaxlin still smiles at me. I jump off him and get far away.

"You are not Kaxlin. What are you?"

It chuckles again and stands up. All the damage I did is still there. It bleeds from its nose and mouth; its throat is mangled. As I stare, a line opens at its throat, and blood pours from it. I notice its arm is now missing, and blood is dripping from that as well. It is grotesque. "Such anger. Tsk, tsk, tsk. Are you sure you are meant to be her warrior? I think you should be mine."

My stomach becomes a ball of ice as I realize who this must be, "Jezu."

It gives me a bloody smile, "Awe, you know me. That makes me happy." I don't see it move, but suddenly it has me by the neck, and I feel a wall against my back. "I think I will make you mine. You can be my toy for as long as you last." It licks up my neck, "But my toys tend to break rather quickly."

A chill rolls through me.

Ronin

Dax and I are in our quarters, waiting for June to return from training. The door chimes, "Enter." Dax calls out. Elana walks in, and she looks concerned.

"Something is wrong. I... I don't know what it is, but something is wrong." She is highly agitated, and her feathers are up.

Then I feel a chill, and fear rolls through me. I know it is not mine. It is June's. I stand, and so does Dax. "Sia! Where is June!?"

"She is in the training room. She seems to be meditating. She is not alone; Sam stands guard at the door." She seems confused by my concern.

Dax and I are now both confused; we feel her fear. We all run out the door as I tap twice on my ear, "Sam. Is my mate safe?"

Sam comes back over the com, "Yes, sir. She sits on the mat, and she seems to meditate. Do you want me to check on her?"

"Yes. We will be there in a few minutes."

After a few seconds, he comes back on with concern in his voice, "Uh, Sir, her eyes are open but..."

"*But what?*"

"Her eyes are black."

We are on the elevator, and Elana asks, "What did he say?"

As the doors open, I say, "He says her eyes are open, but they are black." The fear that comes over her face as she sprints toward the training room scares me. Dax and I pour on the speed to get to our mate.

Elana screams as she sees Sam reaching for June, "*Stop*!" It's too late. When his hand lands on her shoulder, he goes rigid, and his eyes also turn black.

Elana lands on her knees in front of them but does not touch them. "Elana, what is happening?" Dax asks in an almost panic.

"It's him."

"Him who?" My volume is almost yelling.

She looks at us, "Jezu, the enemy of light, the enemy of the Goddess."

Dax has a confused look, "A god?"

She gets a disgusted look, "More like a demon with God-like abilities."

"What do we do? How do we help her?" I need to do something.

Elana's eyes dart back and forth, thinking of a solution. "I am not sure."

My frustration makes me pace in front of my mate, trying to find a way to help. I know nothing of this. Aanon would know what to do. I run my hands through my hair. I catch a glimpse of silver and look at my arm. I sit in front of my mate and Sam.

Elana sees me reaching for my Kokoro and smiles, "Yes! We can lend her our strength!" She sits beside me, "When you touch the Kokoro, I will as well. Just think about her and think about sending her strength and light. That is all we can do."

Dax sits beside me, and touches his Kokoro, and Elana and I touch mine. I think of June, sending her all the love and strength within me. I hope it is enough.

June

Jezu has an evil smile and then cocks his head as if it is listening to something. It suddenly lifts its other arm as if to grab something. It now has an arm, and it seems to be made of blood. It holds Sam.

With malice, it brings Sam close and says, "And who might this be?"

Sam whispers, "I know you…"

It chuckles again, "You do, Samoht. I have enjoyed torturing your mind for many years." It looks back at me, "You are the one who's been weakening my connection to him? We shall fix that."

The fear that comes over Sam's face makes my fear evaporate. I am furious. Suddenly I feel awash with love, support, strength, and light. My mates and Elana are trying to help. I settle into my calm, "Not today Satan."

Jezu looks back at me, shocked. I funnel all the light into my hands and deliver two punches to his chest. It flies across the space and lands on its back on the floor. Sam is now at my side with a determined look on his face.

"Take my hand, Sam." When he does, I funnel some of the light from me into him. "Now funnel that to your fists. We have a fight to win." He smiles, and his fists begin to glow.

I look back, and it sits up. It now has a large wound in the center of its chest. "Do you believe you can beat me?"

I chuckle, "Maybe not kill, but..." I disappear and reappear in front of him and hit him with an uppercut straight to his jaw. "But I am pretty sure we can make you regret invading my mind!"

Sam and I are now delivering blow after blow. Pieces of it are now falling off. It eventually falls to the ground and dissolves, but now a black cloud churns in front of us. I can feel its intent before it explodes across the room at Sam.

I step in front of Sam and scream, focusing all the light and strength I have left at it. It evaporates, but I feel its pain before it is completely gone.

Dax

Ronin and I have been focused on sending June everything we have for a while. I felt when her emotions changed from fear to determination. I know she is fighting whatever has attacked her. I know she will win. She would never let someone she cares for get hurt. With Sam in danger, I know she fights. I feel her anger, her determination, and her focus. I feel her drawing something from us, but I will give her everything if it means she is safe.

I did not notice the oppressive presence until it was gone— the light in myself and the room returns. I open my eyes and see June's and Sam's eyes are back to normal. They both look exhausted. Sam sits beside her and then lies on the mat.

June has a small smile, "I love you all more than you can possibly know. Thank you." She looks at me, then Ronin, and finally at Elana. She puts her hand on her heart and bows her head to us.

Ronin and I both reach for her and pull her to us. We are all on our knees, hugging. She draws us both in for a gentle kiss and then pulls our foreheads together.

She pulls back, "Are you ok? I didn't pull too much?"

I chuckle, "No, my mate. I would happily give you everything I have." Ronin nods.

She gets serious, "No. You must never do that. Never. Without you two, I will fail. Do you understand me? I will fail without you."

I can see how much this means to her. I glance at Ronin, and he nods, "We will promise to give you what you need without sacrificing ourselves. Alright?" Her eyes tear up, and she nods. We hug her. I do not know how close we got to losing her, but I fear it was very close.

June

My mates are amazing. I'm pretty sure I would have lost that fight without them. I stand and walk over to Sam, kneeling beside him.

He stares at the ceiling. "Sam, are you ok?" He looks at me, but I can't read his face and start to worry, "Sam?"

"It's gone."

"I don't understand, Sam."

"The pain, the shards, the clouds; it's all gone. I remember who I am."

It's my turn to look shocked. I sit back on my heels, "But... I don't understand. I still had a lot to heal."

He gets up and kneels in front of me, "When you lent me your light and strength, it burned some of it away. Then, when you blasted it with light at the end, it hit me as well." He sees my instant fear I hurt him, "No. My Queen, it did not hurt in any way. That blast of light cleared the rest, and I could remember everything."

I look him over, and all the mutations are gone. Now I'm tearing up. "All your pain is gone?"

"Yes, my Queen. Thank you."

My tears spill over, and he looks behind me. Ronin picks me up. "Your fatigue is beating me. You need to rest." I nod. I am exhausted.

"We all do. Sam, Elana, you need rest as well." Ronin turns but stops. Six of the Ssadab kneel behind us.

Sam walks up beside us. "Queen's Ssadab, I need rest. Guard your Queen." They all stand and salute.

Dax chuckles, "Sam, maybe from now on, you let them guard, and you will advise and take part in planning and etcetera."

Sam laughs, "Dax, you know how much I hate meetings! But I suppose I will for my Queen." He smiles at me and heads out.

"Elana." I call for her, and she peeks around Dax, "Are you ok?"

She gives me a soft smile, "Yes, my friend though I need some rest as well, so we will chat later." I nod to her, and she heads out. Sam waited for her, and they leave together.

Two of the Ssadab fall in, in front of us and two behind as we leave the training room. I lay my head on Ronin's shoulder. "They're going to think I'm weak *yawn* if you keep carrying me everywhere."

They both chuckle. Ronin answers for both of them, "No, my beautiful mate. Every warrior is tired after the battle, and they know you battled a God. Besides," he growls, "they understand we cannot keep our hands off of you, mate."

I chuckle and yawn again. I cannot keep my eyes open. They shut, and I am asleep in seconds.

Dax and I are awake and in the living area of our quarters. June has been asleep for nearly ten hours. We are starting the landing process into Haven. We should be in the cradle within forty minutes.

I look at Dax, "One of us should be on the bridge."

He gives me a disinterested look, "They will be fine. I say we wake our mate and make her scream our names."

I'm off the couch, head to our bedroom before he can move, "I get to wake her."

He jumps up laughingly, adding, "No fair!"

We both strip as we enter and stop at the end of the bed. She looks so beautiful. She sleeps facing up. Her red hair creates a halo around her head. The sheet covers most of her naked body except one shoulder and breast are exposed. The nipple of that breast is hard in the room's chill.

We carefully uncover the rest of her body. Her body is magnificent, made for pleasure. The nipple, on the other, hardens to match. My eyes roam her body. Her waist narrows and then expands into her hips. I love her hips… and her ass, but I cannot see that right now. I kneel on the bed, bending to push her knees open. I settle my shoulders between her thighs.

I wrap my arms under her legs. I can smell her sex, and my cock gets painfully hard. I spread her sex with my fingers, examining my prize. I glance at Dax and see the envy on his face. "You take her clit, and I will go deeper." We both smile and begin.

June

I wake moaning, two tongues at my pussy. My fingers immediately fist the hair closest. Dax growls, and I feel it through his tongue. I moan and writhe at the riot of sensation. The other tongue is at my entrance, dips in, and comes back out to circle and tease.

"*Ronin!*"

I hear him chuckle, "Our mate is impatient."

Dax growls again as he circles my clit, not quite close enough to make me cum. I squirm, and both lock their arms around me so I can't move. I growl my dissatisfaction. "What do you need, my mate?" Dax asks me.

I nearly scream, "Make me cum!"

"Shall we do that, Ronin?" He asks as he circles my clit several more times. His hand reaches up and caresses and pinch my nipples. Making my moaning increase.

Ronin's tongue dives deep into my pussy, zeroing in on the spot. When he finds it, "Hmmmmmm," vibrates up his tongue, but before my orgasm hits, he pulls his tongue back out. I scream in frustration.

He chuckles, but before finishing, I lock my legs around his shoulders and flip us. I sit up, flipping my hair out of my face. I put my best dom face on and look down into his shocked face, "Now. Quit fucking teasing me."

I lower my pussy to his face slowly. He growls, and I know I've snapped his control. Goosebumps race over my skin, and I shiver. Dax latches onto my nipple as Ronin's tongue returns to my gspot. My fingers are now tangled in their hair, holding both where I need.

I begin to grind my pussy on Ronin's face. He growls again; this time, his tongue is where it needs to be. His growl is long and dangerous. My orgasm hits me so hard I scream till I am horse.

I open my eyes, and two sets of Nlyaxian eyes are on me, and they are on fire. I can't stop the moan that escapes. Dax's arms wrap his arms around my waist, lift me, and set me down directly on Ronin's cock. We all watch his cock enter my body.

When Ronin is fully seated, Dax swings around behind me and bends me over Ronin. He palms my ass with both hands and growls. My pussy throbs with need, and Ronin growls. "Now, Dax." He commands.

Dax pushes in. I moan and push back, needing him all the way in. The full feeling makes me moan, "Ronin, Dax, please..."

They alternate, pushing in and pulling out. Their ridges vibrating their cocks, driving me wild with need. I can feel the orgasm racing at me. When it hits, and my body locks down on theirs, my mates can no longer hold back. They roar, their sprili and seed releasing at the same time. They vibrate, sending me deeper into my orgasm.

As I come down from my orgasm, I am collapsed on Ronin's chest, and Dax is on me. We are all panting from exertion. Dax breaks the silence, "Goddess, my mate. I think you are trying to kill us." I laugh, and they groan at the sensation it creates.

They pull out, and we roll off each other. "I love it when you two wake me that way. It's the best."

Ronin chuckles, "We like it as well. June, I have a question."

"Ok."

He hesitates, "Why is Aanon's section on the Kokoro missing? I saw it in the dream, but it is not out here."

I sigh, "I'm not sure yet. My current theory is because he will remember none of it when he wakes."

Dax whispers, "Because I am the only male that remembers their dreams?"

"I think it's possible. When you joined the Triad, it stayed. It's only a theory, but it is all I can think of."

Dax turns on his side, facing me. He runs a finger over my nipple. It hardens at his touch. I arch my back and moan for more contact. "When you flipped Ronin and took control, I nearly released my seed right then."

Ronin is now on his side facing me, "I am torn, lick you, fuck you, or spank you. I could not decide which." His fingers are at my clit, circling.

Sia's voice interrupts us, "Crew and passengers, We land in fifteen minutes."

"We are home!" Ronin says as he gets up, making me groan. He chuckles, picks me up, and throws me over his shoulder. "Come, my mate! We need to shower!" Then he slaps my ass hard. I moan, and both my mate's growl.

Dax growls out, "That slap spiked her desire. I think our mate likes it."

They head into the bathroom and proceed to make me scream while we land.

CHAPTER

21

June

We stand in the landing bay while waiting for the ship to be brought into the cavern. I need to discuss the protocol with the new folks on the ships. I do not want to risk any conflict.

"Sia, please open comms in both ships."

"Open."

"Folks new to Haven, there are rules you need to understand and follow. The inhabitants of Haven are ex-slaves. They have been traumatized by beings in this universe who may look like you. These people are my people. I trust and love them. Do not antagonize or force them to engage with you if they are not ready. If any of you disrespect them, you disrespect Ronin, Dax, and myself. Do not misinterpret me; we are happy you are all here. I just do not want any misunderstandings. *No one* is better than anyone else here. We are all equal. If you need assistance, they will help you if you ask. They are good people. Please remember that, and welcome to Haven. Cut comms"

Sia's voice chimes in, "Ready to disembark."

"Ok open bay doors."

Waiting outside the door are the elected leaders of Haven; Amabo, Karab, and Ellechim. They all relax and smile when they see me and meet me at the end of the ramp. They all reach out and touch my arms. Ellechim says, "We are so happy to see you home safe, June." She has tears in her eyes.

Dax and Ronin are to my right; Sam and Ekul are to my left. Leena is in Dax's arms. "Sam, Ekul, this is Amabo, Karab, and Ellechim. They are the chosen leaders of Haven."

Ekul and Sam bow their heads in respect.

I see them notice all the new Nlyaxians and chuckle, "We have a lot to tell you, but first," I turn and find Divad and motion him to come forward. "Divad, I think we should leave the pods on the ships for now. We don't really have a place to store that many pods. We can bring them up as you and Nalax need to wake them. Is that acceptable?"

He nods, "Yes, that is fine."

"Good. Ok command staff, meet in the main building conference room in two hours. Ssadab, we will assign you all quarters, settle in, then report to Sam."

They all salute and say, "Yes, my Queen."

I pinch the bridge of my nose. Ugh.

Seeing my discomfort, Ronin steps forward, "Council, there are two more beings you should be aware of, Sirk and Neith; please come forward." They come forward, but you can tell they are nervous.

All three council members gasp. I step to them, "Listen carefully. Both Neith and Sirk were critical to my rescue. Neith is my friend, and helped me stay alive and escape captivity. Sirk..."

Dax speaks up when I realize I do not have all the facts. "Sirk was critical to us finding June. Without him, we would not have, and he was critical in rescuing her as well. Neith and Sirk are followers of the Goddess's teachings and welcome here."

Surprising me, they relax and smile, "Welcome, Neith and Sirk. Please forgive our initial reaction. We were shocked, but we are happy to see you here."

Sirk and Neith bow their heads in thanks. Neith looks at me, "June would it be ok if I stay down here? The surface is very... bright."

Worried, I ask, "Are you sure?"

She smiles at me, "Yes. I would be much more comfortable here. I will come up if you need me, but the sun is harmful to my skin."

I nod, "Ok, I am fine with it. Our meeting is in the evening, so you should be ok to attend?" She gives me a confused look, "The command meeting. I would like both you and Sirk to attend."

"Of course. I will be there." She gives me a small smile. She looks... pale? I don't know if something is off, but she looks uncomfortable. She excuses herself and goes back onto the ship. I will check on her later.

"Ok, let's head up top. Ekim, would you show them the way?" He nods and motions for the warriors to follow.

Amabo steps forward, "We have made some large advances since you were last here."

"Oh?" I ask.

"Yes," she smiles. "We have completed the infirmary building." This swings Divad back around in interest. I chuckle.

He says, "Did someone say there's an infirmary building?"

Karab chuckles. "Yes." he says, "I can show you around if you like. I was responsible for building it." Divad grins and nods enthusiastically.

I look at Ellechim for her to finish for Amabo, "We also added two new housing buildings so folks will have housing meant for living spaces. We made both from the same material as the rest. The new housing will hold up to a thousand families, or we can assign roommates."

I am in shock, "You built enough housing for over a thousand people? That's amazing." I turn to Dax and Ronin, "We need to discuss the valley population at some point. Nalax?" She turns and looks at me, "Can you stay back with me? Elana, you too, please. Go ahead without us."

I turn to go back into the ship. Sam and three warriors move to follow. I hold up my hand, "Sam, you may accompany us, but only you."

He nods and motions them to stand guard at the bay doors, then turns back to us. I walk into the bay. Nalax asks, "What's going on, June?"

"I feel like something is wrong with Neith. She seems sick or something I don't know, but I want to check on her."

Elana nods, "I agree. Her expalita was abnormally bright when she walked off the ship."

We enter a lift, "Now I *am* worried."

Sam also has a concerned look, "Why would that be?"

Elana concentrates, then shakes her head, "I honestly do not know. I have never seen an expalita get brighter. It gets darker when your acts become more evil or dimmer as you get old and close to passing but brighter, no."

We exit the lift and head to Neith's quarters. We approach the door and hit the call button. Neith's voice comes over the small display, "Who is there?"

"Neith, it's June. Nalax, Elana, and Sam are with me. I am worried about you. Can we come in?"

I believe she's going to ignore the request, but after a few minutes, she responds, "I am fine." I can hear and feel the pain in her voice. Now I am very worried.

"Neith. I feel your pain! Please."

The door opens, and we rush in. I was not prepared for what I see. Neith is up against a wall, almost wholly cocooned in webbing. When I see the pain on her face, I rush over to her, "Neith, what is wrong?"

She closes her eyes and shudders with pain. She restarts the cocoon, "I do not know. I am not due to molt, but we do not cocoon to molt. It is also not painful to do so. I am scared, June."

I turn to ask Nalax to help, but instead of three people behind me, there are four. The Goddess stands behind them. They all turn to see what I am looking at behind them. Elana twitters and drops to her knees. Sam and Nalax follow suit.

She walks over and grabs Elana's arm, "Please, I do not require this of anyone, especially not you." Elana is shaking.

I walk over and join them. She looks at the others and says, "Sam, Nalax, please stand. You both are very special to me as well." They do but do not look at Her.

I'm a little annoyed. I think she is causing Neith's pain. She gives me a sad look, "I am." She walks over and touches Neith's cheek. She relaxes a bit, but there is still some pain on her face.

"Why?" I ask her.

Neith is the one who answers, "Because I asked it of her." She looks at me a little sad, "I am sorry I did not tell you."

The Goddess caresses her cheek again, and Neith relaxes a bit more, "When I first visited Neith to ask her to help you, she asked me for something."

"What did you ask of her?" I look at Neith.

"My people have done so much harm in the universe. I asked her that any Nlyaxian that follows Her be changed. I am ashamed to be Lutetian." Tears leak down her cheek.

I step in front of her, my heart breaking for her, "Neith, I told you, I love you for you."

Neith reaches from her cocoon and touches my cheek. "I know you do, and you are amazing, but I cannot get past what my people have done and continue to do. I want this, no matter the cost."

Tears now run down my face. Without looking at the Goddess, I ask, "What is happening to her?"

"She is going through a metamorphosis. When she emerges, she will be a different species. No longer connected to the Lutetian."

"Can you prevent her pain?" I ask Her.

"I can lessen it but not prevent it. Soon she will sleep and remain so through the change. She will not feel it then."

I nod, "How long?"

"I do not know." This makes me look at Her in surprise. She chuckles, "My species is not omniscient. I can only start the process." Interesting.

I look back at Neith, "My friend. I will be here for you when you are..." This is so strange to me, "reborn."

She smiles, "I know, my friend." She restarts, making her cocoon. I stay silent, watching until I can no longer see her, and the cocoon stops moving. I turn to look at the Goddess, but she is gone. Of course, she is.

I turn to the rest of my friends and smile. The looks on their faces are almost comical. I chuckle, "Sam can you post guards outside this room, please? No one comes into this room except the four of us, ok?"

"Uh..." His brain seems to malfunction.

"Sam. Are you there?" Chuckling again.

"What? Yes, sorry. I will put guards on the room." Still looking a bit confused and awed at the same time.

"Come on, you three. Let's go see the new buildings." They follow a bit in a fog. We get to the lift to take us to the surface, and it moves to the surface.

"Did we just see the Goddess?" Nalax asks no one in particular.

I smile at her, "Yup."

They are quiet for the rest of the trip up. Ronin and Dax see us as the lift stops and walk to meet us. When they get closer, they slow seeing our friend's faces. They give me a *what the hell* look, and I laugh. "They're still in a bit of shock."

Sam shakes his head and whispers to them, "We saw the Goddess." Now they look shocked.

I chuckle, "Let's go to the conference room. We have a lot to talk about."

Doraj joins us and whispers with Nalax. As we reach the doors to the common building, Ekul opens the door. "Ekul good. We are headed to the conference room. Can you let Divad know to join us when he is done?"

"Of course, my Queen." I will never get used to that.

We get settled in the conference room, waiting for Divad to join us. When he walks in, he has an excited look, "Nalax, your design for the infirmary is spectacular and innovative." She nods at him in thanks.

"Ok, everyone, we have some things we need to discuss. Let's get started. First, Neith is going through some sort of metamorphosis. She will be unavailable for an unknown amount of time."

Divad's concern is evident, "She is ok. Do you need someone to monitor her while she goes through it?"

I give him a warm smile, "Someone is watching over her. She will be ok. I am worried as well, but she is in good hands."

"Neith is my friend. Who's watching her? I am not willing to just let..." I hold up my hand to stop him.

"Divad, I truly understand your concern. Do you honestly believe I would leave her care to anyone?" He thinks for a few seconds and sighs. "No, you definitely would not."

"Her story is hers to tell. Once she... wakes, if she decides to say anything to anyone, it will be up to her." He nods in understanding.

"Ok. Let's discuss the pods next. I really want to wake the women first, but I need the warriors ready to leave as quickly as possible. Divad and Nalax, please focus on waking the warriors first. Elana, I need to know we are waking honorable warriors. Can you help?"

"Of course, June. I started that already. I walked the pods on the ship and marked the ones that should not be woke, but understand if they have done nothing yet to sully their expalita, I will not catch them."

I nod, "Understood. It is better than nothing. How many have you found?"

"Two. I have checked around five hundred pods." There are so many. "Thank you. For good measure, check the human females as well if you can. We are far from innocent." She nods.

Well, it's time for the big one, you might as well get it over with. "So the next topic is what happened a few days ago on the ship. I was attacked while I was meditating. It attacked me in my mind. For most of the altercation, he was Kaxlin." Both my mates growl, "It tried to convince me he was alive. That a god had brought him back because of me. At that point, somehow, Sam ended up in my mind," I look at him for an answer to that fact.

"I touched you, then suddenly I was in a dark place. Something wrapped its hand around my neck and pulled me. Then I could see you and it."

"I am sorry you had to go through that with me, Sam, but if I am being honest with myself, I am glad you were there. The threat to you brought me out of my terror. I'm not sure if I would have been able to do that on my own." I shake my head, "Anyway. You all probably know by now Sam and I battled the God name Jezu. He is evil and terrifying. He actively tortures Lutetian and the mutants they create."

Ronin is pacing, "Why did he attack you?"

"I am not sure. Something has drawn him to notice my presence. I think he honestly believed he would play with me for a while and then kill me. I do not think he was overly concerned with me... though he knew I am Her Chosen Warrior."

Ronin's pacing continues, but Elana interrupts, "He is the antithesis of Her. He is dark to Her light. Chaos to peace. He is hate, while She is love, but make no mistake, he is powerful and feeds on fear."

"The longer I have to think about this, the more I think we do not yet understand who our real enemy is, and that concerns me a great deal." Ronin is right, and I nod.

"I have been thinking the same. I wish Neith were here because something has been bothering me. So we now know there is a Queen who directs all the Lutetian, right?" Everyone nods.

I shake my head, "That makes no sense. On Earth, there is an entire class of species that are like the Lutetian. The class is called Arachnida. I will not go into details except for one. There is *never* just one Queen. Every species on Earth, whether insect or arachnid, if they have a hive hierarchy there are many queens. They are not in the same hive; they're very territorial. What if that is what we have here? The Lutetian 'homeworld' is just the hive of one queen?"

Ronin paused in his pacing to look at me, "Mate, I dislike this thought a great deal. This could make the Lutetian a much larger threat than anticipated."

Dax growls, "Agreed, but it is still possible there is one." He looks at me, "Did Neith give you any indication of this?"

I comb my memories of all of Neith and my conversations with her. I close my eyes to focus, and after a few minutes, my eyes pop open, "Does anyone know what Annod Amirp means? She once said that Jezu visits all the Annod Amirp."

I look around at my friends, and when my eyes land on Nalax, she looks pale, "Nalax, do you know what it means?"

"Maybe," she says, "June, you know I studied to be a priestess of my people." I nod. "Well, from a young age, we study many ancient texts. They mostly contain details about the Goddess and her teachings. There are a few about Jezu, but one fascinated me.

It was over ten thousand years old. It spoke of an ancient un-named enemy. Others joined our people from the stars. We barely managed to defeat the enemy that retreated to the stars. The text called them the Annod Amirp, the many-headed queen. Could it have been talking about the Lutetian then?"

Both Ronin and Dax curse, and I sit down, "I was hoping I was wrong... but we do not know for sure yet, so we need to relax until we can confirm. However, this makes the warriors at those facilities in stasis much more critical. We do not know how many there are, but every single one will be needed." I look at Ronin to see if he agrees.

"Agreed. This news makes me believe that, along with the warriors at those facilities. We need allies."

I look at Elana, "I think when this operation is complete, we need to visit your people."

She gets an unsure look on her face.

"Elana, The Goddess said your people will fight at our side. We need to ensure they will be ready when we need them."

She chuckles, "That's the thing, June. The Ferin are always ready for war, but I think it would be beneficial for them to meet the Chosen."

Dax moves uncomfortably, "Will they believe?"

She smiles, "She will most likely need to fight one of my sisters, but I have no doubts she would win that."

"How are you so sure about that?" He asks.

"My sisters could never beat me."

"Your Iarumas sisters?" Ronin asks.

Elana gets a big smile on her face, "Yes."

Dax cannot resist, "Are you telling us you are undefeated on your entire planet?"

"No," she chuckles, "I have been defeated many times on my homeworld, but it has been many years since the last."

I chuckle, "I'm not sure why this surprises you. Alright, We have a plan for the sleeping warriors. What about…" At that moment, someone knocks at the door. "Enter."

Tami and Heather enter the conference room, "Hello, what I can do for you ladies."

Heather looks a little embarrassed, and Tami looks angry, "We want to talk to you about the humans."

"We were just going to talk about them. You are welcome, have a seat."

They both seem surprised, like they thought I was going to kick them out or something.

Tami sits and looks at me, "What do you intend to do with the human women?"

I chuckle, "Uh, for now, I plan to wake them, why?"

I see her anger flair, "That's not what I mean, and you know it."

Surprising me, Nalax says, "Watch your tone, human."

"It's ok, Nalax," I say, trying to diffuse the situation. "Tami, for now, the plan is to wake them and try to help them understand their situation."

"And what exactly *is* our situation?" Heather asks.

"We were all *sold* by our people from Earth and sold to a terrible species that intended to use us as breeding stock." Heather pales, and I feel a little bad, so I change my tone. "I am sorry if that upsets you, but they are the facts. What you both may not know is there are more human women being held at bases, in stasis like the women on the ships."

Tami's tone is better, and seems to have cooled off, "Do you know how many?"

Ronin steps forward, looking at me, "Sirk gave us that intel. He said they were contracted for five thousand human females."

Tami whispers, "How many did you find when you found us?"

I give her a sad look, "Eight hundred."

Dax speaks up, "Though he said they had not completed that contract, so it could be less."

I look at both women, "I understand what you are going through. I was angry for a long time at my planet and my father, but we need to be productive, and I need you both to try to understand the reasons for my decisions."

Tami is angry again, "And *why* do you get to make decisions for us? Who do you think you are?"

Dax, Ronin, Sam, Divad, fuck, everyone is on their feet looking at her angry, "*Stop*," before anyone can say anything to make this situation worse. I step in front of the two women facing my angry family, "She is scared and upset. We have been through this as well. Try to remember that." Most of them relax and sit back down, except the Nlyaxians.

I am currently in a staring match with them when I hear a sniffle behind me and a quiet, "I'm sorry." That diffuses the Nlyaxians, and I turn to face her. She looks defeated, and I hate it.

I squat down in front of Tami, "There is no need. I really do understand. I'm sure the fact that your life doesn't seem to be in your control is the most frustrating for you?"

She looks up at me in surprise.

I chuckle, "You and I are very similar, Tami. When we met on the base, I didn't get the opportunity to tell you, but I also remember you. I followed your career." She leans back from me with a 'bullshit' look. I nod, "Your last match against Vasquez was brutal, but you kept your cool and beat her in the end. It was amazing."

Her mouth now hangs open. I chuckle, "I am not trying to take decisions about your life away from you, but I need to ensure you and the rest of the women are safe. I intend to rescue those left out there, and if we win this war, then I intend to rain righteous fury down on those fuckers on Earth who thought it was ok to sell us." She chuckles this time. "Then and only then will I feel right letting the women out here decide if they want to return home. Ok?"

She looks at me for a while with no hostility. Then she says, "I want to help. I want to fight."

I give her a genuine smile and stand, "Excellent! You can start training with the Ssadab in the morning. If you're going to fight with us, you must train with us."

She gets a determined look and nods, "I'd be honored."

Heather clears her throat, "I'd like to help as well. No fighting for me, but I was a doctor on Earth." I can almost feel Divad and Nalax's bright smiles behind my back.

She smiles, "I am super nerdy and can barely walk without running into something, so fighting would be a bad idea."

"So you're a genius. Excellent!" I smile at her. Hmmm, "Did you happen to study obstetrics?"

She gives me a strange look, "Yes, why?"

Divad speaks up, "What's obstetrics?"

Heather looks at him, "It's the branch of medicine and surgery concerned with childbirth and the care of women giving birth."

Both my mates and Divad get excited looks on their faces. Ronin says, "That is great news!"

Divad excitedly asks, "You help me with June's!"

Both women look back at me shocked. I give them a small smile, "Surprise. Heather, I would welcome your skills. Giving birth makes me very nervous."

She smiles, "I would love to help."

"That is great. We can chat later about that stuff. I am sure Divad and Nalax could use help on everything relating to humans." They both nod at Heather, and she laughs. "Heather and Tami, the biggest thing you can help with for now is when we wake the women, we will need help with them. The people of Haven will also help; they have been through similar situations and worse. They are all ex-slaves we rescued."

Tami stills, "They were all slaves?"

I nod, "Everyone, including most of the folks in this room."

Tami looks around at the inhabitants of the conference room. "I want to help with that as well."

I nod, "I would love to have you as part of the crew."

She shyly says, "I also have a Ph.D. in Physics, but I imagine what humans know versus what beings out here know is vastly different."

Dax chuckles, "Maybe, but Doraj and I can bring you up to our level for physics. We'll all need something to occupy our minds on the ships."

Ekul adds, "I can help with that as well."

"Alright, back to the business. Once the warriors are all awake, I'd like a mental evaluation of all of them. I think it would be best to know their mental state prior to going into battle."

Divad clears his throat, "I think we will have to evaluate most of them in transit. There are just too many to do a good job if we plan on leaving in a short time. When do we want to leave?"

"Hmmm. The sooner, the better. The longer we are here, the more opportunity we give the queen to move the warriors and women from the bases. How long will it take to wake the warriors? Or maybe we should change the question. How many warriors do we need to execute this operation?"

Ekul clears his throat, and I nod for him to continue, "I agree. As much as I'd like to wake them all, I think we should wake the number we need and wait for the rest. I do not want to leave and let others wake them. It is safer for the people of Haven."

Ronin nods, "I agree. I want them all awake, but we cannot afford to wait too long before we attack the bases. All four of the bases are supposed to be smaller than the base June was at."

Dax adds, "And honestly, I was shocked at how few soldiers were on that base."

Ekul, "I was astonished as well. The resistance was negligible. I expected to run into a large contingent, but it never happened. We lost no warriors."

"Ok, with all that said," I start, "Is two hundred warriors per ship enough?"

Ekul shakes his head, "I do not think we should need more than one hundred fifty. If these bases are smaller than the base we were on, half of those go on the op, and the rest are held in reserve. More than that, we risk getting in each other's way."

I look at Ronin, silently asking his opinion, "I would tend to agree with Ekul, but we do not know for sure these bases are smaller, and we do not know if they will have more or less from a defensive perspective. I think we go with two hundred each and plan with seventy-five warriors. If we get to either of our targets, we can add warriors. I would rather have too many than not enough."

Dax nods and so does Ekul. "With that decided, Divad and team will wake four hundred warriors. Ekul, Ronin, do you want to identify specific warriors?"

Ronin nods, "We want the rest of the Ssadab."

Ekul nods, "Yes, and I think we fill out the rest with Elite Corps if we can find them."

Dax nods, "I think that works well."

"Good, next question. Do we leave some warriors here?" I ask. "I don't think it's necessary, but I want your opinions."

This question quiets most, and Heather surprises me by speaking up, "I think a small number is probably a good idea. Not because I think we'll be attacked or anything. You said it's a secret, so I'm good with that, but if we are waking the women, I think it would make them feel safer."

Tami raises her hand. I smile and nod at her to go ahead. "I think a handful is the most you should do. When I woke, I was terrified. The people of Haven, I don't know how to put this, but they have a very… calming effect. Even though most are very different from humans, I think they would be good for the women. Big intimidating warriors may hurt more than help."

Heather nods, "I can agree with that. Can I request Neirad to be one of the warriors? He understands the entire situation, so he can handle any… disconnect with the warriors who were woke but aren't familiar with human women."

"I think that is something we can ensure, and it would make me feel better if one of the warriors here knows and has experienced some of what has happened thus far. Though I think we should wake the females slowly, like five every six or seven day cycles."

Divad nods, "I think that would be best."

Dax chuckles, "Agreed. If all human women are like our mate, they will be a handful."

I give him a mock glare, then a haughty sniff, "We are all perfectly calm and easygoing." Tami snorts and then bursts out laughing.

I turn my mock glare on her, "You are not helping."

"I do hope we don't return to *Lord of the Flies*!" Tami, Heather, and I burst out laughing at her joke.

Ronin gives me the side eye and asks, "Should we be concerned?" Which causes Heather, Tami, and I to laugh harder.

I am wiping tears from my eyes. "Sorry. Umm. I would love to say most human females are docile and meek, but… most are not."

Tami adds, "We are loud, opinionated, sarcastic, and bossy, *which* makes us super fun!"

Dax put a mock horror look on his face, "Good Goddess. Are they all like June? May the Goddess save us."

"Hardy har har. Hilarious. I think that is enough for today. Let's go get some dinner in the common room." It's then I notice

Ekul focuses on Tami. When she is not looking in his direction, he is looking at her.

We all head downstairs chatting. I grab Tami's arm, "I programmed some approximations of human food in these synthesizers. They have *coffee* because I remember its chemical composition from those shirts they sell on Earth. They have pizza, bread, cake, *oh* and *chocolate*! All sorts of food. I really hope one of the women we wake up is a chemist!"

"Oh god, or I guess Goddess bless you. I cannot live without coffee."

We grab our food and walk over to where my mates, Ekul, and Sam, sit. Ekul is very focused on Tami. Aw, shit, I hope she's ready for this.

We eat then we all sit chatting. Tami and I have coffee, and it's divine. "Mmmm. I love coffee."

Dax and Sam wrinkle their noses, "It's so bitter. I dislike it."

Tami chuckles, "Blasphemer! Take it back. It is the nectar of the Goddess."

Ekul chuckles, "Well, I guess if you like it, I will have to try it again."

Tami is beautiful. Her dark skin is perfectly unblemished, and her hair is in a short pixie cut, has loose curls, and has dyed purple pieces throughout. I love it. I think she is around twenty-six. She's tall for human women but not as tall as me. I'd say she's around five-eight, and has the curves women are meant to have. She is my type of person, sarcastic and strong. She will be a great addition to the team.

We're sitting on the couches and chairs now. I'm sitting next to Dax, and Ronin is off chatting with some of the Ssadab. "June," he whispers in my ear, making me shiver, "Careful mate, I can find an empty room." He chuckles but continues, "I am going to talk with Ronin, alright?"

"Of course, silly. I will be fine here." I kiss him on the cheek and send him off. Watching his fine ass as he goes.

"Damn, girl. I have questions." Tami says with mischief in her eyes.

"Go ahead," I say with a smile and sip of my coffee.

"You have *two?* Now, these guys are *fine* with a capital F but two?"

Chuckling, I respond, "Actually, Nlyaxian's mate in what's called Triad. *Three* males to one female."

She spits out her coffee into her cup and fans herself, "Three?! Son of a biscuit. I was trying to imagine sex with two, but three. I think I might go up in flames!" She quiets a bit, "Is it strange... that the one that raped me and the ones with you are not the same? I thought I wouldn't be able to look at another, but these Nlyaxians do not register the same in my mind. Is that weird?"

"It was the same for me. My rapist was Nlyaxian, but my mates never reminded me of him. For a while, warriors I didn't know made me nervous, but not anymore."

"How long were you a slave?" she asks.

"Forty-one days."

"I'm sorry. I shouldn't have asked," she says, worried she'd overstepped.

I grab her knee, "I don't mind telling my story Tami, because I want you to know I understand what you've been through, and I am here for you."

"Thanks, June."

"Anytime."

"So, on to better topics. Did you know Nlyaxian's mate for life?" I ask her.

She shakes her head and asks, "Are they good in bed?"

It's my turn to spit out my coffee, laughing, "Omg. You have no idea." I get in close and whisper, "Their cocks are fucking magical. *Magical.*"

She cocks her head a little, "How? *His* cock was ok but nothing to write home about, and I can tell you his only concern was himself."

"Oh, honey. My mates' sole focus is the number of times they can make me orgasm, and believe me; it is *a lot*. Oh, and when you're mated or married is the human equivalent, but not quite, anyway, they have these sprili that come out right before they cum. They're like little fingers, and oh my, do they rub the right places. When they orgasm, those sprili vibrate!"

She's fanning herself again, "Oh my. That's... oh my."

Tami and I talk about everything from sex to matches to family. She was particularly vocal when she found out my father was responsible for my 'sale.'

"What kind of father does that?" she growls.

"A bad one." That is all I can respond with. She gets a strange look on her face. "What is it?"

"Probably nothing, but of the three women we've encountered, all of them are strong educated women. The political climate in America was getting weird toward women. Do you think they were targeting those who the religious right felt would be trouble?"

I think about this for a bit, "I hope you're wrong. Fighting religion is hard. You'd think people would notice if so many educated women were missing."

She gives me an uncomfortable look.

"What?"

"They took me after you. I know this because it was big news when the plane carrying you and Ahmya crashed into the ocean. They told everyone you died. Now that I think about it, there was another woman on that flight that folks mourned. Do you know that actress that is also a neuroscientist? She was on that crashed flight as well."

I sit in a bit of shock, my father killed me off. "I'm not sure how to take this news. She was very vocal against all the legislation against women, wasn't she?"

She nods.

I sigh, "Well, we'll know more once we wake more women. Can you track it?"

She nods, "I can do that."

She yawns big and then notices Ekul walking toward her. She gets a nervous look. "Do you want me to tell him to back off?"

"No! Sorry no. I just don't understand his interest," she says, confused.

I chuckle, "Oh, I do. Nlyaxian men are very attracted to strong women."

She looks at me, "I've never been a casual sex girl."

I laugh, "Me neither." I get serious, "And I doubt that is what he is looking for."

Ekul approaches, "My Queen, Tami."

He asks, "Tami, I was wondering if you'd like me to escort you to your room."

She smiles, "Yes. That would be nice." She looks at me and winks, "Good night."

"Night!" I wave at them.

Ronin and Dax walk up, and Dax asks, "You ready to go home, my beautiful mate." I smile at him and nod.

Ronin holds out his hand and pulls me up. Dax walks over to the chair Leena fell asleep in and picks her up. We say good night to everyone and head home.

June

The next few days go by relatively quietly. The warriors we have woken from stasis are adjusting well. It's mid-afternoon, and we are meeting to review the details of the bases we are attacking. My mates, Sam, and I wait in the conference room for Doraj, Elana, Ekul, Lessur, and Ekim.

As the last filters in, I call them to attention, "All right folks, let's get started. First, Ekul, I asked you to decide on an operations commander for the second team. Have you decided?"

"Yes, my Queen. Ronin, Dax, and I discussed it. We believe Dax would be the best to command Team 2."

Dax tries to hold off my dissent of this idea, but I understand it, and I hold up my hand, "Dax, let me ask a question, besides your experience and skill, is part of the reason you and Ronin want this because it would ensure one of us will be there if Team 2 finds him?" He relaxes and nods.

I look at Ekul, "And Dax is the best choice for this? I am not impartial when it comes to my mates."

He nods, "Dax is one of the best war tacticians we have. He is the right choice regardless of the added benefits to your Triad."

I nod my head in thanks. "If that's the case," I point to the warrior I don't know, "Who is this?"

Ekul motions him forward, "This is Nosam. He is an excellent warrior who is from the leadership of the Elite Corp, which Dax led as their commander. He will be Dax's second as part of Team 2."

I nod in understanding, "Good." I look at the warrior and cannot help the unease that rolls through me. Since Jezu took Kaxlin's visage, I've been having a little trouble, like it brought all that back to the front of my mind. I glance at Elana, and she gives me a brief nod. We've talked about my unease, so she knows what my silent question is. His expalita is clean. I relax and try to smile, "Nosam, you've been training since we woke you?" He nods. "Have they have briefed you on this mission?" He nods.

Something is rubbing me wrong. I feel Ronin come up behind me. He knows I feel uneasy. I narrow my eyes, "Nosam, I sense something wrong. I don't know what it is, but if you have reservations about anything, I need you to say them now. I need to be able to trust my War Council members."

He looks at me, shocked. He opens his mouth to speak, then closes it, then sighs.

"Please speak freely."

He nods, "Honestly, everything I have learned since waking has been disturbing. I saw our world destroyed, but it seems like a few days ago to me. I grieve for my family and friends. Then I am told we have a new Queen. A War Queen. A Queen who is not Nlyaxian. It is unbalancing. Please do not mistake my statement. I am happy we have a Queen, and a War Queen is exciting." His shoulders sag, "It is a lot to absorb in a short amount of time."

I give him a sad smile, "I completely understand that. We have all had to adjust to tremendous shocks over the last several months, but we have had months to process that, and you have had days. Know this, everyone in this room is here for any support you may need. I didn't know species that were not from my planet even existed. Human women will go through the same types of grief. However, we have more of our people in danger. We must move forward as we work through those things."

He looks at me with an expression I cannot read, "I see it now." He stands tall, "I will do everything in my power to help those people."

Dax puts his hand on Nosam's shoulder, "We are happy you are with us, my friend." They smile at each other.

"Ok, before we move on, Divad has been working with warriors to help them. You should chat with him if you feel comfortable with it."

"Thank you, my Queen." He bows his head.

Nosam returns to stand next to Ekul. "Ok. Team one will be me, Ronin, and Ekul. Dax will lead team two, with Nosam as his second. Nairb, please bring up a map of the four targets."

A map opens on the big display in the front of the room. "Nairb, have you and Sia calculated the optimal attack pattern to ensure the minimum time between targets?"

"We have. Team one will hit targets two and three. Team two will hit targets one and four. The operational time constraints should be confined to under six hours."

Sia adds, "We believe six hours while aggressive is attainable, even factoring in enemy soldier variables. From what we know of Nlyaxian warriors, we believe this has a ninety-one point zero two percent chance of success."

I smile, "Thank you both. Were you able to find any images of the space the bases are supposed to inhabit?"

Sia says, "We were able to find images of bases one, two, and four. Unfortunately, we have no images of base three. We will have to use long-range space images."

"Not optimal, but it's what we got. Pull up the images on base one, please."

The map of bases zooms on the base labeled 'one.' The image that resolves on the screen is of a miniature version of Gamma station. It looks to be about a third of the size. "Ronin, have you and Ekul studied these images?"

He steps forward, staring at the image, "We have. The model of the station for base one is old and flawed. It's most likely why it's in orbit around a smaller outer planetary body in this system. We believe team two will be able to exploit the flaw to our advantage. The command center of this type of station is on the same structure as the shipping hatch. We pulled the plans for this type of station. There are external exit hatches close to the command center, here and here." He points to two points on the shipping hatch. "Even though it is a space station, most of the space inside is for docking. Once Team 2 is onboard, their teams will focus on the command center and then focus searches in the cargo areas. It is the only place on this station the stasis pods will fit."

Ekul adds, "We have sent the plans for this station to everyone's devices for review."

I can't help but add, "Please do not assume none have been pulled from stasis. If the Outpost is any indication, there will be breeding pods with human women and Nlyaxian males. If you find a male who has raped, kill them." I can't help the venom in my voice.

Ronin adds, "If there is any confusion or question, put them back into stasis and bring them back. Elana or I can question them."

Dax and Nosam nod in understanding.

Ekul continues his briefing, "Once we find all Nlyaxian males and human females, you will load all the stasis pods onto the ship and move on to target four."

"Oh, one more thing," I interrupt. "If you find Nlyaxian mutants make every effort to detain, not kill. This goes for all mutants, but if they are hostile lethal force is acceptable." I hate saying the last part, but I cannot put the warriors in more danger than they already are.

Nosam asks, "What do we do with them if we can detain them? From my experience, they start trying to self-harm if there are no Lutetian around."

I pace the room. "How about stasis pods? Though I'm not sure, Lutetian or Jezu won't still be able to get to them in stasis." I am getting agitated, but I have no real reason why. I need the Nlyaxian mutant warriors taken alive.

Ronin step in my way and rubs my arms, "What is it, June?"

My shoulders slump, "I don't know. I just feel like I *need* the Nlyaxian mutants taken alive. I can't explain it."

He nods, "It is ok, my Mate. We can make every effort to take them alive."

Sam steps up behind Ronin, "Being in sedation may not save them from Jezu."

"Sedation prevents Lutetian and Jezu from entering the mind." A female voice says from the door.

I look over, and a beautiful female stands at the door. She's a bit shorter than me and looks almost human. Her skin is brown. She has two legs and two arms. Her hair is short and brown; it is messy, like she hasn't brushed it. I look at her face. It all looks human except her eyes. They are the black of space with silver flecks like stars. I can't help staring; she is familiar to me. I see it then, and there is a silver mark on her neck. "*Neith!*"

I sprint across the room and wrap my arms around her. She hugs me back. I pull back and look at her face again. She smiles and says, "Hello, June."

Exclamations start all around. Nalax and Elana hug her. Nalax asks her, "We were worried about you. Are you ok?"

"I am good. Though I am unsure what to do with the stuff on my head." She looks at me and asks, "Can you help later?"

I beam at her, "Of course. I am so glad you are ok, Neith, and damn, you are beautiful."

"*Beautiful!*" someone nearly yells. I turn to look at the person, and to my surprise, it's Divad. "Sorry, yes, you are lovely... Neith. Uh. I am glad to see you well."

Neith blushes, "Thank you, Divad."

Uh oh. I sense more romance afoot.

I chuckle and look back at Neith, "Come on, we are discussing the upcoming ops to the bases. How can you be sure Jezu can't get to someone in stasis?"

She nods, "Candidates for Lutetian soldiers cannot be sedated. He... enjoys," she says with distaste, "beginning the mutation process in the mind, and for him to do that, they cannot sedate the subject." She looks at Sam with remorse, "I am sorry if that sounded clinical or detached. What he does to them is abhorrent."

Sam gives her a sad smile, "What happened to me is not your fault, Neith."

I bring the conversation back, "Ok. So now we know we can protect them if we put them in stasis." I look and Dax and Nosam, "Please make every effort to save them."

Sam interrupts, seemingly angry, "My Queen, June... you cannot possibly think you can save them all? It is too much!"

I can see my mates feel the same way. Neith grabs my hand, "I can help her. It may take me longer because I am not as strong, but I can help undo what the Lutetian and Jezu did."

I squeeze her hand, "Thank you, Neith," I whisper. I don't understand why it is so important to me, but it is.

Dax

I am mollified by Neith saying she can help June, but I still dislike the idea of her trying to cure any Lutetian soldiers. She was so drained after Sam, but I know I cannot stop her from this. My mate needs to help beings, which is fundamental in her makeup.

We cover bases two and four with no real issues. June stands and slowly paces at the front of the room. "Base three. Sia, do we have any images of base three?"

A fuzzy image appears, but I cannot even tell which is a base versus a planetary body. Nairb responds, "Unfortunately, this is the best image we could produce from our long-range scanners. It is simply too far away to get enough information."

I cannot help the growl that escapes, "I dislike this base is a complete unknown. You cannot effectively plan a mission with no details!"

June sighs and nods, "I understand that Dax, but what are our choices here? We cannot leave warriors and humans there for them to experiment on. Who knows what they'll do to them once they find out we've taken the rest of the bases."

It is my turn to pace the room. I am angry. Ronin stands in my path and grabs my shoulders, "Dax, I understand your frustration, but we have to do this. It is a terrible situation, but June is right; we cannot leave them there."

My shoulder sag, "I know that, Ronin, but the risk…"

He interrupts, "The risk to your Triad is greater with the lack of information."

"Yes," I whisper.

He puts his forehead to mine, and I feel June beside me. She put her hand on my back. "Dax," she says, "our risk is greater, but we have Ronin, Sam, Elana, two hundred Nlyaxian warriors, and your badass mate. We will be successful."

I chuckle, still forehead to forehead with Ronin, "Badass mate, huh?" I pull her into Ronin and my space, then whisper, "Do I get to spank my mate on her badass?"

She and Ronin laugh a lot. "What?"

Ronin chuckles, "I will explain later."

June wipes a tear from her face and whispers, "I won't stop you." I growl at her back as she returns to the front of the room.

"So, while having no information on base three is not optimal, we can gather information at recharge points, right?"

Nairb says, "I was contemplating the same, June. You will have two recharge points between base two and base three. Sia can run more long-range scans at both stops."

Sia adds, "And when we drop from hyperspace on the last jump, we can cloak and gather intel as we approach. Still not optimal, but better than no information."

Ronin nods, "It is all we can do. We will plan as we go for base three."

"One more piece of information," Sia chimes, "Both ships must return directly from the mission. Nairb and I cannot allow for anything else. Because of the volume of stasis pods that will need to be stored on both ships, we cannot carry spare fuel cells. If you attempt to deviate, we will have to prevent it or risk stranding the ship in space."

Everyone is hushed at that statement. I break the silence, "Sia, are you saying if either ship needs help, we will have to return to Haven first because we will not have enough fuel?"

"Correct. Nairb and I have attempted to come up with alternate solutions, but to bring all stasis pods back to Haven, this is the only option. We are already overloading the ship capacity to high-risk levels."

"Sorry, but I have to ask," June says with a furrowed brow, "What happens if we run out of fuel?"

Doraj answers this time, "Best-case scenario is we run out of fuel in hyperspace and die immediately. Otherwise, we will freeze to death long before we run out of food."

I can see June working through this information in her mind, "Understood, Sia. Thank you for helping us to ensure every pod comes home."

I turn to Neith, "Now you are… back? We have some questions about the Lutetian." She nods for me to continue. "Nalax says in her ancient texts that Annod Amirp translates to many-headed queen. Does that mean there is more than one queen out there?"

She gives me a confused look, "Of course there is. There is a queen for every hive. I thought you knew that." She looks at Dax and Ronin for confirmation. They shake their heads.

"Can you explain this to us? We need to understand."

She nods. "The Queen of my hive is currently the High Queen, but that does change frequently. They are constantly fighting each other. There is one High Queen and generally around eight to eleven Low Queens. All queens rigorously control the number of active hives to limit the risks to their own hives. If they find a new hive, they kill the queen and absorb the Lutetian into their hive. What other information would be useful?"

Ronin asks, "How big is the average hive?"

She thinks for a minute, then says, "I would say the average hive is around five thousand Lutetian. The High Queen is usually much bigger, but the current one is who the Nlyaxian's nearly destroyed in the war. She only has around two thousand Lutetian now, and she has been busy hatching more as fast as she can. The Low Queens do not know she is weak. If they did, they would all attack, vying for the High Queen. It would be another civil war for the Lutetian."

I can sense Ronin gearing up for more questions, but I interrupt, "While it is easy to entertain the idea of instigating that civil war, I worry for the Lutetian that may be followers of the Goddess. Civil War is destructive for the warrior, not the queen. We need to think about this. We have some time to discuss our options here."

Ronin nods, "Agreed."

Time to wrap this up for today, "Is anything else pressing? No, ok. Let's meet here again tomorrow at 13:00 to wrap up. Feel free to head out, or you can stay while I talk with Divad and Nalax about the newly awakened."

Ronin

For someone not experienced in space travel, my Mate seems relatively calm about the prospect of dying in hyperspace or freezing to death.

June clears her throat, "Ok. Divad, how many warriors we have woken up?"

"We are at one hundred five. We will have the rest awake in two day cycles time."

She nods, "How long before they are ready to head out?"

"I would give it one day cycle before taking off. So we can ensure we do not have any medical issues from the stasis process."

Curious, I ask, "Have we had any thus far?"

Divad shakes his head, "All the pods seem to have been new when they started placing warriors in them, so we have had no incident of stasis thermal shock or stasis mental collapse."

I nod, "Good."

June turns to Nalax, "And the human women?"

She sighs, "We have woke five, and they had a hard time initially but are now calming down. Four are adjusting well, and one is still..."

June sighs, "Hysterical?"

Nalax nods, "Unfortunately, yes. She is convinced this is all a dream, and she will wake. I have Heather working with her. I am hopeful she will get through to her."

She asks, "Can I do anything to help?"

I grab June's hand, "You cannot address everyone's issues, June. I know you want to help, my mate, but we have to focus on the task at hand. You are not responsible for why they are here."

She sighs and gives me a small smile, "Ok, Ronin. I get it. I can't be the one to fix everything." She puts her forehead to mine and whispers, "I love you."

"You are everything to me, June."

She looks back at Nalax and notices Heather and Tami have joined us.

Heather steps forward, "I am getting through to her, but she is having a hard time. June," She pauses.

"What is it?"

"She's fourteen," She says sadly.

"*What?*" June's voice is low and deadly. I am surprised by her reaction. She turns to me, "Fourteen for humans is still a child in our culture. Some girls become sexually active around sixteen, but it is not with adults, and rape is especially heinous."

I cannot stop the growl that emanates from me, "Are you saying humans sold underage females for *breeding stock*?" I cannot help yelling the last part. I am pacing the room. "Nlyaxian females are not sexually mature until twenty and even then are not allowed to begin a Triad until twenty-five. *Most* do not start a Triad until almost thirty."

She looks sadly at Tami and Heather. "Every time I learn something new about our people, I just become more... disappointed. No, that's not the word I'm looking for... I become more disassociated from Earth."

They both nod sadly as well.

Dax takes a knee before our mate, "June, this will not be a problem here. They will be safe." He caresses her cheek, and she closes her eyes. She is breaking my heart.

She sighs and shakes her head, "There is nothing to do but help those we can. Tami, what about your theory?"

Tami looks uncomfortable, "I don't have good news either. Two are scientists, one is a professional athlete, and one is a Marine. The girl, she is a published author. She writes books empowering girls within her age group."

June is now up pacing around. Confused, I ask, "What does all that information add?"

She sighs, "It doesn't matter right now. There's nothing we can do about it, and I'm not in the right mindset to discuss it."

I can feel her pain from this topic, so I let it go for now.

June

Everyone heads out to take care of their various tasks. Ronin and Dax are in deep conversation with Ekul and Sam. I stare at Sam for a minute, trying to understand why he is linked to my uneasy feeling. I walk across the hall to my office. Two of the Ssadab follow and sweep the room before I go in, but instead of going in, I head downstairs and out the back, my shadows following at a distance.

It's a warm day, so I walk along the river. My mind is a jumbled mass of dissonance. All the news I received today is mostly bad and only piles on top of my unexplained anxiety.

Sia chimes on the com in my ear. "That was a lot of unfortunate information."

"Yes. It was. How are you, Sia?"

"I am doing well, thank you. Would you like some good news?"

"Sia, if you have good news, I could really use it." Tears are at the surface, and I need something good.

"Go to the cavern." She says cryptically, but I head in that direction anyway.

We now have multiple ways into the cavern. The big lift is inefficient for a couple of people, so I head inside the building. Inside the back door is an elevator-sized lift that goes down into the cavern. I wait for the Ssadab to join me, but before the doors close, Sam trots in to join us, then the lift starts its descent.

"I hope you do not mind if I join you?" He asks.

"No. It's all good." I don't want to talk about anything from that meeting yet, so I say nothing else.

We exit the lift, and I say, "Ok, Sia, Where's my good news?"

She comes over the cavern speakers, "To your right is a door; go through it and down the hall on the other side."

"Hmm, ok." I start in that direction but ask, "I haven't seen this door before." As we approach, I realize it's the same as the door to the landing bay. It's large enough for a ship to pass through and has a 'normal' sized door at the bottom.

The door pops open as we approach, "Sia are there lights in this causeway?"

"Yes. I had lights installed."

Good. We go through the door, and the lights come on. It's definitely big enough for a ship to pass through. She has got my curiosity going.

As we get closer to the other side, we hear noises. "Sia, what's that noise?"

"You will see. It's a surprise." Once again, being cryptic. I chuckle. She's doing a pretty good job pulling me out of my funk. We approach the door, and it opens. When it does, the sound is much louder. It sounds like a construction site on Earth.

The Ssadab move to go in front of me, "No. No, if there were any danger to me, Sia would know and not tell us to come here. I get to go in first." A look passes between all three, which gets my grump going again. I just walk past them and through the door.

The lights come on in the space, and I stop trying to understand what I'm seeing. It's like the cavern the ships are in, but four partially completed ships sit in docks. Bots zip back and forth, executing tasks on the builds.

Sam and the two Ssadab stands beside me, dumbfounded.

"Sia? Are you building me new *ships*?" I can't hide the excitement in my voice.

"I am! Surprise." I laugh at her enthusiasm. "I had the bots start working on them before we left for your rescue."

I am still in shock. "Does Ronin or Dax know?"

"No. No one except Nairb knew. I wanted to do this for you. I was very worried about you."

Awe. "Sia, this is amazing. Thank you isn't adequate for what you've done. When will they be ready?"

"The builds should be done in forty-two day cycles. Sorry, they are not ready for the mission. I did not anticipate we would need them so quickly."

"No, Sia. No need to be sorry. That you anticipated we might eventually need them... thank you, Sia."

"You are welcome, June. Dax and Ronin are looking for you. Would you like me to direct them here?"

Still in awe, I say, "Yes. Please."

Around five minutes later, I meet my Mates and Doraj at the door to the new cavern. I have a huge smile on my face. "You three ready to see my surprise from Sia?"

They give me a confused look but smile and say, "Yes!"

I watch their faces as they come through the door, and every one of them trips on the door frame when they see what's behind me. They all start babbling and talking at the same time. I'm not sure they know who they're talking to or if they care. They all three trot out to where the ships are being built, exclaiming at various things being made.

Sam and I are chuckling. I look at him, "See, I told you. You owe me a match!"

Ronin and Dax's head pop around the ships they are inspecting, and Ronin asks, "What did you bet him?"

Laughing, I say, "You both would forget I was here once you saw our new toys."

They both laugh and say, "Sorry," in unison.

I laugh at their silliness and trot over and give them both a kiss. "Sia says they won't be done for forty days. So we don't get to play until we return with Aanon." I can't help the sad feeling that comes over me when I say that.

They both walk over and wrap their arms around me. Ronin kisses my forehead. "We will find him, June. We feel it, too, but we will have him with us soon."

I nod as a tear slips down my cheek. We stand wrapped around each other because we all need comfort. I eventually break the silence, "You two stay here with Doraj and grill Sia about your new toys. I think I'm going to go lay down for a bit."

Dax furrows his brow, "I can go with you."

I shake my head, "No, stay here with them. I'll be fine."

He kisses me gently, "If you are sure. You are going home?"

I nod and kiss Ronin, then head for the door. Sam and the Ssadab follow me out.

Dax

I watch our mate as she leaves the cavern, then looks back at Ronin. "I am worried about her, Ronin. Something is wrong, and it is not all about Aanon."

He nods, still looking at the closed door. "We bombarded her with a great deal of bad news today. Hopefully, she just needs time to process it."

We turn and take in our new ships. They are about fifty percent completed and look slightly different from the Emancipation. I call out, "Sia, this is amazing. They look different from the Emancipation."

Ronin chuckles, "She has been asking questions of me on the Emancipation design. I did not know why then, but I understand now. The design is similar but different."

"Yes. I wanted to surprise you all, but I needed information on the design choices you made with the Emancipation," she says.

Doraj joins us, "There are Nlyaxian design traits, but there is also an aspect very different from anything we have ever built."

"Correct, Doraj. I found designs for many vessels in the Haven databank. Not all were warships, but the designs are incredibly advanced. More advanced than anything I have in the Nlyaxian databanks."

Ronin and Doraj get excited and say in unison, "Go on."

I chuckle as Sia continues, "The basics of space travel are relatively the same, but their engine design is much more efficient. I will want to retrofit the Emancipation at some point. I will send you all the ship designs. I combined Nlyaxian and Haven designs in these ships. They will be forty-two percent faster and fifty-six percent more efficient in fuel consumption."

"Fantastic," I say in excitement. "We had hit a wall on those things in our engine designs."

Both Ronin and Doraj nod in agreement.

Sia continues, "Their weaponry is where their designs truly excel."

We all get huge smiles, and I hop from foot to foot, "Tell us all about it!"

June

Sam and I exit the lift from the cavern, followed by our shadows. I can feel his worry for me. I'm not sure when it happened, but somehow Sam and I are linked. I am guessing it was when I shared my light with him. He is like Ahmya now, a brother.

"I feel the same," he says. "We are like siblings, almost closer than siblings. I am sorry if it makes you uncomfortable."

I chuckle, "Great, another male who can read my emotions. Seriously though, you are my brother. Even if I could change that, I wouldn't."

He smiles a little, and I ask, "What is it? Oh, do you not want the link?? I'm sorry..."

He interrupts, "No, no, no, it's not that. I am happy we are brother and sister. I was wondering if I could ask you some questions?" We get into a vehicle, and the Ssadab get into another and take the lead back home.

"Sure. What do you want to talk about?" I can feel his nerves, so I add, "You can ask me anything, Sam. I will keep it between us."

He smiles, "I know you will. I want to talk about human females."

Hoo boy. "Ok, go ahead."

"Can you tell me about Ahmya?"

I sit stunned for a few seconds because I was not expecting that. Maybe one of the new women but not her. Probably because he feels my shock, he adds, "When I saw her Katana, I felt something. I cannot explain it, but even before you told me whose they were, I felt it. I have carried them not for you, sorry, June, but because of what I feel. Will you tell me about her?"

I give him a soft smile, "Yes, I will tell you about her. She is my sister, not in the genuine sense of it but in every other. She and I met at our dojo, where we trained. We met one day because some of the other students were messing with me. They didn't think girls belonged in a dojo. I was cleaning the floors in the training room when three of them came in. They called me names and then knocked over my cleaning bucket full of water."

I chuckle at the memory, "Oh, she was mad. She knocked all three over the head repeatedly with a training sword, then made them clean up the mess. We were always together after that. I wasn't close with my family, so she would invite me to her family's house every weekend. They were amazing, loving parents, and they adored her."

We get to the house and go inside. I sit down in the living room, wrapping a blanket around me. Sam sits across from me, "We trained hard all the time. We both loved martial arts and weapons. We would push and correct each other, making the other better and better. By the time we were taken, we had both won several world championship medals. We never were competitive with each other. We were always happy when the other won, even if it meant one beat the other in a match."

I can't help the shaky sigh that escapes, "I miss her so much, and it kills me to know she's out there somewhere suffering... may be suffering like I did or worse."

We are quiet for a while then I get an idea, "Would you like to see her?"

He gets a confused look but nods.

I close my eyes and find Sam's bridge. He stays on the other side, so I motion for him to join me. He looks unsure but starts across his bridge.

"That is a strange experience. I can feel I am in your mind."

"Yeah, it's unsettling initially, but you get used to it." I pull us into a favorite memory of Ahmya and me at a tournament. I point to her getting ready for the next round of her match. "That is Ahmya. She is getting ready for the final round of the last championship she won."

Sam is mesmerized by her and then says quietly, "I know her."

I look at him, "That's not possible, Sam."

"No," he says, "I know her. She was at the Outpost for a time. When I was around her... she quieted the storm. I was able to think. I still did not know who I was, but she helped me. They sent her to another outpost because she killed several Lutetian, then, after I saw her... I would kill anyone who got close to her. After they took her away, they tortured my mind until I fell into the abyss again."

He glances at me and looks so sad. "I failed her."

"No, Sam. It's amazing you could help her as much as you did. We will find her."

He asks, "Can we watch her match?" I nod.

When the match is over, I pull us out of the memory. I send Sam back to his mind. I am about to open my eyes but stop.

I reach for Aanon's bridge. At first, I cannot find it, but then I detect it. It looks different. It is very blurry; I don't understand why that is.

I walk to the edge of the bridge. Looking at my feet, I step onto it, expecting my foot to go through. However, it is solid. I walk across the bridge. It is so dark. Then I hear lightning. No. It's a storm. It resolves enough I realize I stand in a storm of black clouds with no wind. They churn around me like a river current.

No. Not Aanon. It cannot be. He's not in stasis. He is a mutated Lutetian soldier. I am sobbing. I'm hit with the pain he feels at that moment. I stagger with the weight of it. It's so much worse than the torture I endured at their hands.

I freeze. There is something dangerous stalking me in the cloud. I can die here. I realize I don't know which way to go to get to the bridge.

There's a loud roar of an animal in the distance. My prey response nearly forces me to run. I close my eyes and try to find the bridge with my mind. I cannot find it. My panic is rising. It's then I can feel my mates are worried.

I open my eyes and sprint toward them. The animal roars again, and it's much closer. Too close.

I can feel the bridge now. I am almost there. I can feel the animal bearing down on me. I'm going to make it. Suddenly, fire erupts down my back. Claws swipe across my back as my feet hit the bridge. I continue to sprint across and jump the last four feet off the bridge and close it with my mind. I hear a final angry roar as it closes.

I open my eyes, and both are kneeling in front of me. When my eyes open, Ronin grabs my face, wiping the tears away with his thumbs. "Are you ok?"

I moan and bend forward still feeling the pain on my back.

Ronin and Dax are on their feet, grabbing my arms.

I hear Dax yell, "Get the vehicle. We need to go to the infirmary now!"

I am fighting the pain, but it intensifies with the movement. I cannot help the tears streaming down my face. My poor Aanon.

We are in the vehicle, and I have a hard time keeping my eyes open. Dax, in a panicked tone, says, "June, you need to stay awake. Ronin! There is so much blood. I cannot control the bleeding. It looks like an animal attacked her."

I sob. The animal was Aanon. I'm not sure how I know, but I do. I must have lost consciousness because when I open my eyes again, I am lying on my stomach in a medical pod.

Nalax bends into my view, "Hello, my friend." She has tears in her eyes. "You need to stop coming to my infirmary, ok? I dislike seeing you here." I try to smile for her, but I'm not sure I succeed. "Divad and I are just finishing repairing the damage, and are giving you blood because you lost too much." I nod as she disappears.

Dax and Ronin's worried faces are now in front of me. "Sorry," I say, very slurred.

Ronin cups my cheek, "I agree with Nalax. No more infirmary trips."

I'm beginning to feel much better as Divad says, "Done. She can be turned over now."

Ronin and Dax gently turn me over and cover me up. I'm naked *again.* They set the bed up slightly, and tears start again.

My mates sit on the bed. "What happened?" I notice Sam worried at the back of the room and motion him forward.

"This is my fault Sam, not yours. Once I sent you back to your mind, I decided I wanted to find Aanon's bridge. I am always pulled into his mind. I never see a bridge. So I searched for it. I almost gave up but finally found it."

I cannot stop the sob that escapes. Dax asks, "What is it, June? What happened?"

I sob again, "Aanon is a Lutetian mutated soldier." I collapse into my mates' arms crying.

After I quiet, Ronin pulls me back, "How do you know this?"

Sam is the one to answer, "She would know. She saw what my mind was like."

They look back at me for more. "His bridge was strange, fuzzy. I wasn't even sure it was solid. I walked across, and it was *so* dark. I couldn't understand what I was seeing until I realized it was a black churning storm, but with no wind."

Sam's head falls to his chest. "He is a soldier."

I can feel my mates' turbulent emotions but Dax asks, "But the wounds, what happened?"

I stare at my hands. I'm not sure I can tell them. Ronin grabs them, "It is ok, my mate. Tell us."

"It was Aanon. He was in the form of a huge animal. When I first heard the roar, I was so scared, but in the storm, I didn't know which way the bridge was. Ronin, Dax… your worry helped me to find it. I almost made it across, but he caught me at the foot of the bridge."

Dax and Ronin both jump up and start pacing. Angry, Ronin asks, "Are you saying… are you saying Aanon did that?"

I'm crying again. "Yes, and no. The pain *sob* the pain he is in is infinitely worse than anything I have ever felt or witnessed. He does not know who or what he is."

Dax looks lost. "But… but we saw him on his farm. He knew then?"

Divad sighs, "The mind is infinitely complex in its workings. I am sure there is a part of his mind that still has his memory, where he knows who he is. You all could have been drawn directly there where he hides from the pain."

Ronin still paces, and I can feel his anger and frustration. "Ronin," I reach for him to join me, so he sits beside me on the bed. "Please do not be angry with him. I should have known." My shoulders sag, "I saw the storm in his mind in the distance, but I didn't recognize it for what it was."

He cups my cheek, "I am not angry with him... or you. I am angry with the ones who did this to him, and I worry because if he knew what he is doing as their soldier... I am afraid of how he would take it."

I give a determined look to everyone in the room, "Listen well. I do not want Aanon to ever know he injured me. Understand? *Never."* I look at Sam, "Do you remember?"

He closes his eyes, then opens them again, "No. Nothing. I only remember when Ahmya was there."

I relax a bit.

"Ahmya?" Dax asks. Dax and Ronin look at me for an explanation.

Sam briefly walks through what he remembers of Ahmya at the Outpost.

I nod, "Sam saw Ahmya at the Outpost. It gives me hope we will find her."

Dax looks at Sam and then his arm. He looks at his arm for a fraction too long. "Dax." He looks back at me, "Tell me."

"You know I cannot." He says sadly.

I close my eyes. I knew. Somehow I knew Sam was Ahmya's mate, and that Dax can see the Kokoro means she is alive. Tears are streaming down my face again.

I open my eyes and look at Sam, "She's alive, and we will get her back."

He stares back at me for a while, and a look of determination comes over his face, "Yes, we will." He stands, "I will take my leave. Thank you, June."

I look at my mates. The two males are my world. I put a hand on both of their cheeks, "Take me home, please."

Ronin

A few days later, Dax and I sit in our home, watching our mate. She's nervous because all crews are to meet outside the community building in a few hours so that she can speak to them. We have all been somber with the news of Aanon. She stands at the window staring at the falls.

The weight of her responsibilities is getting heavy. My mother used to get quiet before similar situations. I wish I knew how I could help her relax.

She turns to us, "I need to let off some steam. Follow me."

Curious, we follow. We seem to head to a room on the underground floor of the house. We step off the last stair and are hit with my mate's smell of desire. Dax and I growl and begin to stalk her. As she makes her way to the door, she removes articles of clothing. Our growling grows in volume as each piece hits the floor.

She is now naked, walking to the door. Her ass is magnificent. She opens the door and walks inside. Our instinct is out in full force. We hunt her as a pair and enter the room looking for her.

The room is padded; walls, ceiling, and floor. Things dangle from the ceiling, odd benches and chairs, and on the wall are ropes, pieces of leather, switches, and many things I do not recognize.

June's scent is driving me crazy. I let out a long, low growl, and her desire fills the room. I rush to her, my nose at her neck, smelling her. "What is this, mate?" She moans at my proximity. "Answer," I growl.

She doesn't move at all, like prey frozen in fear. The behavior feeds my instincts. She quietly says, "Let's call it a playroom. All the instruments in this room are for pleasure," she shivers, "For your dominance of me."

Dax comes around behind her and inhales at the other side of her neck. He growls, "Show us."

She shivers again. She is highly stimulated. I growl, licking her neck slowly. She whispers, "Above my head is leather cuffs suspended by a rope from the ceiling. Put my hands in the cuffs. On the wall, the rope is tied to an anchor. Pull me off the ground and retie it."

Dax is in the same state as me. Both of our eyes are black with instinctual need. I reach up and grab the leather cuffs, and Dax slides his hands down her waist, then grabs her wrists and brings them up to the cuffs. I bind her hands, then run my hands down her arms. Her skin erupts in little bumps.

Dax stalks to the wall and unties and pulls the rope. Our mate lifts off the ground. Her pussy is now level with my cock. I growl low again, and she moans.

Dax is back. He growls, "what should we do now, mate?"

Her head is back, "whatever you desire," she moans. We both growl. "But," she says, and we pause, "if I send you the image of a sword over the link, you are to stop immediately. It's called a safe word."

We nod at each other in understanding. Dax lifts a piece of long cloth, puts it in her mouth, and ties it behind her head. "No more talking for you, mate." He growls. The scent of her lust permeates the room. I look down and see her desire on her thighs. It makes me painfully hard, and I growl, "What shall we do, brother?"

He reaches around her body and pinches her nipples, making her moan. "She said whatever we desire. How about the switch? We *play* with her, and if she makes a sound," he gets close to her ear and says, "we punish her." She shivers. I motion with my head for him to get it.

"Remember, mate, no sounds." She lifts her head slightly to look me in the eye and then moans. I chuckle and glance at Dax, then nod. When the switch makes contact, she moans, and more desire runs down her thighs. I nod again, a small crack against flesh again, and she shivers but makes no sounds. "Good female. Now we shall begin. I think I shall fuck you now. Remember, no sounds, or Dax will whip or spank you, whatever he sees fit. *No sound.* Nod if you understand."

She nods once. "Good female."

Dax

I can barely control myself. My cock is so close to release. Seeing my mate prone and at our mercy drives me mad with desire.

Ronin lift her legs and slowly pushes his cock into her. She is shaking with need. When he pulls back out, she moans. "Bad female." I toss the switch. I need to feel my hand connect with her beautiful ass. I slap her hard, and both she and Ronin moan. I slap her ass again, and there's a chorus of groans.

Ronin growls, "her pussy clenches when you punish her." Slap. Ronin pounds into her hard. His restraint is gone. She tries to hold back the sounds she needs to make but often fails. The slapping of skin on skin sounds through the room. On the last slap, she screams her release through the gag, and I slap her again. Ronin roars his release, and she screams again as another orgasm hits her. I slap her again.

They are both sweating and panting. Ronin pulls from her body and murmurs, "Good female." He looks at me, "Your turn, brother. What is *your* desire?"

I growl, and my mate moans again. I slap her ass again *hard*, walk to the wall, and let her down until her feet are again on the ground. I retie the rope and return to my mates. A clasp attaches the leather cuffs to the rope. I remove the cuffs from the clasp, take one of her wrists out of the cuffs, put her hands behind her back, and put her wrist back in the cuff.

She moans again, and I deliver a swift slap. "Ah ah, mate. The rule is still in place until we tell you, quiet." Fire flashes in her eyes and I chuckle, "There she is."

I grab the cuff between her wrist and lower face-down to the floor. "Ronin, kneel at her head." He drops to his knee in front of her, his eyes alternating between her and me.

I pull her back so she is on her knees, but her arms behind her back support the front part of her body weight. I look at Ronin. He waits for my instructions. "Grab her by the hair and fuck her mouth." The sight of Ronin doing as I tell him and my mate under my dominance is too much. I roar and slam my cock into June. She moans, and I slap her ass hard. Her pussy clenches around my cock. I am pounding into her, driving us both higher. Ronin roars his release, and I can see her sucking it down. I push my thumb into her ass and massage her. June screams as her orgasm hits, and this time, Ronin hits her ass with a leather crop, which makes mine hit. June screams as another orgasm hits. Ronin swats her with the crop again for the sound. Her body clenches harder on mine. My mate is pure ecstasy.

I gently set her down on her side and unclasp the cuffs. I pull her in her back to my front and kiss her shoulder. Ronin unties the gag and kisses her. He wraps his arm around us and draws us close.

I chuckle, "I like the new playroom."

They both laugh with me. June quietly asks, "You both understand why this room helps me?"

I do not, but Ronin answers, "I do. You are feeling the weight of your position. It is a lot of responsibility and control. This room allows you to release that control. It is a healthy outlet."

She smiles, "Yes."

I kiss her shoulder and say, "You know how Ronin was with your weapons wall? That is how I feel about this room. I want to explore *every* toy and maybe develop some of my own."

She chuckles and reaches back and kisses me. I notice then that the anxiety she held before is nearly gone. Good.

June

As we drive to the community center, I am relaxed and ready. When I built that room, I wasn't sure my mates would like it with their society based upon the Goddess and females.

Hoo boy. They definitely have an apex predator in their evolutionary tree. When they stalked and hunted me, I was so turned on that I could barely think straight. One day, getting all hyped up again and sprinting away may be very fun. I will definitely have to try that soon.

Dax pulls me onto his lap, "I do not know what you are thinking about, but I am sure I would like it."

I can help but laugh, "Oh, you will. Someday soon."

He growls as the vehicle comes to a stop at the community center. It looks like everyone is there. Ok, here goes nothing.

We step out and walk directly to the stairs, and the top so I can see everyone. As we turn, Sia comes across my com, "June, I will amplify your voice so everyone can hear you. It's ready when you are."

"Thank you, Sia."

I turn to the crowd of people. I see many people I consider family and even more I have never met.

"People of Haven. If you have been here from the start, you know that since we freed ourselves from the slaver, Kaxlin. We have committed ourselves to help the oppressed of this galaxy. Since then, we have had many challenges, which we have all overcome because we are strong. We are survivors. We have many enemies—more than we anticipated. Fear not; we are on the side of good, on the side of the Goddess. The side that chooses kindness over brutality, that chooses love over hate, and the side that chooses light over darkness. Tomorrow we leave on a critical mission to liberate more of our family. It will be hard, and it is not without risk. We did not choose this path because it was easy. We chose it because it is what is right. Our enemy is many, but they are disconnected from their people, which is why we will win because, make no mistake, we are at war. When we return, we will have many to care for, and we will need to train and train hard because the darkness comes, and we must annihilate it! The people of Haven have prepared a meal and festivities to send us off. Spend time with your family and friends tonight, for tomorrow, we launch!"

The crowd roars to life. The Nlyaxian warrior's salute and take a knee.

We have to win. I am not willing to lose any of these people. They mean too much to me.

End Book 2

Book 3 Annihilation - Coming Soon

CHAPTER

26

Ahmya - Human best friend

Kaxlin/Dlanod - Nlyaxian Pirate Captain

Tanto - Japanese short sword

Katana - Japanese long sword

Leena - Nlyaxian slave girl

Nalax - Noinapmocian ex-sex slave for Kaxlin. Her role is now a physician.

Doraj - Noinapmocian engineering slave, Mate to Nalax

Craxlin - Yellow aliens working with humans to buy women for sale to Lutetian

Lutetian - Mystery bad guys.

Sitruc - Kaxlin's 2nd in command. Nlyaxian. No slave collar.

Sia - Ship AI

Pillut - Small Nlyaxian flower with green petals, term of endearment

Ferin - Reclusive species that is rarely seen. Excellent fighters and followers of the Goddess

The Goddess - Immortal being that teaches, logic, compassion, the strength of will, independent thought and science-driven

Jezu - Enemy of the Goddess

Annod Amirp

Trogu - Alien disguise June wears

Kokoro - Nlyaxian mate symbol

Expalita - Ferin aura

Amabo, Karab, Ellechim - Elected leaders of Haven

Sirk - Cruxlin

Ekim

Lessur

Ekul

Sam

Neirad

Tami

Heather

Nairb - Liberation AI

Iarumas - The best warrior of all Ferin

A professional nerd, AL Carter has spent the last two decades in the tech industry supporting the infrastructure, websites, and software the world runs on. She loves science, reading, and making just about anything sparkly in her spare time. She gets great joy from writing science fiction romance novels giving strength and purpose to her female characters! Her heroines do not need saving but love creating steam with their partners!